HOT AND BOTHERED

JENNIFER BERNARD

1

MOST DAYS, NOTHING DISTRACTED BEN KNIGHT WHEN HE WAS AT the controls of a plane. He did his best thinking when airborne, thousands of feet above all the crap. Up here, he felt at peace with himself, and with the world in general. He often flew with a big grin on his face. His passengers, mostly honeymooners, loved him for that.

But today it was a struggle to keep that smile on his face. Actually, it had been for the past few weeks—since Julie deGaia had returned to Jupiter Point. Since she'd had the *nerve* to come back. Skipping into town the way she'd skipped out—without a word.

Just thinking about her made his hands tighten on the yoke of the Cessna 206, and the plane dipped. He and Julie hadn't even spoken yet, and he was already all hot and bothered.

Luckily, the honeymooning couple currently buckled into the passenger seats didn't notice. They were supposed to be enjoying the spectacular scenery of Jupiter Point from five thousand feet above ground. Instead, they had their tongues down each other's throats.

Get a grip, Knight. He was over Julie, after all. He shouldn't be so bothered that she was back. And he had a job to do. He was supposed to be showing these honeymooners a good time— though they were obviously doing just fine on their own.

"If you look out the window to your right, you'll see the observatory. We have the West Coast's most powerful infrared telescope right here in Jupiter Point; we're pretty proud of that." Ben adjusted the attitude of the 206, revealing the panorama of green hills, the highest peak topped with the sprawling observatory. "As you probably know, Jupiter Point is famous for its stargazing. You can see a lot with the naked eye, but it's also worth taking a trip to the observatory."

The bride, Susie, pulled away from their kiss and peered out the Plexiglas window. "Oh, I see the telescope sticking out! I bet they saw us kissing, Chuck."

"Then let's give them a show," Chuck said, tugging her back toward him.

Oh boy, Ben wasn't sure he could handle another make-out session. "Not to worry, that telescope is focused on outer space, not us," he said. "Stars, planets, celestial objects. That sort of thing. So, what would you two most like to see on this trip? Wildlife, dolphins, scenic views...we have a little bit of everything here."

"Just give us your best tour," said the groom—Chuck—gruffly. He was probably fifteen years older than Susie, and to Ben, he seemed like kind of a jerk. A wealthy one. "We're paying you good money for this flight."

"That you are," Ben agreed amicably. "How about we take a spin over some of the offshore islands? You can get some great shots for your honeymoon album. Hang on tight, I think I spotted a pod of dolphins."

He straightened the wings and trimmed the plane for level flight.

"Where? I want to see!" Susie pressed her face up against the window, her attention now completely on the scenery.

Chuck gave Ben a nasty look.

He whistled to himself, ignoring his irritated passenger. He was still the captain of this ship, no matter how wealthy his passengers were. And besides, Chuck would thank him later, when the thrill of a dolphin sighting translated into hot honeymoon sex.

"There they are, to the right of Sand Island. There are several sets of binoculars back there, feel free to use them."

Both of them picked a pair of binoculars and aimed them out the right Plexiglas window. "What a pretty island!" Susie exclaimed. "I see a beach. Can you swim there?"

Ben didn't answer right away. He was thinking of the last time he'd swum on Sand Island—with Julie deGaia, when he was eighteen and she was seventeen. And how she'd looked in her simple black racer-back one-piece. She was a strong swimmer; every summer he'd known her, she'd worked as a lifeguard. She didn't go for bikinis, but it didn't matter to Ben. To him, she'd been the sexiest thing on the planet in her plain old Speedo.

And now she was back in Jupiter Point. Sneaking into his thoughts at random moments, completely uninvited and definitely unwelcome.

Distracting him. Damn it.

"Hello?" Susie was saying.

He jolted back to the moment, the drone of the engine, the vibrations of the little craft...the poor deluded honeymooners, who thought their love would last forever.

Not that he wanted to rain on their parade. They were paying his bills, after all.

"Sorry, I was checking a gauge. Yes, the beach is swimmable," he said. "Go ahead, take some photos. We have a good patch of air here."

They started clicking away with their phones. He stayed quiet, letting them do their thing. God, he loved being up here. This was why he loved flying so much. While his hands and most of his brain dealt with the controls and gauges, the rest of his mind was free to wander wherever it chose.

And of course...it chose Julie.

He'd run into her for the first time since her return at the 7-Eleven, near the Slurpee machine. She looked the same, yet not the same. She'd always had a quiet kind of beauty, not the sort that jumped out at you. Her brown hair might seem ordinary at first, until you were lucky enough to touch it and discover how incredibly silky and fine it was. When they were together, he'd tried to define her eye color—kind of gray? Kind of blue? Kind of "lake water"? She'd laughed when he came up with that, but he stood by it.

Like the sappy kid that he'd been.

He and Julie hadn't spoken to each other at the 7-Eleven. He'd been there with another woman, Lanie, who'd wanted to stop in for cigarettes. He hated smoking, and had already decided this would be their last date. But as soon as he spotted Julie, a wave of forgotten anger rushed over him, and he'd put his arm around Lanie.

Screw Julie. She'd left him without any word, any explanation. *Twelve years* of no explanation. He was pissed. He couldn't even force his *face* to be nice to her.

Julie's greeting froze in mid-smile. Then that smile slid away, melting like a snowman under a hot sun. She'd watched every moment of Lanie's cigarette purchase. As if she was forcing herself to do so. Then a boy in glasses, with a wild black shock of hair, had tugged at her arm. She'd jerked to attention and finished getting the kid his Slurpee.

The look on her face as she'd turned away pissed him off even more. As if *he'd* done something wrong. As if he was the one who had disappeared from town without so much as a goodbye.

"Hey. Hey! Pilot!"

Chuck's gruff voice pulled him back to attention.

"Sorry." He pretended to fiddle with the comms controls. "I can hear you now. What's going on?"

"Where's the champagne in this tin can? We're thirsty."

"Right behind you, there's a cooler."

Grumbling, the man turned in his seat. He probably wasn't used to getting things for himself. To him, this little plane was probably slumming it. No flight attendant, no white-glove service. Ben would love to tell him to shove it. But Knight and Day Flight Tours was a brand-new business, and both he and his brother Tobias had invested all their resources into it. He couldn't afford to be blowing off wealthy and well-connected clients.

"Want me to pour some for you, too?" Susie leaned forward and tapped his shoulder.

"Ah no, that would be a serious FAA violation."

"We won't tell," she teased. "Right, Chuck?"

"Wrong." Chuck was messing around with the champagne bottle. "What is this, a screw-top?"

"Small plane," said Ben easily. "Can't have corks hitting something essential."

Chuck unscrewed the top and poured two plastic flutes of champagne. The couple lifted their glasses, but when they tried to clink, a bumpy patch of air made them miss.

"Control your plane, pilot," Chuck growled.

"Just a little turbulence. We'll be out of it in a few. Carry on with that toast. Here's to a happy life for you both!"

They tried again, and again missed.

The perfect metaphor for romance, if you asked Ben.

But Chuck apparently wasn't used to glitches like this. "You're doing it on purpose, pilot."

Ben pulled back on the yoke to gain a little altitude, where they'd encounter fewer bumps. "Turbulence is part of flying. Kind of like marriage."

"Excuse me?" Chuck gave up on the toast and downed his champagne.

"Turbulence in marriage. It's a thing, or so I hear."

"Not married, huh?" Susie leaned forward against the seat belt, her flute clutched in one hand. "Why not, a handsome guy like you? I bet the girls around here are crazy for you."

"Yeah, but he's probably smart enough to stay single."

Susie made a face at her husband.

Okay then. So much for romance. Not that Ben believed in it anyway. It was a goddamn mind-altering drug, and he wanted nothing to do with it.

"So, no girlfriend either?" Susie was asking.

"Nope. Not right now."

"Just haven't met the right girl yet, huh?"

"Something like that," he muttered. Of course, that wasn't the problem at all. The problem was that he *had* met the right girl. He'd just never recovered from it.

HE'D MET Julie through Savannah Reinhard. During the summer after his sophomore year, Savannah had invited him to her house —more like a mansion—to play tennis. The Reinhards were the richest family in town, and Savannah was their only daughter. Ben had no idea how he'd caught her eye, but all of a sudden he was scrambling to return her wicked overhand serve on the private tennis court next to the Reinhards' infinity pool.

It was mixed doubles; her partner was her teacher, a tennis pro. Ben's partner was Julie deGaia, who was a year younger. He'd seen Julie around town, and knew that she lived with the Reinhards. Julie's mother was the Reinhard family's private macrobiotic, vegan, gluten-free chef. Even though she was essentially a servant's daughter, she and Savannah were best friends.

They were nothing alike. Savannah commanded everyone's attention with her black hair and wild laughter. Whereas Ben wouldn't have noticed the quieter Julie if they hadn't been paired up on the tennis court.

Once they started playing, that changed. First, he took note of her pretty legs flashing past on her way to scoop up a shot he missed. Then they exchanged high-fives after a hard-won point. She smiled at him, and his heart jumped.

As they played, Julie managed to sneak in a few secret pointers. Things like, "Here, take my racket, it's strung a little tighter," and "Savannah really loves to win, just so you know," or, "Your shoelace is coming untied. No bloodshed allowed on this court."

By the end of the match, a lopsided victory for Savannah and her tennis-pro partner, all Ben wanted to do was find a way to talk to Julie some more. To be honest, Savannah scared him a little. She seemed to look right through him, or size him up in a way that made him uncomfortable. But Julie, with her sympathetic smile and funny comments, put him at ease.

When a servant delivered a tray of lemonade after the match, he sat next to Julie and asked her what she planned to do that summer.

"Ugh," Savannah pouted. "She's going to be a full-time lifeguard and I won't have anyone to hang out with."

She probably meant to suggest that Ben should hang out with her. But that wasn't his conclusion.

"Stargazer Beach?" he asked Julie. "I like to go running there when the tide's out."

Their eyes met, and it felt like a zing of lightning flashed through him. Their connection was so complete, so thorough, so electric and undeniable, that not even Savannah could make it go away. She shifted her attention to her tennis pro and left Ben and Julie alone.

Ben had never asked a girl on a date before. He didn't even know how to do it. At that point in his life, girls were just prettier friends to him. The whole "dating" part of life was foreign territory. So, he asked if she liked to swim, and told her they had a creek behind their house, and a tire swing that you could only use if there'd been enough rain recently.

Then it turned out she liked basketball, too. "I'm like a grasshopper, I can jump almost twice my own height," she'd informed him.

So, a week later, she rode her bike three miles to Ben's house for some basketball and a dip in the creek, and that was it. He was in love. *They* were in love.

Or so he'd thought. So everyone had thought.

"PILOT!" Chuck was barking at him. "Pay attention."

Jesus, he'd never been this distracted during a flight. *Get it together, Knight.*

"My beautiful wife is about to throw up all over your no doubt highly leveraged plane, so do you think you could even things out a bit?"

"Hashtag SOS," Susie gasped.

"Poor baby." Chuck seized the moment and put his arm around her. "I'm here, honey-buns."

Oh boy. More kissing on the horizon.

Enough with the distractions. Time to play tour guide again. "To your left, we're now passing Stargazer Beach."

How many times had he and Julie made out in the lifeguard shack after hours?

And now she was back and he couldn't think straight.

"Up in the hills there, you can see the Seaview Inn, which is a great place for a sunset dinner."

Like the time he and Julie had scraped enough spare change from his old Dodge truck to drive up the hill and sit on the terrace, sharing one order of crab cake appetizers. It was so good that they'd spent the next ten minutes thinking up crazy ways to finance more of their meal. Trade the Dodge for a main course? Pick bouquets from the inn's garden and sell them to dinner guests? Let Julie sing for their supper with her pretty voice?

The elderly couple at the table next to them was so amused,

they'd told the maître d' to serve Ben and Julie whatever they wanted.

Nothing in life had ever been as fun as being Julie's boyfriend. And it never would be, because his innocence had been completely destroyed.

And now she was back. And he was completely distracted.

"As you probably know, the reason we can see it so clearly is the unique topography of Jupiter Point. All those air currents that we've been bumping around on keep the air quality up. We have strict controls over the lumen levels to prevent light pollution. A little turbulence is a small price to pay, right?"

Glancing at the mirror that allowed him to see the interior, he saw the honeymooners were back in mash mode, kissing like fiends.

He fell silent, letting them have their moment. Maybe Chuck and Susie would make it, after all. Maybe there was a tiny part of him that still wanted to believe in love. Maybe Jupiter Point would work its honeymoon magic. It seemed to work on everyone.

Except him and Julie.

2

JULIE SHOVED THE SQUEEZE HANDLE OF THE MOP ALL THE WAY TO the hilt. Water spurted into the mop bucket, with a few drops splattering onto Felix. He looked up from the book he was reading and sniffled.

"I'm sick, and now you're trying to murder me with mop water." Her godson shoved his glasses back onto his nose.

"You seem so uncharacteristically cheerful. Are you sure you're sick?" she asked dryly. On a scale of one to ten, he was maybe at a three in terms of sickness. She figured he needed more of a mental health day than anything else. Nothing wrong with that.

"Too late now. You can't take me *back* to school," he pointed out.

"Oh yeah? Try me."

"They wouldn't take me. I have even more germs now."

She pushed the mop across Mrs. Murphy's living room floor. The bookstore owner was the first Jupiter Point resident to book her "Green and Pristine" cleaning services. Most of the others seemed to be holding back, waiting to see if she was going to stick around.

Which was a good question. She loved this town. But so far, Felix hated it.

And then there was Ben, who seemed to hate *her*.

He had yet to say one word to her.

"There are other places I can take you," she told Felix ominously. "Where you'll be babied and coddled and fed chicken soup by servants and—"

"That's not funny. You promised."

Since Felix looked so alarmed, she relented. "Of course I won't take you to your grandparents. I told you I wouldn't leave you alone with them until you're ready. But Kiddo, I hope you can be ready soon. There's no reason to be so scared of them."

"Mom says they're monsters."

"That's just a figure of speech. You know how your mom is. She loves to make things exciting." Sometimes Julie felt like a civilian casualty of Savannah's ongoing war with her parents. "But I promise you that they're not monsters. They took me in when I didn't have anyone to take care of me. Would monsters do that?"

Felix blinked at her behind his glasses. Savannah refused to say who his father was, but clearly, he carried the near-sighted gene. None of the Reinhards wore glasses. But he'd definitely inherited his wild black mop of hair from Savannah. "I guess not."

His phone beeped. Julie had mixed feelings about an eleven-year-old having a cell phone, but it gave Savannah a way to keep in touch with Felix when she was shooting a movie, as she was now.

He read the text and snorted. Probably a meme. Savannah communicated best with Felix via memes, especially when she was away on a film set. She loved making him laugh.

Julie reached the armchair where Felix was curled up. "Okay, kid, why don't you jump over to that couch. And don't forget the floor is hot lava."

"I'm not six anymore," he grumbled, before gathering up his backpack full of books and climbing onto the couch.

He was just settling in when the jingle of keys sounded at the front door. Mrs. Murphy bustled in.

"Julie, I'm happy I caught you before you finished up. I've been hoping for a nice chat after all these years."

Julie barely kept herself from a massive eye roll. Of course that was why Mrs. Murphy had hired her. Perfect chance for some gossip. When it came to the Jupiter Point grapevine, Mrs. Murphy was the root of all information. She was never malicious. She just wanted to know what was going on.

She plopped onto the couch next to Felix, who blinked at her. "I'm Elaine Murphy. And who might you be?"

"Felix Reinhard," he said.

"Reinhard. So your mother is—"

Julie stepped in. She didn't mind getting the third degree herself, but Felix shouldn't have to. "Felix, can you run out to the car and get me some more vinegar?"

Felix shot her a reproachful, knowing look. When she and Savannah got into fights over Felix, Julie always made a point of sending him out of the room on random errands.

As soon as he was gone, Julie stuck her mop in the bucket and faced Mrs. Murphy. "Felix is Savannah's son. I have no idea who his father is, but I don't believe he's from Jupiter Point. Savannah is currently shooting a movie, and as you probably know, Adam Reinhard has been ill. He wanted to spend some time with his grandson, so I volunteered to bring Felix to Jupiter Point for the semester. I can clean houses anywhere."

Julie figured this was the most efficient way to get the word out, rather than explaining to everyone individually who Felix was and why he was here.

"So, you and Savannah..." The older woman trailed off delicately.

"Me and Savannah what?" Julie squeezed the water from the sponge mop again.

"Are you..."

Julie stared at her blankly. What exactly was Mrs. Murphy getting at?

Then it clicked.

As did the opportunity to tweak her—just a little. "Savannah and I are a couple, absolutely," she said solemnly. "All those pictures of Savannah with movie stars and so forth? It's all a front. Don't be fooled. We're lesbian lovers, always have been."

Finally, Mrs. Murphy burst into laughter. "Okay, you had me up until the end. Always have been? I don't think so. Not with how you and Ben Knight were. You were the most lovey-dovey couple I've ever seen, and that's saying something, considering all the honeymooners who come around here."

The mention of Ben sent a deep pang of pain right into Julie's solar plexus. She focused on her yellow latex gloves, giving herself time to recover.

"I'm Felix's godmother," she explained, dropping the joke. "Almost more like an aunt."

"Well, you and Savannah did grow up together, so that makes sense. Something tells me you're a lot more than an aunt to that boy, though. Savannah never was especially reliable. Do you know how many times she had me order books, then lost interest by the time they arrived? I had a whole 'Abandoned by Savannah' section in the bookstore. I just hope the boy doesn't fall into that category."

Julie picked up the mop bucket and backed out of the room. They'd been chatting so long that the floor was dry. "Of course not. Savannah loves Felix. But she's such a big star now, so in demand. Whenever she's on location, Felix stays with me."

Mrs. Murphy followed after her. "Well, I'm sure he's lucky to have you. He seems very attached to you."

Of course he was. Julie was the most consistent person in his life, other than Savannah, and he craved routine. In her opinion, he was one step away from an anxiety disorder. But she didn't want to tell Mrs. Murphy all that.

"I've been wanting to ask you about something," she said quickly, before the bookstore owner could ask her anything else.

She brightened. "What's that?"

Julie screwed up her courage. "I wanted to ask about Robert Knight."

"Ah. Jupiter Point's only unsolved murder." She gave Julie a shrewd look. "Ben's father. You must have known him pretty well."

Mrs. Murphy truly was a mastermind when it came to interrogations. She should have been a spy, not a bookstore owner.

"Not well, no. I was shocked when I heard what happened. Have they made any progress in solving the case?"

"You'd have to ask Chief Becker. He doesn't tell me anything." Mrs. Murphy sniffed, as if insulted that the town's police chief didn't confide in her. "But there was a big story in the newspaper recently. Merry Warren interviewed all the Knight brothers."

Well. She'd definitely have to check that out. She could probably find it online. If she couldn't talk to Ben herself—since he clearly didn't want to—she could read his words in a newspaper.

"As a matter of fact, I heard that Will Knight is now investigating the murder himself. So you could always talk to him."

Julie swallowed hard. Seeing Will would be almost as hard as seeing Ben.

Which had happened exactly three times since she'd gotten back. The first time was at the 7-Eleven, where he'd been wrapped up with a stunning blond. Ben had scowled at her so hard, she'd worried his head might explode.

Originally, she'd intended to talk to him right away and find out what had gone wrong twelve years ago, why he'd stood her up. But his frown had stopped that plan in its tracks.

Then she'd spotted him at the hardware store with his older

brother Tobias. She'd ducked behind a shelf of plumbing parts before they could notice her. Then she'd spent the next ten minutes peering between copper pipes and white plastic elbows as they'd shopped for lumber.

If Ben had been alone, maybe she would have tried again to talk to him. But two Knight brothers at once? She couldn't bear it. The brothers had been like another family to her, at a time when she felt utterly alone in the world. Even though the Reinhards asked her to stay after her mother died, there were always strings attached. She always felt like a guest, maybe one step removed from a servant. But with Ben and his family, she never felt that way.

The third time she'd seen Ben was at the cemetery. She'd gone to visit her mother's grave. He was kneeling at his father's, eyes closed, in silent communion with his murdered parent.

Again, she'd fled before he could see her. The guilt was too much.

Because there was a strong possibility that she'd encountered Robert Knight's killer on her last night in Jupiter Point.

That encounter was the reason she'd stayed away until now. And one of the main reasons she'd come back.

Twelve years was long enough to keep a secret like that. Someone needed to know. Not Ben, since he obviously didn't want anything to do with her. The police chief? Could he be trusted?

Mrs. Murphy was asking her something. "I'm sorry, what was that?"

"I was saying that we could really use you at the theater. We're putting on *Grease* this year. I remember what a lovely voice you always had. The church choir sure missed you after you left."

"Oh no. I definitely don't have time for anything like that. I'm still settling in." Besides, she wasn't ready for anything that public. She still wasn't entirely sure it was safe to be back in Jupiter Point.

"Well, I sure hope you stay a while. You've done a spectacular job here." Mrs. Murphy surveyed the living room, where the floors radiated a soft glow and the windows sparkled. Julie smiled proudly. "Green cleaning" hadn't exactly been her first choice for a job. But she liked creating order out of messes. She liked setting her own hours and choosing her own clients. Green cleaning had been very good to her.

Felix loped back into the room with his odd, stiff-legged stride. Her heart swelled at the sight of him.

Sure, the arrival of Felix had upended her life. But he was worth it.

"Julie, you have to help me." Savannah's call had come at night, waking Julie from a deep sleep in the little Reinhard guesthouse.

"Savannah? What's going on?"

"You can't tell my parents anything. Promise."

"Um." Julie sat up in bed and rubbed the sleep from her eyes. "They barely know I'm alive, you don't have to worry about that. But where are you?"

"I'm at a hotel in Benson. I need you to come here. I'll explain when you get here. Bring a suitcase."

"Benson?" Why was Savannah in the next town over? "A suitcase? What are you talking about?"

"Please! And don't worry about money. I'll cover everything."

None of it made any sense. Julie had her last final the next day. She and Ben were planning a camping trip to celebrate the end of her junior year. She couldn't go to Benson.

"Just come. I need you!"

The edge of panic in her friend's voice really scared her. Savannah never panicked. She was always so bold, so defiant, so rebellious. And she'd done so much for Julie. If not for Savannah, she'd be in a foster home by now. Savannah was the one who'd insisted that Julie stay with the Reinhards, even after the car accident that took Mama.

"Okay. I'm coming." Julie took down the address and threw some clothes into a bag.

But she had to tell Ben what was happening, and she tried his phone. No answer. Probably had it turned off.

So she got into her mother's old sky-blue VW beetle and drove out to the Knight house.

And that was when everything had gone off the rails.

She'd told no one except Savannah what had happened. But now it was time. *Past* time. She was going to tell the whole story to *someone.*

Felix helped her pack up her cleaning supplies while Mrs. Murphy reeled off the list of who was performing in *Grease.*

Maybe she should tell Mrs. Murphy her story so *everyone* could hear it. Then she wouldn't have to face Ben. Because once the Knight brothers heard the entire thing, they'd probably think she was a coward and want nothing to do with her.

3

"You need to fucking talk to her," said Tobias bluntly. That was Tobias's style, direct and to the point. With his deep-set dark eyes and fearsome physique, he played the intimidator well. But he'd do anything for his brothers—including tell them when they were being idiots. "We have a business to run here. Planes to keep in the air. Honeymoons to not ruin. You need your head in the game, bro."

"You're right, and I will. The next time I run into her, we'll talk." Ben propped his boots on the desk, where he and Tobias were going through applications for a mechanic. So far, they'd been getting by on their own, but they needed a full-time airplane mechanic to take care of their little fleet. They also needed someone to take bookings, and possibly another pilot.

A pile of fuel receipts caught his attention; he had to organize the damn things. Their need for an assistant was getting dire. Honestly, they needed an assistant to help them hire an assistant.

"I thought you were over Julie like, ten years ago."

"I was."

Tobias glanced at him with a raised eyebrow. "Was?"

"*Am.* Was and am. Still am." He shuffled through the receipts. "Even more so now. Much more."

Tobias looked as if he was trying not to laugh. "Got it. Loud and clear."

Will, their oldest brother, pushed open the door of the little office. At his heels was Chase Merriweather, Merry Warren's half-brother, who was Will's new intern. He had the look of a golden retriever in human form; Ben always pictured a playful, eager puppy whenever he saw Chase.

"We have to talk." Will dropped his long body into one of their metal folding chairs.

"That seems to be a theme today," Ben said gloomily. "What is this, an *Oprah* episode?"

Will shot him a puzzled look. "This is about Mom and Cassie. I heard from them today. It's happening. They're going to come here for a visit."

They all got very quiet for a moment.

They'd gone twelve years without seeing Janine Knight or their sister Cassie. Mom had always been fragile and volatile. Sky-high one day, deep in the dumps the next. And Ben had always been the son closest to her, the one who could coax her out of her dark moods.

And then had come the night of the murder. The night Ben had the task of telling his mother her husband was dead. And he'd fucked it up.

That night...he'd never forget it, never forgive himself.

After that, she'd fled Jupiter Point, taking Cassie with her. The four Knight brothers had scattered in various directions. Ben had joined the Air Force, Tobias had joined the Army. Only Will had stayed to take care of their youngest brother, Aiden, who was barely eight at the time.

Ben missed his mother fiercely, but at the same time, his stomach churned at the thought of seeing her again. He cleared his throat. "How long are they coming for?"

"To be determined. Cassie says she thinks Mom can handle it, but she's not sure."

Ben grunted, fiddling with the pile of resumes.

Will glanced at him curiously. "Got something to say, Ben? You never really talk about Mom."

Because there was nothing to say. Informing your mother that her husband had just been stabbed to death in the kitchen...yeah, everyone did that kind of thing. And Mom's terrifying reaction— that was totally normal.

"It's all good," he said, with an approximation of his usual carefree manner. "I hope she comes. I miss her." That much was true. There'd been a huge hole in his heart ever since she'd left.

Will nodded, moving on. "I got something else too. I think I found something about Dad's murder. I tracked down—"

"*We* tracked down," said Chase proudly.

Will raised a skeptical eyebrow, but nodded in agreement. "Chase and I tracked down all the surviving soldiers who were with Dad during his last mission. I thought one of them was dead, but it turns out he's been living under a different name."

"Why?" Tobias frowned at their oldest brother. "Why a different name?"

"I'm not sure. I'm still trying to locate him."

"*We're* trying to locate him," Chase corrected.

Ben and Tobias exchanged an amused glance. Having Chase around was like living with a puppy still being trained. No better trainer than Will, in Ben's opinion. Will had raised Aiden, so he had the proven parenting skills.

"One thing," Will added softly. "The last known address of this particular soldier is only a hundred miles away. He's probably changed his name again, and moved again. But it does raise the possibility that the killer is more local than we thought."

Silence settled over them all. The idea that someone local— someone from Jupiter Point, the most peaceful, charming tourist town you could imagine, whose biggest claim to fame was stargazing—the idea that someone from around here could have committed murder was shocking.

But no place was immune to evil deeds or to misfortune. Ben knew that. He'd learned it when his world had fallen apart at the age of eighteen, and then again in the Air Force.

He cleared his throat. "Any other leads you guys have found?"

Chase shot him a grateful look, thrilled to be included in the "you guys."

"There were a few anonymous tips called into the police station back then. I'm going to sift through them."

"*We're* going to—"

Will laughed and squeezed Chase's shoulder affectionately. "Actually, I'm going to tackle the tips on my own. I have another fun job for you."

An uneasy expression came over the kid's face. "Like when I filed all your notes? And organized your desk? Got your computer up and running?"

"No, an actual fun job. I have a line on Cindy Tran, who used to work with me at the Sheriff's Department. She disappeared and I'm worried about her. I heard she might be in Las Vegas, so off you go."

Chase did a few air pumps while Will headed for the door. "Anyway, think about the best way to welcome Mom and Cassie back. Ben, you always knew her best, see what you can come up with. I'll be gone for a few days, then we'll come up with a plan."

The door fell shut behind them. In the sudden quiet, Ben looked over at Tobias, who wore a dark scowl as he stared at his phone.

"Worried about Mom?" Ben asked him.

"No, I'm trying to decide if Sarah wants a pink bike or a red one."

Tobias and his new wife, Carolyn, had recently adopted her younger sister, Sarah. Watching big tough Tobias turn into a father figure for a little blond pixie was hilarious.

"Pink seems too on-the-nose girlie," Tobias continued, rubbing the back of his neck. "But some girls really like pink. I shouldn't *not* get her pink just because it's too predictable. Seems kind of unfair, in case that's what she wants."

As he spoke, his frown got more and more dire. That frown was the reason Ben ended up taking most of the flights. No honeymooners wanted to be scowled at.

"Have you tried asking her?" he suggested.

Tobias directed his glare toward Ben. "You make it sound so easy."

Ben lifted his eyebrows at him. "It's pretty easy. You just open your mouth and let the words come out."

"A-ha." Tobias pointed a big finger at him.

"A-ha, what?"

"Pretty much exactly what you should do with Julie, that's what. If it's so easy, what's stopping you?"

Now Ben was the one scowling, while Tobias grinned like a maniac. And there they were, right back where they'd started. Go figure.

"I ought to kick your ass," Ben muttered.

"You could certainly try. But that wouldn't help straighten things out with Julie."

"She fucking left town without a word. What's there to straighten out?"

"This is Julie. *Julie.* She's a sweetheart. Something must have happened. Did you try to reach her?"

"Of course. She never answered her phone. Savannah never called me back. I even went and knocked on the Reinhards' front door."

"What'd they say?"

"Not much," Ben muttered. He could still remember the pitying look on Priscilla Reinhard's face. He must have looked pathetic, begging for answers about why his girlfriend had kicked him to the curb. "They promised to pass along her new phone number and address when they had it. I tried again before I left for Miramar. The housekeeper said they hadn't heard anything. And that was it."

Tobias leaned back in his chair and clasped his hands behind his neck. His gold wedding band caught the light, and Ben actually wanted to punch him. How'd *he* get to be the lucky one with a happy family?

Ben was supposed to be the one already married with kids. It was *always* supposed to be him and Julie. How had things gotten so screwy? A year ago, all the Knight brothers had been single. Then Will had fallen head over heels for Merry, a reporter at the local newspaper. Tobias had fallen deeply and suddenly for Carolyn Moore, an art history teacher.

Now Ben was the single one, flirting his way through Jupiter Point. And Julie was back and—

Stop it.

Love is a mind-altering substance, Ben reminded himself. *No need to be jealous. The single life is the way to go.*

"The Reinhards were always jerks," Tobias said. "The only decent thing they ever did was let Julie stay on after her mom died. You know there's only one way to get this straightened out, brother."

"Swear to God, if you say 'talk to her' again, I'll—"

"Talk to her."

"Ah hell."

4

Julie kept Felix out of school for another day. She didn't have any other cleaning jobs lined up yet, so she decided to show him around the charming little historic downtown. Her pride had been piqued by Felix's constant complaints that her hometown was boring.

"Did you know that Jupiter Point is famous?" she asked him as they strolled down Constellation Way.

"So what? My mom's famous."

"True. But Jupiter Point's famous for stargazing."

"My mom's a star."

Yeah, so far this wasn't going very well. "Not that kind of star, grumpy." They passed the Milky Way Ice Cream Parlor. "Do you want to try the best ice cream sundae in the galaxy?"

"That's stupid. How can they know if it's the best? No one's tried all the ice cream sundaes in the entire galaxy."

She stopped in the middle of the charming street, with its ironwork lampposts and cedar-shingled storefronts. The Reinhards had wanted Julie and Felix to stay in the guesthouse where Julie had lived with her mother. But Felix flat-out refused, and Julie knew him well enough to pick her battles. So, they were staying in a little studio apartment just a few blocks away, paying by the month. Every few days she took him to visit the Reinhards. It never went well. Tomorrow was their next scheduled visit.

Was that the problem here? Was he anxious about seeing his grandparents?

"Felix. Kiddo. What's wrong?"

Felix hung his head and stared at his sneakers, which sported a cartoon depiction of a detonating bomb. "Nothing."

"You can't fool me, sweetie. How long have I known you?"

"Since before I was born."

"Yup. Now cough it up. What's bugging you?" She decided to throw out some possibilities. "Is it school? Do you miss your mom? Is it your grandparents?"

He screwed up his face at her. "When can we go back to LA? We're only five hundred ninety-two and a third miles away."

Julie smiled at his accuracy. Felix was always meticulous with his facts. When he got into something, he learned it to the nth degree. They called it "pulling a Felix."

"You know, you could try giving your grandparents more of a chance. That's why we're here. Family's important." *Take it from me*, she wanted to say. She had no more family, just a faraway father who never called her. Savannah and Felix were the closest thing she had to family.

"But they said that you—"

Before he could finish his sentence, someone called to them from one of the charming little shops. "Julie deGaia, get your butt over here!"

She swung around to see her old friend Suzanne Finnegan. She'd known Suzanne well in high school, but she hadn't stayed in touch with her. In fact, all her old Jupiter Point friendships had fallen by the wayside.

She guided Felix over to the shop, with its gracefully lettered sign reading Stars in Your Eyes. She and Suzanne shared a hug, then she introduced Felix.

"This is Savannah's son, Felix. My godson."

"Nice to meet you, Felix." Suzanne's blond hair was pulled into a twist, making her look grown-up and professional. "I'm Suzanne. I knew Julie waaaaay back in the day. By the way, any kid who steps into my shop gets a lollipop."

"Dentists give lollipops," Felix told her, with his usual gift for moroseness.

Suzanne smiled brightly. "That's true, and I always thought that was strange. Why would you get your teeth cleaned, then get them all sugary? Not that I ever complained. But it's okay, you don't have to take a lollipop. You can just sign my guest book. I'd love that even more."

Suzanne herded them through the front door into a comfortable office space filled with cream furniture, a Keurig, a rack of brochures and a desk bearing a vase of fresh tulips. On the wall, the store's name was written in flowing script, along with the tagline, "Where honeymoon dreams come true."

Julie's honeymoon dreams seemed a million years ago. They'd all involved Ben, and maybe a convertible with the top down, and dancing on a beach in the Caribbean, or wandering through a cathedral in Italy...they'd changed depending on the day. The only thing that hadn't changed was that Ben was there.

Speaking of Ben...there he was.

A picture of him, anyway. On a flyer. Next to a small plane, wearing a bomber jacket, grinning widely.

As if drawn by a magnet, she drifted toward the brochure. *Knight and Day Flight Tours*, it read. *See Jupiter Point from the sky. Offering a wide variety of tours, from wildlife to scenic. With a combined fifteen years of military flying experience, the Knight brothers are proud to be Jupiter Point's only flightseeing service. Call now to book your trip of a lifetime.*

Tobias was in the photo too, standing right next to Ben, but she paid no attention to him. It was Ben's beloved, familiar face that captured her attention and wouldn't let go. She knew that face better than her own. Its smooth planes, its slightly crooked nose from when he'd gotten hit by a basketball. The way one eyebrow was just slightly higher than the other, giving him a quizzical look. His laugh-lined eyes, always so full of heart and love. His mouth, so kissable. His hair, so touchable. He used to forget to comb it for days; she'd run her fingers through it and get stopped by knots.

But in the photo, he looked different. He had a hardness to him, an edge, a cynical curve to his grin. It reminded her of the way he'd glared at her in the 7-Eleven.

Also, his body had changed. In high school, he'd been fast on the basketball court, wiry, with quick reflexes, but not especially muscular. He'd been a boy. Now he was all wide shoulders and lean strength, powerful and fit. He looked like someone you didn't want to cross.

"Ben and Tobias are really doing great with their new business." Suzanne startled her out of her reverie. "They just opened it a few months ago and they're practically turning customers away."

"I'm not surprised. Ben loves to fly. He started accruing hours toward his license when he was sixteen."

"Well, I'm sure glad he kept with it. Everyone wants a flight tour on their honeymoon now. I can barely remember the days before they opened up. You should go by there and check out their operation. Have you seen Ben yet?"

"Yes, of course I've seen him." Julie felt her face heat up. Maybe "spied on him" was a better way to put it. "From a distance."

"Well, that's got to change. You and Felix should come over for dinner. You can meet my little girl, Faith, and I'll invite Ben and—"

"No. Please, don't do that." Julie cringed just thinking about it. How awkward would it be to sit across a dinner table from Ben, as if they were nothing more than two long-lost acquaintances? She couldn't bear that.

"Why not? You can meet Josh, my husband. He's a hotshot, which means he's going to be gone soon, fighting wildfires. So we should do this soon, before he starts training and never has any time for a social life."

"Who's Ben?" Felix piped up.

Suzanne stared at him, then turned her wide-eyed gaze on Julie. "You haven't told him about *Ben*?"

Julie bit her lip. What exactly was she supposed to tell an eleven-year-old about the most passionate relationship of her life? One that Felix's birth had pretty much screwed up? "I'm sure Felix will get a chance to meet Ben. It's a small town. People run into each other all the time."

Then again, they'd been pretty good at avoiding each other so far. Why stop now?

"Does he fly that plane?" Felix was asking in a tone of awe.

Well, wasn't *that* interesting? A temporary break from sullenness, thanks to a plane that looked like a kid's toy.

"He does. Him and his brother," Suzanne told Felix. "Pretty cool, huh?"

"Are you calling me cool again?" Ben's laughing voice filled the little office as he swung through the door. Julie whirled around, her elbow slamming against the rack of flyers. It teetered backwards. She grabbed it to keep it from falling, and wound up with a handful of glossy brochures.

At the rattling noise made by the rack, Ben looked her direction. As soon as he spotted her, the smile instantly dropped from his face. His expression turned blank, the blue-gray of his eyes shifting from summer to bleak winter. He shoved his hands into the pockets of his flight jacket.

"I, uh...we should get going," Julie stammered. My God, he looked so furious with her. "Felix, come on."

But Felix wouldn't budge. He was staring at Ben. "You're the man in the plane. The one in the picture."

Ben relaxed enough to smile. At Felix, not at her, Julie noted. "That's me. Knight and Day Flight Tours."

"You're Ben. They were just talking about you."

Oh God, worse and worse. Julie's face felt like fire, she was blushing so hard. Luckily, Suzanne stepped into the awkward moment.

"I was just telling them what a great addition Knight and Day Flight Tours is to Jupiter Point. How did the flight with the Coopers go?"

Ben looked blank for a long moment, then laughed. "Chucky and his bride?"

Julie snorted. Ben had taken her to one of the *Chucky* movies once. But horror movies were not her thing, and she'd spent the entire time with her head buried in his side. He'd wrapped his coat around her and covered her ears at all the scary parts. When she couldn't take it anymore, she'd fled to the lobby. They'd gotten into a big fight that night because he'd thought the movie was ridiculous and hilarious, and she'd thought it was just plain horrifying.

Of course they'd made up. So it had all been worth it.

All those memories flitted through her mind in the brief moment between when Ben said "Chucky and his bride" and when he glanced in her direction. Right away, she saw that he was thinking of the exact same occasion.

Suzanne laughed. "I hope you didn't call them that to their faces. He could buy and sell Knight and Day about a hundred times over."

"No, he couldn't." Ben gave that gentle, stubborn smile that had always been Julie's favorite of his smiles. "Because we'd never sell to him." He shrugged. "The flight was just fine, if you don't count them making out in the Cessna."

Felix made a gagging sound. "Ew."

Ben laughed and reached down to offer Felix a high-five. "You said it, dude."

It seemed to happen in slow-motion, Ben's hand descending to touch Felix's palm. He didn't know anything about Felix, obviously. Didn't know that he was hostile to strangers, that he didn't like to be touched. He rarely even let Julie hug him. Only Savannah got that privilege.

Felix shied away before Ben's hand could reach him. He knocked into Julie, who stumbled backwards, causing the rack of flyers to teeter again.

Ben looked horrified and, more than that, confused. He snatched his hand back, then started forward as if trying to help, then jerked back again, as it occurred to him that more physical contact probably couldn't help the situation.

Instead, he brushed past Julie and stabilized the rack of flyers. A few fluttered to the floor. All along the side of her body closest to Ben, Julie felt his presence. Sweet fire swept across her, something she hadn't felt in so many years. Since the last time she'd seen Ben, actually.

"Are you okay?" he asked her.

She nodded, her heart pounding. "Yes. Sorry about—" She broke off. How to explain Felix's issues? She couldn't, not like this, not right in front of him. Besides, now she was lost in his eyes. For the first time since she'd gotten back, he was looking at her with concern, not scorn.

Felix's hand closed on her wrist. "I want to go, Julie." He tugged her toward the door.

Yeah, they should get out of there before he had a meltdown. Even at eleven, they still happened occasionally, and she could feel it coming.

"I'm sorry about the mess," she told Suzanne. Her glance flicked to Ben but it felt like looking into the sun. She couldn't do it for too long. He was too beautiful to her, and too lost.

"Seriously, don't worry about it. It's no big deal. Ben probably came with a new batch of flyers anyway, right, Ben?"

He nodded, offering her a smile. And in that tentative, gentle curve of his lips she saw the old Ben. The sensitive, thoughtful boy who had claimed her heart because he *saw* her when no one else did.

Then they were outside and the door of Stars in Your Eyes was closing firmly behind them. Julie freed her hand from Felix's grip. "Kiddo, take it easy. What's the big rush?"

"I don't like him," Felix declared. He marched down the brick sidewalk. Julie hurried after him.

"You mean Ben? He didn't know that you don't like to shake hands. How could he know something like that?"

"I don't care. I don't like him. He's mean."

"Well, I hate to say this, Kiddo, but you're wrong. Ben Knight is the last person in the world anyone could call mean."

On the other hand, he'd stood her up. He'd ignored the message she'd given to the Reinhards after she'd left, the one Priscilla had personally delivered to him, word for word. Julie had made her write it down just to make sure. So maybe he *was* mean.

Except he wasn't. She knew him down to his bones. He was the most caring and loving person she'd ever known.

She looked down at her hand and realized she still held a fistful of flyers, a blizzard of photos of Ben, staring right back at her with those eyes full of smiles.

"He was going to hit me."

"That was a high-five, Felix. And you know it was. I think you should give Ben another shot."

The stubborn set of his jaw didn't offer much chance of that.

Then again, did it matter? She and Ben had been over for about a thousand years. She sighed deeply as they passed one pretty storefront after another. On the bright side, Ben had spoken to her for the first time. He'd even smiled at her. She'd gone just as weak in the knees as ever.

On the other hand, she'd made a fool of herself, and Felix had decided he didn't like Ben.

She'd heard that Will Knight was out of town, but as soon as he returned, she'd meet with him and tell her story. In the meantime, she'd better go back to avoiding Ben.

5

HOW HARD COULD IT BE? JUPITER POINT WAS A SMALL TOWN IN feel, but it had a big enough population that it should be possible to avoid one particular person. Ben spent most of his time in the air, for heaven's sake. Avoiding him shouldn't be a problem.

Besides, Knight and Day Flight Tours was located outside city limits, on a stretch of grassland along the coastline. It was a good half an hour drive away, in a direction she never went. She could do this.

And yet somehow, she kept running into him.

She stopped in at the Fifth Book from the Sun to pick up a check from Mrs. Murphy, and there he was, in the Books About Nature aisle. He was looking for a book on local wildlife so he could work some more details into his flight tours.

She knew that because she'd slipped behind a shelf of mysteries, hoping he hadn't noticed her. Mrs. Murphy hovered near him, pointing out various books that would be helpful, and slipping in sneaky little questions between recommendations. It went a little bit like this:

"Now *this* book will tell you everything you need to know about the sea life around here. Speaking of sea life, have you been to Stargazer Beach lately? I remember how much time you spent there when Julie deGaia was a lifeguard."

Julie slapped her hand over her mouth to keep a spurt of laughter from bursting forth. Mrs. Murphy truly was a master of prying information from people.

She heard the laughter lurking in Ben's voice when he answered. "It's not really beach weather now, is it? But I heard we might have an early spring."

Pretty good deflection.

But this wasn't Mrs. Murphy's first rodeo. "Well, it's not spring yet, thank goodness. The Reinhards haven't even held their Winter Ball yet. By the way, have you heard their grandson is visiting? Have you met Felix yet?"

Wow. Truly masterful.

"Yes, very briefly," Ben answered. The laughter disappeared from his voice. She could tell he felt guilty about scaring Felix, even though it wasn't his fault. She should have explained her challenging godson's behavior, so Ben didn't take it personally. She could *still* do so, if only she had the guts to step out from behind the Mystery and Suspense aisle. But if she revealed herself now, it would be obvious she'd been hiding back there.

Instead she tiptoed backwards out of the shop and hurried down the street, wrapping her sweater tightly around her against the brisk breeze. It wasn't quite time to pick up Felix from school. She decided to stop at the Sky View Gallery and Espresso Bar for a quick shot of courage, since obviously she was sorely lacking in that department.

A beautiful silver-eyed woman smiled at her in greeting. "Julie deGaia, right? Remember me? Evie McGraw."

"Evie. Of course. Good to see you again." Drawn by Evie's warm, welcoming manner, she stepped toward the counter, which held a gleaming espresso machine with Italian writing on it. The gallery was filled with photographs ranging from local scenic panoramas and images taken by the observatory telescope, to honeymoon selfie-style shots. "Is this your place? It's beautiful."

"Thank you." She smiled proudly. "It's finally paying its own way, and I'm pretty proud of that. It was touch and go for a while. What can I get you?"

"An espresso would be perfect. I'm a big fan of speedy caffeinating."

"I hear that."

Julie took a stool and looked over her shoulder just in time to see Ben striding past, a few hardcover books gripped in one hand.

She quickly turned aside, hoping he hadn't spotted her.

Evie set a dainty white cup filled with foamy espresso on the counter in front of her. "Hiding out?" she asked sympathetically.

Busted. Julie took a sip of the invigorating liquid and let out a sigh. "I suppose you could call it that." Under Evie's sympathetic gaze, her defenses melted. "I intended to see Ben as soon as I came back, but I don't think he wants that. I got the hint pretty quickly. Now we're pretty much on the same page. Keep out of each other's way and no one gets hurt."

Except it did hurt. This was *Ben.* Her favorite person in the world back then.

"Hey, you don't have to explain anything to me," Evie said, wiping her hands on a towel. "I know how hard it can be facing a difficult situation. In my family, we have a long habit of avoiding uncomfortable things. It took me years to break free of it."

Julie eyed her over the edge of the cup. "What inspired you to make a change like that?"

"Well, keeping a secret can be crushing. After a while, it becomes harder to stuff it down than to let it out."

A lump formed in Julie's throat. *Exactly.* That was why she'd come back to Jupiter Point, after all.

"Also, I fell in love," Evie continued, smiling. "My husband is Sean Marcus. You might remember him. He's a hotshot now, so when he sees a crisis, he just plunges right in as if it were a wild-fire. He helped me find my own courage."

Feeling lonelier than ever, Julie tossed back the rest of her espresso shot. "Well, I think I'm on my own, and always will be, the way things are going." She set the cup down and paid with a five-dollar bill. "It's great to see you again, Evie. I might come back some time and browse for a photograph or two."

"Come back anytime."

On her way out, Julie glanced at the photos displayed on the simple cream walls of the gallery. And there he was *again*. In a photograph, piloting a plane. The photo was snapped from the backseat, so the only part of the pilot's face to be seen was the back of his head and the corner of his jaw, which was outlined against the bright blue sky outside the plane. But she knew it was Ben. She'd know him anywhere, in any context.

Was he haunting her? Was she going to see him around every corner in Jupiter Point?

She paused to look more closely at the photo. She had no pictures of Ben. When she'd left Jupiter Point, she hadn't intended to *move*. She'd assumed she'd be back as soon as Savannah didn't need her anymore. Then Savannah had fallen deep into post-partum depression, Felix had turned out to have issues, and then he'd gotten diagnosed, and they'd never stopped needing her. The Reinhards had eventually gotten rid of her things. And all she had left of Ben was her own memories.

If she was going to have a photo of Ben, this one would be perfect. His back was to her and he was flying away. It would be a good reminder that Ben was part of her past, not her present or future.

She turned to Evie, who was clearing her cup off the counter. "Evie, do you think I could put this photo on hold?"

If Evie was surprised, she didn't show it. "Sure thing. I'll give you a good price on it, too. Local discount."

"Thank you." Julie glanced at her watch, then hurried out of the Sky View to collect Felix from school.

LUCKILY, Felix was in a great mood. He'd been invited to a birthday party at the ice skating rink. Felix was a klutz on skates, but he loved the frosty air of a rink. He could spend hours slowly circling, clinging to the walls. Of course, Julie was thrilled to take him to the party. This was what he needed—a chance to connect with the kids here, to find out how different life was in a slower-paced town like Jupiter Point.

It was the last place she would have expected to see *Ben.*

But of course, with her luck, there he was, helping a dimpled little blond girl skate for the first time. The girl was younger than the kids at the party, and she and Ben were at the opposite end of the rink. Julie shrugged it off and focused on helping Felix with his skates, then assisting the birthday boy's mother in the snack room.

As she blew up balloons and taped up streamers, she kept an eye on Felix inching around the rink. When he drew close to Ben, the little girl spotted him. Smiling incandescently, she tried to skate toward Felix. Halfway to him, she fell on her butt and burst into tears.

Ben skated after her, then helped her up and brushed ice crystals off her snow pants. Felix watched the entire episode patiently. As soon as the girl stopped crying, he showed her his method of staying upright on skates.

Ben straightened to his full height and watched, arms crossed over his chest. From the snack room, Julie feasted her eyes on him. She didn't care about the vanilla buttercream cake. All she wanted was to watch Ben on the ice, the way he glided close to the two kids, dropping an instruction now and then, the way his wool sweater clung to his muscles, the way his jeans cupped his ass.

Her heart ached and she realized, crystal clear, that she was not over Ben. Not even close.

The birthday boy's mother—Candy—caught her looking. "That's one of the Knight brothers. I'm pretty sure he's the single one, too. I can handle things here if you want some rink time."

"No no. I'm good here." She picked up another balloon and blew air into it. *Stare at the red latex, not at the hot guy on the ice. Don't think about how adorable he is with that little girl.*

This was a serious problem. If she kept running into Ben like this, she'd be in love with him all over again in no time. These little glimpses of him in his real life, relaxed and casual, were torturous. In another world, he'd be giving *their* child skating lessons. It was the kind of life they'd always known they wanted, filled with ordinary, everyday joys.

But that world never came to be. Instead, she lived in this world, where she and Ben circled each other like planets whose orbits kept colliding.

Something had to give. She had to talk to him. But not here. Not when Felix was attending his first Jupiter Point birthday party.

The next time she ran into him, she'd definitely take the bull by the horns and initiate a *real* conversation. *"Hi, Ben,"* she'd say, *like a normal adult. "I was thinking we should get together and talk. We should be able to carry on a grownup conversation, right? Like maybe over a butterscotch sundae at the Milky Way like old times. No? Too nostalgic? Okay, how about we go to Neptune's Oasis, where I waited for three hours until I realized you'd stood me up?"*

Ugh. *Gah.* Why was this so hard?

She blew a little too hard on the balloon and it burst out of her hands. Zooming across the table, it narrowly missing the birthday cake. The air fizzed out of it with a high whine until it landed in a pile of red limpness on the floor. Honestly, she couldn't think of a better visual metaphor for her and Ben.

Maybe she shouldn't wait for Will to get back. She'd try the police first.

~

First thing the next morning, as soon as she'd dropped off Felix, she drove to the Jupiter Point Police Department. Before she could lose her nerve, she strode to the front desk, where a sergeant in uniform was fielding calls and logging in visitors.

She stared at the signup sheet, wondering how strict they were about names. "I was hoping to talk to Police Chief Becker," she told the sergeant.

He barely glanced at her. "He's on vacation. But if you want to file a police report, I'm your man."

Her heart sank. Why were the law-enforcement types around here so hard to pin down? "How long will he be gone?"

"Two weeks." Finally, he looked up. "We got a whole bullpen full of police officers here ready to serve and protect. What's this about?"

A door behind him opened, revealing a brief glimpse of a large open-plan room filled with desks and uniformed officers, some talking to each other, some on the phone.

How could she be *sure* they could be trusted?

No, she didn't want to talk to any of these police officers. Especially if she had to sign in. That was too public, too risky.

"I'll come back to see the police chief," she told the sergeant politely. She practically ran out of the station house to her car. Her heart was racing. The fear was still with her, she realized, even after all these years.

Her hands shaking slightly, she started her car and headed for work. She'd finally booked her second job in Jupiter Point. The manager of a condo complex had hired her to clean the lobby.

Fifteen minutes later, she had a dust rag in one hand and a bottle of natural lavender-and-vinegar glass cleaner in the other. As she sprayed down the large mirror, she heard footsteps rattling down the staircase, along with the sound of a whistle.

Are you kidding me?

She recognized that tuneless hiss. Ben was such a notoriously bad whistler that it had been a running joke between them. She'd claimed that everything he attempted sounded like Queen's "We Are the Champions." His whistling hadn't improved one bit in the past decade.

She glanced in a panic around the little foyer. The only place to hide would be behind a potted ficus. He'd spot her in a second. *Don't be such a coward*, she told herself fiercely. *Or such an idiot. It's just Ben.*

So, she straightened her spine and stood her ground as he burst through the door into the foyer. He saw her right away, pure surprise lighting his face. In what felt like no time, he took in her spray bottle, her dust rag.

Her face burned. Back in the old days, she'd had any number of dreams. Singing, songwriting, recording. Never once had she talked about cleaning lobbies for a living.

She opened her mouth to say hello, when someone else came through the door into the foyer. A woman wrapped her arms around Ben from behind.

"You win," she said, laughing. "I should know not to ever bet against those long legs of yours."

The woman was young and beautiful, with magenta-streaked hair and a skimpy workout top. Ben was wearing workout clothes, too, light cotton sweats and a Knight and Day t-shirt. They were on their way to jog, or hike, or bike. And the woman was touching Ben's chest and the muscles of his stomach.

Julie's own stomach turned over at the sight. She still remembered the feel of Ben's skin, so rough in some places, so tender in others.

But from the way the magenta woman was touching Ben, she knew a lot more about his body than Julie did.

Not surprising. She'd left Jupiter Point a virgin, after all.

"What are you doing?" Ben asked in surprise. "Do you work here?"

"Just a little light cleaning," she chirped, as if there was nothing more delightful than polishing mirrors. As a kind of punctuation, she waved the spray bottle. The tension coiled inside her transferred to her hand, and a spritz of cleaner erupted into the air. Right at the magenta girl's eye level.

She coughed, eyes watering, and waved the droplets away from her face. "Jesus. Blind a girl, why don't you?"

"I'm so sorry." Julie looked around for something to wipe her face with, but all she had was the dust rag. She held it toward her. "I've only used one side of this. Would you like to dab the cleaner off with the other? It's completely natural and nontoxic, don't worry. It's lavender. Practically like cologne."

The girl rubbed her face against Ben's t-shirt. "Uh, no thanks. I think I'll live. Ben, come on. That 5K isn't going run itself."

Ben was still staring at Julie, a puzzled look on his usually carefree face. "You're a cleaning lady?"

"See, that's a little bit sexist. If I was a man, would you call me a cleaning man? Or a cleaning gentleman? I prefer the term 'cleaner.' In fact, I own my own business, Green and Pristine. I even have employees back in LA." Jeez, why was she getting so defensive? Screw that. "Anyway, I've been hired to clean this foyer, and I'd better get on with it."

Especially because it would be the last time she cleaned it, that was for damn sure. No way was she going to take another chance on running into Ben in a way that put her at such a disadvantage.

"Well, it, uh, looks great," Ben said. She could tell he wasn't sure exactly what to say.

"Actually, you missed a spot." The magenta girl pointed at the mirror, where a grease mark blurred her reflection. She broke into a jog and grabbed his hand. "We gots to go, yo. Come on."

Ben gave Julie a helpless smile as he was dragged toward the exit.

She tried to smile back, but it didn't come out right. Of all the embarrassing ways to run into Ben, this was definitely one of the worst. Not that there was anything wrong with cleaning. But she was wearing a faded old bandanna around her head and her usual cleaning outfit of paint-stained coveralls and yellow rubber gloves. Charming.

After the two were gone, Julie returned to her work. As she dabbed viciously at the spot on the mirror, she glared at her own reflection. "Your life choices suck," she muttered to herself. "Weren't there any other professions handy? Why don't you just let Savannah pay for everything? Is her guilt money not good enough for you?"

The sound of a throat clearing made her jump around. Ben stood just inside the front door, clearly trying not to laugh. "I... ah...dropped my keys."

She gestured at the earbud dangling around her neck. Generally, she kept one in her ear, leaving the other ear free in case someone needed her attention. Right now, no music was playing, but he didn't need to know that. "Sorry, didn't hear you. I was, ah, singing along."

Better than talking to herself.

He nodded solemnly, as if he knew perfectly well she was covering. "Great. I always loved hearing you sing. I'm not surprised that you decided to go for it. Don't let me stop you."

She stared at him. *I'm not surprised you decided to go for it.* What the heck did that mean?

The magenta-haired girl poked her head around the front door. "You coming, Ben?"

No time to ask him. She put both ear buds in and focused her full attention on the mirror. Of course, he was there, too, his big frame reflected back at her.

In the mirror, Julie watched him bend down to pick up the keys. His strong thighs flexed, his t-shirt tugged against the long ridge of muscle along his side, and his ass made her mouth water.

Sweet Lord, he'd grown up fine.

Get a grip. Scrub, scrub. Bob her head to the pretend music. Smile vaguely as he jogged out the door. Inhale that familiar scent that was one hundred percent Ben. Sweetness and sweat, sneakers and fresh air, boy and man.

Oh God. She was so screwed.

6

FOR SOME REASON, BEN'S BLACK MOOD—THE ONE INSPIRED BY Julie's reappearance—lifted. Maybe it was because she was so obviously flustered every time she laid eyes on him. It was fairly adorable to watch her hide behind red balloons and non-functioning earbuds. Whatever was going on in her mind, it wasn't thoughts about what a loser he was, and how glad she was that she'd left him behind.

Meeting Felix had put things in an entirely different light. Was he special needs? Or simply a challenging, eccentric kid? A little of both or neither? In any case, they obviously had a close relationship. Watching her with Felix changed everything. It softened him toward her. He wanted to know more now, not from a place of hurt feelings, but from friendship. What had her life been like since she'd left Jupiter Point? How did Felix fit into it?

At the rate they were randomly running into each other, the perfect moment would arrive when he could have a civilized conversation with her.

But after all those chance encounters, he didn't see her for another week. Valentine's Day brought a flurry of tourists to Jupiter Point, and they all wanted to get airborne. Tobias was busy with his

48 JENNIFER BERNARD

new family, so Ben took on the bulk of the flights. When he wasn't in the air, he was holding interviews with mechanic candidates, or helping Moira train for her race, or working on new flyers, or trying to get their accounting system straightened out, or any one of the thousand details that went with starting a new business.

Not that he was complaining. This was what he'd dreamed of every day while he was in the Air Force. To come home, work for himself, and fly for the sheer joy of it. At the back of his mind, he'd also thought about starting a family. But he couldn't think about that now, not until he got this unfinished business with Julie taken care of.

But that was never going to happen if he didn't *see* her. She wasn't on social media. Suzanne refused to hand over her phone number without Julie's permission. He was completely dependent on a quirk of fate throwing them together. And after a couple weeks of running into her constantly, suddenly she was nowhere to be seen.

Maybe she'd left again.

That dark thought brought back his bad mood, to the extent that he even glowered at a couple celebrating their anniversary. Tobias caught him in the act and drew him aside.

"Dude. I'm the frowny one. Not you."

"Frowny?"

"Sarah's description. You get the point. It's your job to smile at the customers, because Lord knows it isn't mine. I thought we settled this."

Ben bared his teeth in a forced grin.

"Better. Still needs work, though. Hey, we're all going for pizza tonight. That ought to make you smile."

Tobias was right about that.

Being surrounded by his brothers always made Ben happy. Now that they were adding on partners—Merry and Carolyn—and more—Chase and Sarah—they didn't all fit into one booth at

Outer Crust Pizza. Instead, they pushed two tables together. The only one missing was Aiden, currently in the thick of his spring classes at Evergreen.

And Mom and Cassie, of course. And the permanently missing member of their family, Dad.

Sometimes Ben thought that Dad wasn't gone at all, because he was right there in the back of his thoughts. Times like these, when they were all together, Ben felt his presence even more powerfully.

They launched into a long, noisy discussion of which combination of pizzas to order. Half meat, half veggie? What about olives, loved by some, loathed by others? What about Carolyn, who liked to eat healthy and avoided cheese? What about Merry's dislike for mushrooms?

"I don't eat anything that could be described as a toadstool," she declared from her spot snuggled against Will's side.

Carolyn stage-whispered to Sarah, "Toadstool-gingerbread pizza, how does that sound?"

"Ewww," Sarah said, relishing her disgust. Ben was amazed by how well she was adapting to her new life, after spending the first seven years of her existence in a wacko compound run by a militia group. Carolyn and Tobias had gone into the compound to rescue her. Ben had flown the chopper up the coast in case they needed a quick getaway, and so he'd actually been the one to whisk Sarah, and several other kids, away from the Light Keepers. That experience had bonded them forever.

Chase took charge of the pitcher of beer and filled glasses for anyone interested. Ben accepted one and took a long swallow. "How was Vegas?" he asked.

Chase startled. "What do you mean?"

"I mean, how did it go?"

"Oh. Pretty good." Uncharacteristically, he said no more. Ben glanced over at Merry for help, but she shrugged.

"I've tried prying the story out of him, but I got nowhere. And if *I* can't make him talk, no one can."

A wave of ruddy red crept up Chase's cheeks. "There's no story," he muttered.

Will snorted, and Chase turned on him. "You said you wouldn't tell!"

Will threw up his hands in a defensive gesture. "Did I say anything?"

"I heard a sound," Chase muttered.

With a roll of his eyes, Will took a glass of beer from Chase. "The good news is, our client is safe and sound. The bad news is, Chase has lost his damn mind."

The server arrived, ready with a notepad. Tobias beckoned him over. "No one can agree what to order, so I'm taking charge here." He rattled off a list of pizzas that miraculously seemed to cover all the possible contingencies.

As he was wrapping up, Sarah climbed onto her knees on her seat so she could see over Chase's head. "There's that boy! From the ice skating!"

Ben turned to look, his gaze arrowing in on the woman who had just walked in. The bells over the door were still jingling, her cheeks still pink from the outdoor air. Her hair was loose around her shoulders, a knit cap keeping it from her face. She wore a cozy red-and-black plaid wool jacket that made him think of curling up in front of a fire in a cabin in the woods.

Maybe naked.

His cock stirred as that vision took shape. She'd stretch out nude on the blankets, all pink and flushed. He'd keep her warm, every inch of her, with his hands and tongue and...oh hell.

Stop it. Just stop. Public place here.

Felix was a half-step ahead of her, bundled up in a sheepskin-lined jacket. He looked over at their table because Sarah was calling his name, but his glasses were fogged from the steamy warmth. It fell to Julie to wave at them, then tap Felix's shoulder to encourage him to do the same. The boy took off his glasses, then carefully took out a piece of cloth from his jacket pocket and cleared the lenses.

He really was a character, this kid.

When he saw Sarah, who was now standing on her chair, grinning at him excitedly, he smiled back and headed toward them.

Julie hesitated. She scanned the table, obviously daunted by the group of Knight brothers and company. For a quick flash, he saw things from her perspective. Will and Tobias used to treat her like a little sister, but what did they think of her now? And the rest of the group were strangers to her.

As for him? They had yet to have a normal conversation.

Maybe this was their chance.

With an out-of-body sensation, Ben rose to his feet. "Come on over, Julie. Meet the crew."

She pulled her lower lip between her teeth, still hesitant. Her eyes shone bright against her flushed cheeks. And a visceral memory came over him of the first time they kissed. He remembered exactly how fresh and tender her lips tasted. It was behind the lifeguard shack at the beach. She'd worn her regulation lifeguard swimsuit, which had revealed just a shadow of cleavage that drove him absolutely mad with lust...

He'd brought her a soda and a bag of barbecued corn chips, because she was a junk food addict at that point. Since her mother cooked obsessively healthy meals for the Reinhards, Julie rarely got a chance to eat junk. Nothing made her happier than a surprise gift of completely nutrition-free food.

She'd grinned and accepted his gift with a hug. The sensation of her sun-warmed skin was like an injection of adrenaline into his veins.

"What are you doing here, Knight?" At that point, they weren't yet boyfriend and girlfriend. They were "hanging out." Which he loved and hated. They joked and talked and even shared a few secrets. But she had those pretty legs, and those breasts, and that skin, and those lips, and he lusted after her hard.

So, he'd leaned forward and touched his mouth to hers, as if it was pre-ordained. Destined. The sweet sweep of his flesh against hers filled his senses. A quick draw of breath echoed in his ears, amplified by the blood roaring through his veins. Her breath? A gasp? Had he gone too far? Ruined everything?

Almost afraid to know, he opened his eyes. She was staring at him, mouth open, touching her lips with her fingertips. "You kissed me."

"Yeah," he said cautiously. "Is that...are you...I'm sorry..."

"I thought you liked Savannah."

"*Savannah?* Why did you think that?" He was almost insulted. Ever since he'd met Julie, he'd barely remembered that Savannah existed.

"Because she's..." She flapped her hand, chasing the thought away. "It doesn't matter." She lifted her chin and leaned toward him. "Will you do that again? It's so much nicer than I even imagined."

He laughed a little, thrills of joy racing through him. "So, you imagined kissing me?"

"Um, yes. A few times. Now shut up and let's try it again. But like, longer this time."

So, they kissed longer, and deeper, and it was amazing and arousing and maddening and satisfying, all at once. After that, they were officially boyfriend and girlfriend.

Until she left.

Ben shook off the memory in time to see Tobias introducing her to everyone at the table. She smiled at everyone, then said, "And this is Felix Reinhard. I think someone here already knows him, right?"

Sarah jumped with happiness. "I do! I do! He helped me skate. What kind of name is Felix?"

"It means 'happiness,'" Felix said stoically. "But there's also

Felix the Cat. A lot of people know about him. It's kind of a stupid name because I'm not a happy kind of person."

Ben's eyes flew to meet Julie's, because that's what the two of them had always done. They'd always shared jokes and found the same things funny. Julie caught her lip between her teeth and amusement filled her eyes.

"You're not happy?" Sarah sounded amazed by that concept. "Why not?"

"Just not. I'm in a bad mood a lot."

Julie stepped in. "Felix is a very honest person. Sometimes he's happy and sometimes he isn't. But he's always himself, and that's a good thing."

Sarah's forehead creased as she worked that concept through her mind. "I know how you can be happy!" She turned to Ben, who braced himself for whatever madcap idea she'd suddenly come up with. "Let's take him on a plane ride!"

"Uh, sure. Anytime. But that's probably up to the parent-in-charge." He lifted an eyebrow at her. Hopefully she could tell that he'd be perfectly happy to take her—them—up for a ride. But he didn't want to exert any pressure, especially considering how Felix had responded to him last time.

Julie looked down at Felix, who twisted his body around to stare up at her. "Would I like it?" he asked her.

She shrugged. "I guess there's only one way to find out. But we'd hate to impose on you, Ben, and—"

"No," Ben interrupted before she could go too far in her bowing-out-gracefully process. "I'd love to take you up. Both of you. All of you. Bring the whole family. Name the day and I'll put it in the calendar."

"That's very generous of you. We'll talk about it, Felix and I. I'll have to get Savannah's permission."

Sarah was so excited that she launched into a long description of her helicopter ride. She kept asking Ben to back her up on the details, so he almost missed a brief conversation between Julie and Will.

"There's something important I need to talk to you about," she told Will quietly, under cover of the general chatter. "Can I come to your office sometime this week?"

Ben didn't catch the rest of their conversation, but he knew one thing for sure. He intended to be at that meeting, no matter what.

7

To Julie's amazement, Felix threw himself into the idea of venturing up in the air in one of the small planes they'd seen in the flyer. It was all he could talk about the next night at dinner at the Reinhards' sprawling Tudor-style estate in the foothills at the edge of town.

Every time Julie brought Felix here, her stomach filled with butterflies. So many memories—the flagstone terrace where she and Savannah used to do their homework, the little cottage where she'd lived with her mom, the woods filled with birch and pine. She knew every inch of the property except for the Reinhards' private quarters, where she was never allowed.

Adam and Priscilla Reinhard were a "power couple" who owned houses in Jupiter Point, the Bahamas, and Dallas. He was an investor, she was a marketing genius, both were lean and sleek and sharp-eyed as sharks. They'd always been generous to Julie and her mother, but she'd never felt comfortable with them. Even as a teenager, and Savannah's best friend, she'd sensed the distance they liked to put between them and those with less money. Not only that, but their generosity came with strings. Julie was expected to help the new cook, clean up after parties, run errands, and so forth. She'd never minded, because without the Reinhards, she would have been adrift after her mother died.

But now, as an adult, it didn't feel right. She'd chosen to stay close to Savannah and Felix. That didn't mean she was his nanny, or some kind of paid caretaker. Yet sometimes she felt that way around the Reinhards.

Like now.

"Have you contacted Savannah about this?" Priscilla asked from the foot of the 1840s Victorian dining table. She had a passion for antiques, in a good investment kind of way.

"I will, of course, but she trusts my judgment when it comes to Felix."

A server came in with a platter of rare, juicy roast beef, its rich scent making Julie's mouth water. When her mother had cooked for the Reinhards, Priscilla had tried every diet from macrobiotic to paleo. So far, this meal seemed fairly normal.

"The idea of Savannah being the final say on anyone's judgement is debatable," Adam Reinhard said in his wry way. His illness had turned his face gaunt and colorless, but he still had every ounce of his acerbic manner. Julie was starting to suspect his ailment wasn't that serious, he was just using it as an excuse to get Felix to visit.

"You shouldn't say mean things about my mom." Felix forked a piece of roast beef into his mouth and chewed in the sloppy way he knew his grandmother despised.

"I've known Savannah a lot longer than you have." Mr. Reinhard always hit back when he felt attacked, no matter the age of his *attacker*. "And if you think that was mean, the ladies have been spoiling you."

Felix stared stonily back at him.

Julie cleared her throat. "I looked at the school schedule, and I think the best day for the flight would be this Saturday. That's only a few days away, Felix. We can spend that time learning everything we can about Cessnas."

"I already started. It's a 206, and it holds six people, including the pilot. It has a flight range of five hundred and sixty-three nautical miles and a cruising speed of one hundred and forty-four knots," Felix rattled off.

They all stared at Felix, while Julie hid a smile. The Reinhards weren't used to Felix's thirst for knowledge yet. When he glommed onto something that interested him, he soaked in details and information like a human supercomputer.

"Six people, you said?" Priscilla asked. "Well then, plenty of room for us as well."

Adam looked at her askance. "Us? Are you referring to you and me?"

"We'll make it a family outing," she declared. Her black hair was now cut in a bob, with one dramatic silver streak allowed to remain.

"I'll have to check with Knight and Day," Julie began, before Priscilla interrupted again.

"I'm sure Ben Knight will be happy to accommodate you." She added just enough emphasis on "you" to make Julie flush.

"This invitation didn't come from Ben. It came from Sarah Moore, Ben's niece. Or sister-in-law, or something along those lines. I'm not entirely sure of the connection. At any rate, she and Felix have struck up a sort of friendship, right, Felix?"

But Felix had now checked out of the discussion. He was probably dismayed at the thought of the Reinhards joining them.

She tried again. "It might be less stressful if it was just me and Felix."

"Ben will be there, correct?" Priscilla nodded briskly. "I'd feel more comfortable keeping an eye on things. With all the baggage between you two, I'm not confident it's safe."

"Baggage? Plane? Good one." Adam gave a bark of laughter.

Julie gave her a puzzled frown. "Ben was a pilot in the Air Force. I'm sure it's perfectly safe."

"Nonetheless, I think it's best. You'd like to get out, right,

Adam, now that you're feeling better?" Priscilla didn't wait for his answer. "It's settled, then."

Julie forced a smile at the older couple. The Reinhards were used to getting what they wanted, which was often annoying. But maybe this plane flight would be a good way for them to connect with Felix, which was her purpose for being here, after all. "Saturday, then. It'll be fun."

Well, maybe. At any rate, with more people around, maybe she'd have less chance of embarrassing herself in front of Ben. Maybe.

BACK AT THE tiny apartment she'd rented, Felix dove into more Cessna research while Julie took a quick shower. The streaming water gave her the sense of being swept back in time by a fast-moving river. Spending time at the Reinhards brought back so many intense memories.

Her mother had been a free-spirit gypsy type who'd used her cooking skills wherever she wandered. But once Julie reached the age of ten, Mom had decided they needed to be in one place. The job with the Reinhards had seemed perfect. When she and her mother had first moved in, Julie had been terrified of the Reinhards. She'd stayed away from the big house and played in the woods by herself, climbing trees and making up adventure stories.

Then one day, when she was eleven and Savannah was twelve, Savannah had "run away from home," which meant fleeing into the woods in tears. She'd wound up huddled under one of Julie's favorite fir trees, near the tree fort Julie had created from fallen branches and moss. So Julie had invited her in. From then on, they'd been best friends. The Reinhards didn't like it at first, but when they discovered that Savannah was a lot happier with a playmate, they relaxed and gave Julie the run of the estate.

She tagged along for tennis lessons, piano lessons, country club outings.

Then came Ben, which was the first serious setback in Julie and Savannah's friendship. But since Savannah always had boys in love with her, and she'd seen Ben as basically a new toy, they got past it. Then Julie's mother had died just before Julie's junior year. Right away, Savannah had vowed that Julie would always have a home with them, her parents be damned.

Julie had passed through that year in a blur—leaning on Ben during her grief—and then had come that panicked call from Savannah.

Which led to the end of her and Ben. Forever.

She turned off the water and toweled dry, squeezing the water from her hair. Thinking about Ben made her stomach cramp. And it made even more memories come flooding back.

Ben had been so sweet when her mother died. He'd held her and let her cry. He'd made her a big card with snapshots and little quotes of things Mom used to say. He'd helped her write the eulogy for the small church service, and made sure all their friends went. He made contact with her mother's family back in South Carolina. He'd even called her father for her. Her father worked for the Coast Guard in Alaska, and she hadn't seen him in years. He'd awkwardly offered to move her up there.

That had at least made her smile.

Ben had done *so much*. He was amazing. She always figured it was because he was so close to his own mother. He knew how to be *there* without being annoying.

This was bullshit, this not talking and avoiding each other. Ben was too important in her life. She had to talk to him.

Before she could think about it too much, she wrapped herself in a bathrobe and went to find her bag. On her cell phone, she looked up the number of Knight and Day. This late, she doubted that he'd be there, but she could at least leave a message.

"Knight and Day, Ben speaking," he answered. His voice had

deepened since she'd been gone. It had more of a sexy edge to it, a playful baritone that sent pleasurable shivers up her spine.

"Um, hi, Ben. It's Julie."

A shocked pause followed. "Hey, Julie."

She couldn't read his tone at all. Damn it, why had she done such a boneheaded thing as to call him? Now that he was on the phone, she didn't know where to start. *I used to love you so much? I missed you? You're so sexy it physically hurts me to look at you?*

Uh, no. "I'm calling about the flight tour. Sarah's invitation."

"Right." Had his tone cooled a bit? She couldn't tell. "Did you figure out a good time? I'll check the books."

"Saturday. Anytime you have open will be fine. But there's something else, Ben."

It was strange how his name felt so right in her mouth. "Problem?"

"It's the Reinhards. They want to come along."

"Ah." Ben had no big love for the Reinhards, she knew. They'd always been standoffish with him. "Well, with Sarah, Felix, you, me and the two of them, we'll have just enough seats. That should be fine."

"Great. Well. I guess we'll see you Saturday."

"See you then." He hung up.

Tears started in Julie's eyes. Oh my God, so *awkward*. Would they ever be able to have a normal conversation? Her hand hovered over the phone. There was so much she wanted to say to Ben. Too much for a phone call. But maybe she could call back and arrange a time to talk. Make an official "date."

Or maybe an "appointment" would be a better term.

She quickly dialed again, but this time she did get the answering machine. "You've reached Knight and Day Flight Tours. Please leave a message."

Leave a message, leave a message... Hi Ben. This is Julie again. I can't stand the fact that we can't even talk to each other. You were my best friend, the only boy I've ever really loved, and I'm so sorry for leaving the way I did, and if you could only understand what happened, I think you'd forgive me, so please can we get together and talk? And by the way, every time I look at you, my heart does this funny flipping thing and I want to touch you so badly it's a miracle I haven't thrown myself into your arms by now.

Yeah, at least he'd get a laugh out of that. Maybe Magenta Girl would get a few chuckles out of it too. Or Tobias, if he was the one who picked up the message.

Just in case she got too tempted, she buried her phone under her pillow and went to play video games with Felix. And get her ass kicked, of course.

8

Friday night, Ben went to Barstow's Brews and played pool with some of the Jupiter Point Hotshots and local firefighters. Moira showed up, celebrating her top-five finish in the 5K. He bought her a beer to celebrate, then maneuvered things so she wound up in a conversation with one of the firefighters. His attraction to her was gone, but he didn't know how to tell her so. Hopefully, she'd appreciate the fine and studly qualities of Luke McCarthy.

No such luck. On his way back from the restroom, she cornered him. "Where's my congratulations kiss?" she purred, pressing against him.

He bent down to kiss her on the cheek, but she turned her head so their lips met. Instantly, he drew back. "Sorry, Moira. This isn't going to work."

"It's your ex, isn't it? The one who squirted me with her little spray bottle?"

"That was an accident, and there's no need to bring her into it anyway. This is about us. You're great, but the connection just isn't there. You must feel it too."

"I don't even know what you're talking about. You're hot, I'm hot, we like the same things. That's a connection."

He looked down at her. She was gorgeous, her hair gleaming deep red in the low light, her toned body poured into a tight sweater and jeans. "I just don't think that's enough, Moira. There's still something missing."

"Yes, and I know exactly what it is. Sex. We should sleep together and *then* talk about whether or not we have a connection."

A month ago, he probably would have agreed. Hell, if he'd met Moira a month ago, they'd probably already have slept together. He found her plenty attractive and easy to be with. Good jogging companion.

But that didn't make a "connection." Maybe Moira had never experienced the kind of relationship he'd had with Julie, that soul-deep, life-changing kind of love.

This was all Julie's doing. Julie's return had brought all of those feelings back—or at least the memory of them. It wasn't about sex, that was for sure. He and Julie had never gotten that far. They wanted to, had planned to, but then her mother had died and their relationship had shifted. He'd become her protector, her support system.

"I'm sorry," he repeated. "I'd rather be clear now than have things get messy later."

She took a step back, her hands lingering on his chest. "You're going to regret this. That fireman's ready to take me home right now."

"You should go for it. Luke's a good guy."

It finally seemed to sink in that he was serious. Her face fell, and she let her hands come away from his chest. "Fine. But you should at least stop lying to yourself. This *is* about your ex. I saw the way you looked at her, and the way she looked at you."

"What way? Like she wanted to spray me with Windex?" He frowned, remembering only that Julie had looked rattled when he'd surprised her in the foyer. Also, she'd looked adorable with her hair bundled into a bandanna and yellow rubber gloves covering her hands.

"I honestly can't describe it." She fluffed her hair around her face. "But you'd better figure it out or your sex life is going to suck. Bye, Ben." She flitted off down the hallway.

Ben shoved his hands in his pockets and stared at the floor.

His sex life already sucked. At least it had since Julie showed up. What happened to the lighthearted, easy-come-easy-go Ben Knight who'd been flirting happily with the single girls of Jupiter Point? And before that, the girls who hung out around every Air Force base he'd spent time at?

He knew what had happened. *Julie.* Julie had shown up, and now he knew he'd been fooling himself. He wasn't really a player, not deep down. Deep down, he wanted to fall in love for real. The way he had with Julie.

But with someone else, not her. Because he was completely over her. And even if he weren't—which of course he was...had been and still was—how could he ever trust her again?

SATURDAY DAWNED BRIGHT AND CLEAR, with a slight west wind at about 5 knots per hour. Ben showed up early at the airstrip and did a quick cleanup of the office. Maybe he should hire a cleaning lady. Correction, "cleaner." He knew a good one, in fact.

But why was Julie working as a cleaner? What happened to her singing dreams? Wouldn't LA be the perfect place to pursue a songwriting career? Wasn't that the reason she'd left Jupiter Point? What had gone wrong?

There were so many questions he wanted to ask her. And now that she was on her way, with the Reinhard clan in tow, he wished they'd already cleared the air.

The group arrived in the Reinhards' Rolls Royce, which looked completely out of place in the gravel lot of the airstrip. Mrs. Reinhard descended from the vehicle like some kind of disdainful queen. She surveyed Knight and Day's tiny fleet through dark sunglasses, making him feel embarrassed that it was such a small operation.

Ben drew in a breath and went to greet them. He shook hands with Mr. and Mrs. Reinhard, but was careful not to make any movement toward Felix. The kid was too fascinated by the sight of the freshly washed 206 perched on the tarmac to give him a glance.

Julie extracted herself from the car last. She wore jeans tucked into boots, and a long sweater belted around her waist. Her hair was pulled into a ponytail, and she too wore sunglasses. But at least she smiled at him as he helped her out of the Rolls.

The touch of her palm against his was electric.

He addressed the little group. "Tobias is bringing Sarah, she should be here any minute. She wants to give Felix the grand tour, so how about some coffee while we wait?"

They all trooped after him into the little reception office, which smelled like coffee from the Keurig.

"Ben!" Julie exclaimed as soon as they went through the door. "You've done such an amazing job in here. Did you guys fix it up yourselves?"

Trust Julie to know the way to his heart. Knight and Day was his pride and joy. "Sean Marcus and the hotshots did a lot of work on it before we bought the place. It was basically abandoned for years, and it was a mess. But then my brothers and I took over after that. I'm glad you like it."

"It's incredible. It really is. Isn't that sign great, Felix?" Their logo, rendered in full color on a big hand-painted sign, consisted of a knight in armor riding a plane.

Felix wasn't quite as impressed. "I want to see the planes," he said. "What kind of engines do they have?"

"Oh Felix, don't pester him," said Mrs. Reinhard.

Ben shook his head. His fascination with planes had begun around Felix's age, though he'd been restricted to the wooden model planes his father had ordered for him online.

"It's fine. I'll take Felix into the hangar and show him a few things. You guys can relax here."

The Reinhards perched on the guest chairs, looking not at all relaxed.

"I'll come with you," Julie said, with a quick glance at Felix. Ben got the message; she still wasn't sure if Felix had accepted him.

He led the way outside to the hangar, where the Piper Matrix was currently awaiting a maintenance check. "In answer to your question, Felix, the 206 has a Continental O-520 engine. This plane here, the Piper Matrix, has a two thousand hour TBO Lycoming. We're probably going to sell the Piper, since it's more of a commuter plane. Hunter McGraw wants to buy it." He turned to Julie. "You remember Hunter, right? He married Starly Minx, the pop star, and they go back and forth from here to LA a lot. This rig would be perfect for them."

"We live in LA," said Felix.

"Yeah, I heard that. Maybe you guys can get a plane too."

"We're not staying here," he said firmly. "It's too boring."

Ben's heart dipped. Why had he thought that Julie might be staying? It seemed so right for her to be here. In the back of his mind, he'd assumed they had plenty of time to work things out.

He glanced at Julie, who was shooting him a wry look.

"Felix is still warming up to Jupiter Point. But I think it's growing on him."

"Maybe he just needs to see it from the air." Ben grinned at the kid, who gazed solemnly back at him.

"I do like the ice skating rink," he said, very serious. "When is Sarah coming?"

"I'm here! I'm here!" Sarah came bounding into the hangar.

She grabbed Felix's arm and tugged him toward the tarmac. "Come see the helicopter that rescued me."

Ben noticed that the boy didn't seem to mind Sarah's touch quite as much, though he still stiffened. The two kids disappeared out of the hangar, and finally, he and Julie were alone.

"Thank you for doing—"

"I'm glad you guys came—"

They both spoke at once, then laughed. Ben shoved his hands in his pockets and breathed in the comforting smell of fuel oil and hand cleanser that permeated the hangar. This was his home turf. His comfort zone. His little kingdom. Nothing could hurt him here, not even an awkward moment with the former love of his life.

"Felix is really excited, even though he doesn't show it the same way other kids might." Julie fiddled with the end of her belt, and he realized she felt just as awkward as he did. To put her at ease, he reached for her arm and gave it a comforting squeeze.

Mistake.

The feel of her body brought too many lost emotions rushing back. He snatched his hand back. "Sorry."

"No. Please, don't be sorry. I mean, I should be sorry. I *am* sorry. Ben, we need to talk—"

He took a step away, his back bumping up against the Piper Matrix. This didn't seem like the best moment for talking. Touching her arm had rattled him, and he was about to have six lives, including his own, in his hands. If *thoughts* of Julie had been distracting him in the air, what would *actual* Julie do? "How about some other time," he muttered.

A quick wince flashed across her face. "Oh sure, I didn't mean now. I just...there's a lot to say. And the longer we wait, the harder it gets."

"It's waited twelve years; how much harder could it be?" He meant the words lightly, but they didn't come out that way. They came out harsh and edgy.

She flinched, and cinched her belt tighter. "Ouch Maybe this isn't such a good idea after all."

And then—ridiculously—he hated that she was backing out of it. "What isn't, talking? Flying? Coming back to Jupiter Point? Acting like you didn't walk out on me when I needed you most? Pretending like everything's normal? You're going to have to be more specific."

Her face went white, and he instantly felt like the biggest ass in the world. Why was he getting so hot and bothered? He was *over her*. None of this should matter to him anymore. "Sorry," he muttered.

She opened her mouth, but nothing came out. Her gaze dropped to the floor. He followed her glance. Concrete stained with old diesel, scuff marks. "Don't be," she whispered. "I guess I deserve that."

No, she didn't. Or maybe she did. He didn't know anymore. A stew of emotions boiled inside him, turning his stomach. Anger —*so much anger*. He thought he was through with that. He'd worked it out in basic training, at the flight academy, in long pounding sessions at the gym, in hundreds of late-night study sessions. But it wasn't just anger haunting him...there was plenty of hurt, too. Not to mention confusion.

What had he ever done to deserve the way she'd treated him?

But still, the stunned look on her face tore at him. This was still Julie, no matter what she'd done twelve years ago. Before, he never would have spoken to her in such a nasty way.

Then again, *before*—he wouldn't have wanted to, because he loved and trusted Julie with all his heart.

Not anymore.

When he looked up, she was studying him closely. "You've changed, haven't you?"

"Of course I've changed. I grew up. Stopped believing in fairy tales."

Stopped believing in love—that was what he really meant.

Stopped believing in miracles, in happy endings, in "everything's going to be okay." Of course everything wasn't going to be okay. Just look at all the terrible things that had happened. How could that *ever* be okay?

She smiled sadly. "There's one fairy tale I believe in. 'Humpty Dumpty.' All the king's horses and all the king's men, couldn't put Humpty Dumpty back together again. I have a feeling that's us, Ben."

Before he could protest the idea of comparing their relationship to a giant talking humanoid egg, Mr. Reinhard charged into the hangar.

"What's the holdup here? If we don't get this show on the road, Felix is going to be taking over the controls himself."

Julie jumped at the interruption with a look of relief, and hurried to join Mr. Reinhard.

Ben took a moment to compose himself, scrubbing his hand across the back of his neck and letting out a long whoosh of breath. Pilot. Flying. Cessna. Happy place. No distractions. Got it.

9

JULIE STUMBLED OUT OF THE HANGAR IN A STATE OF SHOCK. OF course Ben was angry at her. He had every right to be. But the look in his eyes—the sheer hurt and betrayal—was far beyond what she'd ever imagined. It was almost as if...

She turned to Mr. Reinhard. "This may come out of left field, but do you remember when Savannah and I first called you from LA, and I gave you a message to deliver to Ben? You never told me what he said in response. Do you happen to remember?"

"Message? Sorry, I'm drawing a blank. That was what...ten, twelve years ago?" He gave her a distracted look, more occupied with Priscilla's arrival than their exchange. She was striding toward them across the tarmac, her heels clicking. "Pris, Julie's asking about some message for Ben, back when Savannah pulled her runaway act."

Priscilla's sharp eyes slid past her. "I have a message for him right now. I'm tired of waiting for him, and I'm tired of hearing every tiny fact about Cessnas from that brilliant grandson of ours. Is he coming?"

Julie stared at the other woman. Had she deflected on

purpose? Was she hiding something? Or just being her typical impatient self?

Before she could ask again, Ben joined them, all business, and quickly got everyone onboard the Cessna and buckled into their seats.

"Felix, you want the right seat? That's where the copilot would sit, if we had one. So I guess that's you today, buddy."

Felix's face lit with delight. Ben helped him with the harness, which meant he had to make some physical contact, though he clearly tried to keep it to a minimum. Julie watched closely, but caught no sign of distress from Felix. Ben had such an easy manner with him, but then again, he did with everyone.

No point in heading down that road, she reminded herself. For the first time, she'd gotten a look past Ben's lighthearted manner and seen how much pain she'd caused him. She was foolish to think that a few words of apology could make up for that. She'd been foolish to come back to Jupiter Point. She and Felix should leave tomorrow, or as soon as the Reinhards had had enough family bonding.

Ben flicked switches and watched the instruments as he spoke into his mic, communicating with an air traffic control tower somewhere. With every action, he explained to Felix what he was doing. He pointed out the yoke, the rudder controls, the throttle. Her godson soaked in every bit of information like a solemn sponge.

He also did his share of showing off. "That's the altimeter, that Garmin 530 is the GPS, that's the air speed indicator, that's the external temperature gauge."

"I thought this was your first time in a small plane." Ben sounded appropriately impressed.

"It is. I studied an instrument diagram."

"Nice. Well, pictures are great, but there's nothing like the real thing in action. You ready?"

Felix nodded seriously. His entire body quivered with excitement.

Ben taxied into position at the end of the runway, then executed a little circle. "That's mostly a formality to make sure no other planes are around," he explained. "All set for takeoff, folks." He added power and the plane cruised down the runway, picking up speed. The entire craft rattled and shook. Julie clutched the edges of her seat and held her breath.

"Here we go." Ben eased the yoke back as the plane gained speed and they lifted into the air.

An incredible feeling filled her up. *Free.* That was how it felt. Free from troubles, free from demands, free from gravity. She laughed exultantly as the low-lying meadows tilted away, replaced by sparkling waves, then the coastline, then a bright flash of sun in her eyes, bluer than blue sky, then sweet puffs of clouds.

"This is amazing!" She shouted into her headset, forgetting that she had no need to yell over the engine noise. They could all hear each other perfectly well through their headsets.

Ben chuckled in response, and for that one moment, they were perfectly in tune. Even though she was in the farthest backseat, along with Sarah, and Ben was all the way up front, they may as well have been alone in the sky. She felt as if he were right there with her, in her ear, in her head, laughing with the same joy that filled her.

New words and melodies came into her head. She hummed them to herself, chasing down the notes as if they were butterflies she was trying to capture in a net. It took all her concentration, and everything else faded away, even Ben.

Da-da-dee, da-da-dum...da dee... She was so enraptured with the bright rush of sky and clouds and waves and music that she almost missed the fact that something was wrong.

Then Mr. Reinhard's tense voice cut through her happy

trance. She blinked back to reality and saw that he was leaning forward, his hand on Felix's shoulder.

"Get a grip on yourself, little man."

Felix was whimpering. Why was Mr. Reinhard touching him? Didn't he know not to do that uninvited? It always made things worse.

Ben seemed to understand. He reached over and pushed the older man's hand away. "Please sit back in your seat," he told him sternly.

"But he's acting like a baby. Felix, stop it. This minute!"

Julie craned her neck, trying to see what was wrong, what the hell was happening. "What is it?" she called. Why did she have to be so far away from Felix? If only she could be in the middle seat, where she could handle the situation.

She tried again. "Ben, what's wrong?" Next to her, Sarah was also talking into the comm, saying things like, "Felix, are you scared? Don't worry, we won't crash." Which was fine, except that Julie couldn't get her own words to be heard through the din. And the worst thing for Felix was too much sensory input. Too much noise, too much light, too much touch—all things that could tip him over the edge.

She started to pull off her seat belt, determined to scramble over the Reinhards so she could reach Felix. But then Ben's firm, commanding voice cut through the noise.

"I'm going to need everyone to calm down and *stop talking*. That means you, Sarah. Right now."

The little girl snapped her mouth shut. Julie was about to ask again what was going on, but Ben forestalled her. "I got this, Julie. Stay put."

She bit her lip, tears of worry stinging her eyes.

Mr. Reinhard spoke again. "I will not have my grandson making a scene—"

And then her headset went quiet. Ben must have cut the comms. The hum of the plane was all Julie could hear. She watched Ben smile at Felix, watched her godson's green face tilt desperately toward him. Ben pulled an air sickness bag from between the seats and deftly flicked it open one-handed. Felix grabbed it and, with a huge convulsion, heaved the contents of his stomach into it. The sour smell of vomit filled the plane. Followed by the scent of urine.

Oh God. The poor kid.

BEN CUT the trip short after that disaster. As soon as they stepped onto the tarmac, the Reinhards began their apologies. Ben walked around the plane, putting chocking the wheels.

"Never have I been so embarrassed," Priscilla began.

"Believe me, we'll be having a few words with the boy," added Adam.

Felix, still queasy, scuffed one foot on the tarmac. He hadn't said a word since he'd emptied his stomach on the plane. Sarah hovered anxiously next to him, but he wouldn't look at her. Felix was an unusual boy in many respects, but he was just as easily shamed as any other kid. When he was younger, an incident like this could trigger a meltdown. *Please, Lord, no meltdown.* Not here.

"It could happen to anyone," Julie reassured him. "That's why planes have airsickness bags. It's nothing to be ashamed of."

Felix stared at the ground, refusing to respond.

Ben ducked under the wing. "She's right. Remember the first time I went up, Julie?"

Not really, but she went with it, for Felix's sake. "It was a disaster, right?"

"Yeah, the only good thing about it is we didn't crash. That's been my motto ever since. If you don't crash, it was a good trip."

"That's a kind way of looking at it, but he peed his pants. We'll compensate you for the cleaning bill, of course—"

Ben waved that off. "We're prepared for that sort of thing. I

have to hand it to Felix. He's a brave kid. No complaints whatso-
ever. I remember when I flew my first mission, I was so damn
scared I cried. Actual tears on my face. Might have been some pee
involved too, it's all a blur now." He crouched next to Felix and
smiled at him with easy kindness. Julie remembered that smile so
well—it had shone like sunlight on some of the toughest
moments of her life.

"How does that ground feel under your feet? Little shaky
still?"

Felix nodded.

"Listen to me. Anyone who doesn't feel a healthy dose of
alarm riding in a metal box held up by air flowing over its wings
is fooling themselves. So don't beat up on yourself."

"It's called lift. It's a difference in air pressure." Felix spoke in a
small voice, but it brought Julie a rush of relief. If he was willing
to talk, he'd be okay.

"You're right. I can tell you've studied how airplanes work.
Actually flying in one is a little different, and the first ride can
really throw you for a loop. I threw up my first time too. Some of
the best pilots, the ones who become astronauts and daredevils,
they have all kinds of physiological reactions. But now you're
prepared. Next time won't be as bad."

"Next time!" Priscilla exclaimed. "Absolutely not. He's not cut
out for flying, clearly. You know he's on the spectrum, don't you?"

Julie could have throttled her. How insensitive could she be?
Anyone could get airsick; why blame it on his atypical neurology?

"All due respect, Mrs. Reinhard, but none of us are 'cut out for
flying.' You don't see wings on us, do you? It's up to Felix whether
he likes it or not. I won't blame him if he doesn't. It's no fun
getting sick. But if he wants to give it another go, I'd be happy to
take him up again."

Ben was still crouched next to Felix, at eye level with him.
Felix finally lifted his head and studied him for a long moment.

Julie held her breath. Felix so rarely gave anyone a second

chance. Once he had a bad experience with someone, he put up his walls and refused to take them down. But Ben was—Ben. Even this new version of him was irresistibly kind and emotionally generous. He might be angry with her, but he'd never take that out on Felix.

Felix's mouth finally lifted at the corners. He stuck out his hand.

After a quick moment of surprise, Ben took it and gave it a brief shake. "Deal, then. You name the time and I'll be there. Just us next time, maybe."

"And Julie," Felix said. "Sarah can come too if she wants."

That was a definite snub of the Reinhards, which they didn't miss. Priscilla turned on her heel and stalked toward their Rolls.

Julie sighed, knowing she'd have to spend some time smoothing ruffled feathers later. Why did the Reinhards never understand that their harshness *affected* people? Especially Felix, who had less control over his emotions than most kids. Would Felix and his grandparents ever figure out a way to get along? It seemed impossible.

"Felix, why don't you go find the bathroom and get a drink of water?" she told him.

Sarah skipped next to him. "I'll show him where it is!" The two kids set off toward the reception office, and Julie turned to Ben.

"I'll clean up that vomit."

"Absolutely not."

"Come on, Ben, it's the least I can do. I'm a professional. I'll have it spit and polished and good as new in no time."

He rubbed his forehead with the heel of his hand. "No, Julie. Don't worry about the 206. Take care of Felix. I don't like the way the Reinhards treat him. Brings back some bad memories."

She laughed ruefully. "No kidding. I was hoping they'd mellowed over the past twelve years, but I think they've gotten worse. Or maybe I have less tolerance for it, especially when Felix is involved. Thanks for handling them so well."

He shot her an odd look, and shrugged. "What's to handle? They never liked me, and I knew it. Never lost any sleep over it. By the way, I think I have a smallish set of coveralls Felix can wear. The Reinhards probably don't want pee on the seat of their Rolls."

She followed him across the tarmac, catching up so they could walk side by side. "What makes you think the Reinhards didn't like you?"

"Well, they basically said it. They said I was getting in your way."

Startled, she made a gesture that made her hand brush against his. Tingles rushed up her skin, a geyser of sensation. She took a step to the side. He didn't seem to notice, though a muscle ticked in his jaw.

"When did they tell you that? This is news to me."

"They told me—" He broke off, then stopped walking and turned to face her. In contrast to the kindness he'd shown Felix, his face now wore a blank mask. "You really want to do this? Dig everything up and dissect it? What does it matter when they told me? It's ancient history. You were gone, and that's really all I needed to know."

She drew in a sharp breath. "So they told you that after I left? That you were getting in my way?" The suspicion she'd had earlier, that the Reinhards might have interfered somehow, came back stronger than ever. "What else did they say? Didn't they give you my message?"

She saw the hurt behind his flat gaze, the muscle still working in his jaw. "Of course they did. That's the only reason I knew about your plans."

Disappointment cratered through her stomach. "So you *did* know about my plans." And yet still, he'd stood her up.

Sarah came hurtling out of the office building. "Felix needs

Miss Julie's help. He needs something to wear. I told him he could just tie my jacket around his waist but he thought that was stupid."

"Coming in just a sec," Julie called to her. One more minute, that was all she needed to sort this out.

But Ben had already turned away. "I'll get those coveralls from the hangar."

And he was gone, leaving only the aftereffect of his presence —faster-than-normal heartbeat, the pulse beating in her throat, hand still tingling from that brief touch.

She let out a long exhale and followed Sarah to the restroom where Felix was waiting.

Maybe he was right, and there was no point in digging up the past and dissecting everything. This wasn't some archeological dig. She had to focus on Felix, not her and Ben's ancient history.

There was only one thing she absolutely had to relive, and that didn't need to involve Ben. On Monday, while Felix was in school, she was going to meet with Will Knight. Once she told him everything, one of her main purposes for coming back to Jupiter Point would be accomplished.

Felix was probably even more eager to go home to LA now. No matter how nice Ben was about it, how could Felix ever forget that he'd thrown up and peed his pants—in front of his grandparents and an adorable little girl? That was the kind of thing you never lived down.

Sigh. She probably ought to go ahead and book their return tickets now.

10

On Sundays, the Knight brothers liked to barbecue. Now that there were women in the family, the barbecues had expanded to include things like fruit salad and dessert. Sometimes even green salad, Lord help them. For some reason, Ben always cooked the burgers even though he was arguably the worst at it.

"Never fear," he told them all as he hunched over the grill behind the farmhouse where Tobias, Carolyn and Sarah now lived. "I've consulted some cookbooks and I think I have it down now. No more charcoal burgers from Ben Knight."

"End of an era." With a beer bottle, Tobias saluted Ben from his lawn chair, where he sat with legs akimbo, hand interlaced with Carolyn's. Only Sarah was missing; she was taking a nap upstairs. They all wore hats and scarves on this winter Sunday, because no bad weather would keep the Knights from their barbecue.

"It was the best of times, it was the worst of times," Ben said, peering carefully at the array of burgers on the grill.

"Where did the best part come in? Must have missed that."

Ben showed him a middle finger, then carefully lifted one corner of a patty. Was it done? It was pinkish-brownish.

The back door opened and slammed shut, then Merry emerged carrying a giant wooden bowl of Greek salad.

"Are those vegetables I spy? Never thought I'd see the day." Carolyn affectionately rubbed her cheek on Tobias's sleeve. Ben felt such deep envy that he lost his breath for a moment. Once upon a time, that had been him, sharing the utter comfort of companionship with Julie.

You've changed, she'd said, her clear eyes scanning his face, showing uncertainty and doubt. That look still bothered him. Maybe some things had changed. But not everything.

"This salad is the result of some serious negotiations." Merry mock-glared at Will, who followed behind her with a platter of garlic bread. "We had to work out a greens-to-carb-to-meat ratio that didn't completely destroy the Knight family legacy."

Tobias and Ben both saluted their older brother, who gave a mocking bow. "I tried to convince her that relish counted as a green, but she wasn't buying it."

Ben flipped the burgers and let the conversation flow over him. It was ironic that his two brothers had found happy relationships before he had. Neither of them had ever seemed interested in "settling down." Yet here they were. And here he was. Still single and manning the grill while they cuddled with their soul mates.

Ben mechanically poked at the burgers, his thoughts drifting in their usual direction—toward Julie. And Felix, too. He was "on the spectrum," according to Mrs. Reinhard. After they'd all left, he'd googled the term and learned that it meant Felix had a certain degree of autism. He'd read all the information he could find, and it definitely explained some of Felix's behavior. His wariness about being touched, his unexpected reactions to things, his intense and obsessive thirst for information when something caught his interest.

Not an easy kid. He tried to imagine Savannah coping with a child that challenging. Hard to picture. Was that why Julie had stepped in to help, the way she always did? Was that why she wasn't a famous singer by now? She'd spent the years helping with Felix, not working the music biz?

"Ben, did you hear me?"

He startled, nearly jarring a burger from his spatula. "Sorry, what?"

"Do you know what Julie wants to talk to me about tomorrow?" Will put a hand on his shoulder, brother-style.

"Uh, no. No idea."

"I got the impression it has something to do with Dad."

Ben's head jerked up. What could Julie possibly know about the murder? She'd disappeared before it happened. She'd never even sent condolences or a sympathy note. "I want to be there."

God, wasn't he trying to *not* get distracted by Julie? This was different, though. Anything having to do with finding their father's killer, he was all in.

"I'll have to ask her. She might prefer a private meeting."

"Fine. Ask her. But you know something? I don't care if she doesn't want me there. She owes me." He slid the rest of the burgers onto the platter and carried them to the picnic table. Will followed him, and the others gathered around as well.

"Maybe you should get that chip off your shoulder. Maybe it's not about you and what she 'owes' you," Will said.

Ben slapped a burger onto a bun. "Are you taking her side?"

"How do you even know there *are* sides? I'm just saying, your damn ego might be getting in the way."

"In the way of what?"

Tobias poked at his burger with a suspicious frown. "What is this?"

"In the way of *what*?" Ben asked again.

"This burger is not cooked," Tobias declared. "This is a travesty. I think I speak for the entire Knight family when I say that I want the old Ben back."

"Well, the old Ben isn't coming back," Ben snapped. "And I want Will to finish his sentence. Getting in the way of what?"

"Love and happiness," Will snapped back. "Love and goddamn freaking happiness. You're playing a part that doesn't suit you. You're not some asshole playing the field, afraid to feel anything. That's just not *you*. And I'm tired of you fooling yourself that it is."

An abrupt silence fell over the group. Ben stared at his older brother. What the fuck? How long had he been thinking that? "Fooling myself? I don't know what you're talking about."

Will squirted ketchup on his bun. "Yes, you do. You know exactly what I'm talking about. You got hurt and you closed up shop. You're not a cynical dickhead who doesn't care about anyone. You care *too* much. And you always will, because that's you who are. You need to stop lying to yourself."

No one dared say anything as Will and Ben stared each other down. From inside the house came the sound of Sarah's footsteps clattering down the staircase. She must have woken up from her nap. What an awkward moment for her to walk in on. Ben scrambled for a change in subject, but his mind was blank. *You care too much.*

Merry took a fork and lifted one edge of a burger. "You know something, Tobias is right. This burger could use a little more flame on it. How about I—"

"I got it." Ben grabbed the platter and carried it back to the grill. "At least there's one thing I can still do right. I can still screw up a burger like nobody's business."

BY THE TIME Monday rolled around, Ben had done plenty of

thinking about what Will had said. He didn't necessarily agree with all of it. But his brother had a point. Maybe he should get that chip off his shoulder—at least long enough to hear what Julie had to say to Will.

She arrived at Will's new office—which was half of the duplex he and Merry had purchased—a little late. Ben watched through the front window as she parked her bright red VW Jetta out front instead of in the driveway, as if she might want to make a quick getaway. In black leggings and boots, with a red sweater hugging her body, she made his mouth water with desire.

He opened the door before she could knock. "You look great," he told her, hoping to start off on a positive note. "Special occasion?"

"Audition, actually. Mrs. Murphy talked me into trying out for Grease. They lost an understudy. I'm here to see Will, is he in?"

"Yes, he's next door. He went to get coffee so I could try to convince you to let me stay for your meeting. Would you mind?"

Her eyes widened and worry tugged her eyebrows together in a frown. Julie had never been good at hiding her emotions; he'd always read them in her eyes like wind on the ocean. She was afraid of something. Filled with doubt. About him? About what she had to say?

Finally, she nodded. "Sure. It's probably better, actually."

Well, that was cryptic.

She stepped inside, bringing the fresh scent of lavender with her. He immediately thought of her spray bottle, and how he smelled lavender and remembered her every time he walked through his foyer these days.

"How's Felix?"

"He's fine," she said absently, tugging off one of her gloves. He noticed that her hands were reddened and chapped. It probably went with the territory of being a cleaner. "He's already plotting ways to avoid airsickness on his next flight."

"Good—" he began, but she interrupted.

"Ben, before I tell you and Will what I came here to say, I want you to know how sorry I am about your father. I cried every night after I heard. I should have said it earlier, but things have been so awkward between us."

Her sympathy felt weird to him. Almost out of place. Wasn't it a little late to be sharing condolences? But he didn't want to start on the wrong foot, so he simply nodded.

Will came through the door then with a pot of coffee and a pile of Styrofoam cups. He and Julie greeted each other warmly, though Ben could tell that Julie was starting to get nervous.

Will had furnished the sitting area with a comfortable couch and armchair arrangement, so he could put potential clients and sources at ease. Sunshine streamed in the bay window, giving the hardwood floors a warm caramel gleam and keeping a hardy jade plant alive. Ben wasn't sure the pleasant atmosphere was working on Julie, even though Will showed her to the most comfortable seat, the armchair. Ben could personally vouch for it, having napped there one evening after a long day of flying.

She perched on the edge of the seat and gripped both upholstered arms, as if it was a rocket ship instead of a La-Z-Boy.

Will set a cup of coffee on the end table next to her, then sank onto the couch next to Ben. "You know I'm not a deputy anymore, right, Julie?"

She nodded. "I intended to talk to the police instead, but then I heard that you're investigating the murder of your father. This has to do with that."

Ben narrowed his eyes at her. "You'd already left when it happened. How could you know anything about that?"

She shot him a look. "I don't mind if you're here; in fact, I want you to hear this. But you can't interrupt me every other sentence. Obviously, I wouldn't be here if I didn't think it was relevant."

Will shoved a coffee cup into his hands. "Ben, you focus on that. Let me do the questioning. Can you do that?"

"Sorry," Ben muttered. "Just ignore me. Carry on."

She drew in a long, audibly difficult breath. "Okay. I think I saw the murderer. In fact, I believe he came after me and threatened me. He told me never to come back to Jupiter Point."

11

Even though Ben had pledged to be quiet, as soon as Julie made that statement, he exploded with a curse, then another one as coffee spilled onto his pants.

In the next second he was on his feet, six feet plus of steaming, furious manhood.

"*What?*" He swung back toward her. "Is he still here? Has he threatened you again?"

Julie gave Will a pointed look. Maybe it wasn't such a good idea to have Ben here after all. She'd thought it would help clear up a few things, answer some of his questions. But she hadn't anticipated this kind of reaction.

Will reached for his brother and tugged him back to the couch. "Want me to kick you out of here, Ben? Because I will at this rate."

Ben turned fierce eyes on him. "She just said the murderer threatened her and you're worried about *me*?"

"I'm trying to get the story, for chrissake. Now sit down."

Ben sat, but he didn't look happy about it. He leaned forward, elbows on his thighs, hands gripped together. "Just tell me if you've gotten any more threats, and I'll shut up."

A sense of warmth bloomed in Julie's heart. Maybe Ben still cared about her. If he didn't, he wouldn't be freaking out like this.

"No more threats. Believe me, I wouldn't still be here if there were. Especially with Felix."

Ben scanned her face, and what he saw must have reassured him enough so he nodded at her. "Okay. I'm shutting up now. Trying, anyway. So, when did this happen?"

"You know, the next time I sit down in the pilot's seat of the 206, feel free to slug me," said Will, shaking his head. "Start at the beginning, Julie. What makes you think you saw the killer?"

She decided that the only way she was going to get through this was to focus on Will. If she watched Ben's reactions, she might lose it.

"I was outside your house, late at night. I'd gotten a panicked call from Savannah, begging me to meet her. But I couldn't reach Ben to let him know I had to cancel our camping trip, so I drove to your place to tell him in person. I didn't want to wake everyone up, so I turned the headlights off and parked out of sight. I snuck over to the side porch. I used to climb up that post to reach Ben's room. I mean, not very often...hardly ever, really. Just occasionally."

"We know," Will said dryly. "Wasn't exactly a secret."

Julie's face heated and she dared a glance at Ben. He looked stunned, and maybe a little disbelieving. She dragged her gaze away from him and fixed it on Will again.

Will, with his stern manner and quiet gray eyes that somehow drew the secrets right out of you.

"Anyway, I never got to the post. A man grabbed me from behind and clamped his hand over my mouth. He said, 'Get out of here or I'll hurt you.' It was more like a growl, like he didn't want me to recognize his voice. He yanked my arm behind my back. It hurt, a lot. He demanded my phone, and I gave it to him. Then he said, 'Now go, Julie. Run, before I change my mind. No telling anyone or you'll pay.'"

"Those exact words?" Will asked.

"Exactly. I'll never forget those words. I can still hear them. I was always good at hearing things and memorizing them, because of my singing."

She flicked a glance at Ben. His face had gone blank, and she couldn't tell what he was thinking.

"I was scared to death because he knew my name. I didn't know if he knew it already, or maybe saw it on my phone. It was just an old-fashioned flip phone, nothing fancy. Definitely not worth stealing. I ran to my car and drove away as fast as I could. But I didn't do what he said. I mean, there was a stranger lurking outside your house. I had to call the police. So I stopped at the Mobil gas station right outside of town and used their phone to call nine-one-one. I told them what had happened."

"You took a big chance," said Will softly.

"Well, I kept it anonymous because he knew my name. They had a cruiser already in the area. I waited on the phone until the dispatcher came back on and told me that they'd checked it out and seen no one. He made me feel stupid even for calling, like maybe I was pulling some prank. Anyway, I was glad the man was gone and figured maybe I'd scared off a burglar or something."

She stole another glance at Ben. His head was lowered, gaze fixed on the floor, hands clasped together so tightly the tendons and veins stood out.

"I kept driving until I got to Benson. Savannah had a hotel room there, which she'd booked under a fake name. That was when I found out she was pregnant. Like, about six months pregnant, but she'd been hiding it really well. I hadn't noticed because I was in such a funk over my mom. She was freaking out because she hadn't told her parents and didn't want them taking over her life the way they always did. She begged me to help her, at least until the baby was born. I couldn't say no—I owed her so much. Her and the Reinhards."

Ben made a sound somewhere between a scoff and a snort.

She ignored him and went on. "Savannah and I holed up in that hotel for two nights, ordering room service and trying to figure out how to make it work. She didn't want her parents involved, but I convinced her she had to tell them. She was going to need financial support no matter what she did, and she still hadn't finished high school. I was still only seventeen, how much help could I really be?"

Ben dug his hands into his hair, as if it were physically painful to listen to her story.

"Anyway, when we finally left the hotel, I saw a note on my car. It was addressed to *me*, by name. And it said that if I made any more calls or came back to Jupiter Point, all hell would break loose."

"Did you save that note?" Will asked sharply.

"I did." She reached into her bag and pulled out the Ziploc bag in which she'd kept the note all these years. The ink had faded, and the paper looked soft and worn. "But it probably won't tell you much. Block letters, ordinary notebook paper. I'm sure my fingerprints are all over it, so if you need to take mine, that's fine." She handed it to Will.

"Pretty good thinking to save this."

She shook her head, the familiar guilt flooding her. "I should have done something before this. But I kept thinking, how did he know I called the police? What if he *was* the police? So who should I tell? And his threats sounded real. He knew how to find me. He knew my car, knew my name. He had my phone. I completely freaked out."

"So, what happened next?"

"We took my car to a junkyard."

"Your mom's Beetle? You junked it?" Ben raised his head to look at her. A quick memory of making out in the front seat of the Beetle flooded her brain. Ben had kissed the inside of her arm for hours, until it felt made of liquid fire.

"We didn't know what else to do. The man knew how to track it. Savannah and I decided Los Angeles would be a good place to go. We figured it was a big city with everything we needed. Jobs, hospitals, apartments. She called her parents and told them she was pregnant. I got on the phone with them, and they begged me to stay with her until the baby was born. They promised to pay for everything, even pay me a salary. They didn't want her to be alone. So I agreed." She looked at Ben, who was still watching her steadily. "But I asked them to give you a message, since I didn't feel safe calling myself."

"What was the message?" he asked slowly, as if he was afraid of the answer.

She flushed. "I asked them to tell you about Savannah, and that I planned to stay with her until the baby was born. I asked them to tell you that I loved you. And I asked them to tell you to meet me on my birthday at the place where I first told you I loved you. I figured even if that bad guy was listening, he wouldn't know what I was talking about."

For a long, agonizing moment, he stared at her blankly. Did he not remember that moment? Could he really have forgotten something that was indelibly printed on her heart for eternity?

"Neptune's Oasis," he finally said.

"Yes." She made a little face. "Water parks aren't nearly as fun alone."

"You went. On your birthday."

"Yes. It's not in Jupiter Point, so I figured I wouldn't be angering the man, if he was still paying attention. My birthday was after Savannah's due date, so I thought I'd be at loose ends by then."

"I was at the Air Force Academy by then."

She licked her lips, dry from all her talking. "It was a stupid plan, anyway. I just couldn't think of anything better. That was before Facebook and all that."

Will cleared his throat. "I'd like to get back to that first encounter, when he grabbed you outside our house. Maybe there's a detail that might help us identify him."

But she barely heard him. She was still captured by the intensity of Ben's gaze. "I'm sorry, Ben," she whispered to him. "I probably should have done something different, or more. But when you didn't show up at Neptune's Oasis, I thought maybe you were done with me. After a while, I called the Reinhards again and asked if they'd seen you. That was when they told me your dad had been murdered, and that you'd joined the military."

Ben looked as ashen and horrified as if he'd seen a ghost. He jerked to his feet. Hung his head. Then said something in a strangled voice and pushed his cup of coffee at Will. "Do your thing," he said. Then strode from the house without another word.

Tears started in Julie's eyes. So much for explaining herself. If Ben still hated her now, there was nothing she could do or say.

"Don't worry," Will said, touching her briefly on the knee. "He just needs to readjust his entire world view, that's all. He'll be fine."

"Are you sure? He seems pretty upset."

"Probably upset to learn he's had his head up his ass. He thought— Well, you two should work things out between yourselves. Can I ask you some questions now?"

She glanced at the door Ben had fled through. Part of her longed to go after him. "Go ahead. I'll try to remember as much as I can."

"Let's start with that night outside our place, when you had physical contact with the man. Can you remember anything like how he smelled, other details like that?"

"It was twelve years ago," she said dubiously. "And I was scared out of my mind. I remember his gloves were leather, and they smelled like diesel. I know he was really strong. I didn't recognize his voice."

"Did he have any kind accent or particular quirk in how he talked?"

"No, not that I remember." She thought back to the terror of that moment, but nothing jumped out at her. Except... "This will sound strange, but he had a really good voice."

Will cocked his head at her, a penetrating look in his gray eyes. "Explain."

"Well, you know I'm kind of a singer. I mean, I like to sing, it's always been something I was good at. Especially back then, I sang in the church chorus and every time there was a musical production, I auditioned. This man had a very resonant baritone. He was disguising it by growling, and he didn't say much. But I did notice." She laughed a little. "Not much of a clue."

"You never know. It's more than we had yesterday."

She twisted her hands together. "I know I should have come forward earlier, as soon as I put it together that your dad was killed a few nights after that man grabbed me."

He put up a hand to stop her. "You have nothing to apologize for. You took a chance calling the police, and that backfired on you. We don't know for sure if this man was the killer, and it's not as if you saw his face." He shook his head. "No. I'm glad you didn't try anything else. Staying away was the best choice. But I have to ask you, what made you come back now? Do you think the man who attacked you is gone?"

"I had a few different reasons," she said. "The Reinhards are one. But the truth is, it's been weighing on me. I really wanted to tell someone in case it wound up being important. I didn't like feeling like a coward."

"You are not a coward, Julie. You did your best with a tough situation, the way you always have."

The respect in his voice sent a quiet thrill through her.

"And...Ben? Is he one of the reasons?" Will asked the question gently, with a hint of a smile. He was a few years older than Ben, and had been off at law school when she left. She'd always seen him as somewhat of an intimidating figure, not lighthearted and playful like Ben.

"Maybe," she admitted. "But it looks like that's a bust. I think he'd rather I just go back to LA."

Will laughed and shook his head. "Don't give up on him yet. Since you got back, he's been acting like a prize jackass. And since we all know that Ben has the heart of a lion, or maybe a panda bear, it must be thanks to you."

She shouldered her bag, preparing to leave. "I'm not sure 'thanks' is the right word."

"It is. Ben needs a wake-up call. Believe me, we're all glad you're back. Now the question is whether you'll stay."

That drew a weak smile from her. Good question. Too bad she didn't have a good answer. "I'll be around at least long enough to answer any other questions you have. Are you going to analyze that note?"

"Yes, first thing. I have a law school buddy in the FBI, he does me favors now and then. I'll let you know if he finds anything. Do you think you'd recognize the man's voice?"

"I doubt it, but I'll keep my ears open." She rose to her feet, then hesitated. "Maybe I should go to the police station and just sit there and listen to everyone's voices."

Will stood as well and looped an arm over her shoulders. "Absolutely not. I'll take it from here. You continue with life as usual. Just let me know if anything else comes to mind. I'll want to interview you again soon, but right now, I have a feeling there's a more important conversation awaiting you."

He gestured at the sidewalk out front, where Ben was waiting, slouched against his truck, hands deep in his pockets.

She drew in a deep breath. "Wish me luck."

"You got it."

Outside, Ben glanced up as she came out the door, belting her sweater more tightly around her. She couldn't read his expression, which made her nervous.

"Come for a ride?" he asked in an even tone.

That made her even more anxious. The old Ben never hid his

emotions. He wore his heart on his sleeve, which was one of her favorite things about him.

But this conversation was a long time coming. It had to happen. "Sure." As he opened the passenger door for her, she hesitated. "But maybe you shouldn't be driving while we talk."

"Babe, I was flying fighter jets eight months ago. I can handle a Dodge pickup."

Right, she'd almost forgotten he'd had a whole different life for the past twelve years. A fighter pilot. Her Ben. Her sweet, tender, openhearted Ben.

She got into the truck and strapped herself in. Ben pulled away from the curb with a squeal of tires. They sped away from Will's house.

She stole a sideways glance at his clenched jaw and white knuckles and decided to hold her tongue. The Dodge rattled down the streets until they hit the highway heading for the foothills.

"Where are we going?" she finally asked.

"To the Reinhards'."

"What for? They aren't even home. Ben, stop. Pull over."

"Those fuckers!" Ben exploded. "I never got any message about your birthday." This was a new side to her gentle ex-boyfriend. The muscles of his forearms tensed into corded bands of steel as he swung the steering wheel to the side. They'd reached the unincorporated area, where farmland replaced the cozy neighborhoods of Jupiter Point. He jerked the truck to a stop next to a field of alfalfa, now fallow. A plume of dust rose up around them, enveloping them in a cloud of sepia. "The Reinhards told me something completely different."

Julie sucked in a breath and slumped against the passenger window. Her worst suspicions, confirmed. "So that's what happened. What did they tell you?"

"That you'd decided to move to LA and you wanted some time to get your singing career going, so I shouldn't bother you.

They told me I'd been holding you back because you were afraid to hurt me. They told me they'd send me your address and phone number when they had it."

The scope of their betrayal hit her like a sucker punch to the gut. "They lied. Every word of that is a lie. You weren't holding me back."

"I didn't think so. But then I started to wonder. They made me doubt myself. They made me think I wasn't doing it right, loving you the way I did."

"Oh my God." She wanted to wrap her arms around him but the air between them still vibrated with prickly energy. "That's not true, Ben. You did *everything* right."

"And you still left." His voice sounded raw.

"I had to! I had to help Savannah. But I didn't intend to leave *you*."

He pushed his way out of the truck and stood in the road, hands clasped behind his head, looking skyward.

She dropped her head into her hands. An ache pounded at her temples. She felt as if a hundred years had passed since she'd arrived at Will's office. In one way, she felt freer. The story she'd been keeping quiet for so many years was out. But she also had a bitter taste in her mouth, worse than any hangover. After all she'd done for the Reinhards, how could they betray her like that?

Of course, they probably thought *they'd* done everything for *her*. Because they were rich and she was penniless, and they were powerful while she was naive...so naive.

The passenger door opened. Ben braced one hand on top of the truck and leaned in.. She'd never seen his face so serious, so intense. This was Ben the man looking her in the eye, not Ben the boy.

"Julie, I need you to know that if I'd had any clue you were at our house that night, that some stranger had hurt you and threatened you, I would have..." He stopped, his jaw flexing, his Adam's apple working. "I can't believe I didn't know he was out there.

With you. My God, Julie. What if—" He kicked at the tire. "He almost got you, too."

"Ben, no. No. It wasn't like that. He was just trying to chase me off." She unhooked her seatbelt and slid out of the passenger seat to stand next to him in the road. The wind swirled around them, causing a lazy drift of dust and debris. She smelled the cooling metal of the truck, the rubber of its tires. And closer, the wool of Ben's sweater, the scent of his skin.

Everything shifted into sharp relief, as if nothing had been quite real until she wrapped her arms around him one more time.

She hugged him to her and whispered in his ear. "Nothing happened. He scared me, that's all. Scared me so much, I made some stupid decisions after that."

Against her shoulder, he shook his head. "No. You did the right thing. I'd take a broken heart any day if it's a choice between that and some asshole threatening you."

She wanted to cry from sheer, sweet relief. Ben didn't hate her. He was touching her, holding her, whispering back in her ear, his heart beating so fast and loud it vibrated through her sweater.

This was her Ben, the Ben she knew and used to love so much.

And for the first time, she was one hundred percent glad she'd come back to Jupiter Point. How else could she find herself standing in the road wrapped in Ben Knight's arms? And have it be exactly where she wanted to be?

12

THE ONLY THING ANCHORING BEN TO EARTH RIGHT NOW WAS THE comfort of Julie's arms around him. He was so angry his head was spinning. The Reinhards had *lied*. Deliberately. And he knew why, too. Because they'd wanted Julie to stay with their daughter, not come back to Ben.

He was furious with the attacker, too, the man who had scared Julie away. And a little bit—maybe just a little—he was angry with Julie. Why had she believed for one second that he would stand her up on her birthday? Why hadn't she found another way to reach him?

He held on to her more tightly. The girl Julie had been slim, almost a tomboy, someone who'd loved climbing trees and swimming in the ocean. The woman Julie was stronger, curvier, with the body of someone who did physical work for a living. But certain things hadn't changed. Her hair still smelled like apples and felt like silk against his cheek.

"We need to go see the Reinhards." The more he thought about it, the angrier he got. "I know what they were up to. They wanted to make sure their precious little girl was taken care of. They didn't care about *us*."

She licked her lips, a nervous gesture he remembered well. It used to turn him on, until he realized it meant she was anxious about something. "They know how to get what they want. They always have. I'll talk to them."

"Not without me," he said firmly.

"I don't think—"

"They lied to me. *To my face.* Come on, Julie. They can't be trusted. You know what I'd like to do? Get them up in the Cessna and do Dutch rolls until they promise to tell the fucking truth."

She gave him a skeptical frown. "Does your plane do that kind of thing?"

"Nope. That's how pissed off I am. Twelve years, Julie. *Twelve years* they've had a chance to correct the record. Not a word."

"You were gone," she pointed out. "And they've had other things to deal with. Savannah had such a tough time after she had Felix. She had severe depression. She checked herself into the hospital a couple times. And then Felix got his diagnosis. It was one thing after another."

"Are you making excuses for them? Why aren't you angrier?"

"I *am* angry. Actually, I think I'm more numb than angry." She took his hand in hers and interlaced their fingers. "The thing is, you're here and I'm here, and I'm just so glad we're speaking again. I don't want to think about anything else."

Speaking. He wanted to do a lot more than speaking. He pulled her against his chest and tangled his fingers in her silky hair. Emotion surged through his heart. She was right—everything else paled compared to the joy of being with her again.

Except...wrong was wrong. The Reinhards had to answer for what they'd done. "Are you saying you want to just let this go?"

She drew back, still within the circle of his arms. "No. They owe us a huge apology. But they've always been like this. They go after what they want. But I can see why they did it, because they were worried about Savannah and Felix."

"That justifies ruining our lives?"

"No, of course not, but Ben..." She rested one hand on his heart. "You weren't there. Felix needed me, more than you know. Savannah was in over her head, and I was too. It took both of us to take care of Felix."

"How did that even work? Did you live with them?"

"At first I did, but then I got my own place in the same apartment complex. But I was still close enough so I could help out, especially after Savannah got cast in her first movie. All of a sudden, she had to go on location and so forth. She tried taking Felix but he couldn't handle the travel. If I hadn't been there, I honestly don't know what would have happened to Felix. He doesn't like change, and he doesn't like strangers."

Ben absently rubbed his thumbs across the rise of her shoulder blades. He got it, he really did. A child had needed her, and Julie would always answer the call. That was who she was. But damn those Reinhards! Just thinking about their lie made his blood pressure rise.

The drone of an engine overhead caught their attention. He squinted up at the sleek craft gliding across the sky.

"Tobias in the Piper Matrix. I think he's taking Starly and Hunter back to LA."

"It's so pretty and silver."

He shaded his eyes from the sun as he watched it. He rarely got to see Knight and Day in action like this, a plane randomly spotted in the wild. Pride filled him as he traced its smooth path across the sky. He'd done that. He'd purchased that plane, formed that business, created the chance to give people the unforgettable experience of flying in a small craft.

Would any of that have happened if he hadn't joined the Air Force? Would he have served his country, taken pride in that, if Julie hadn't left?

The truth was, if he'd known about Savannah and Felix, he would have told her to go, to do what she had to do.

But that was the problem. He *hadn't* known. Thanks to the Reinhards.

"Okay, back to the villains. It's not just about their lies. What about you? What about all the things you used to talk about? Singing? Songwriting? College, for chrissake? What about your future? Are you *always* going to be catering to the Reinhards? All the generations?"

She shook his hand away from her and stepped back. "Are you talking about Felix? Don't call him that."

"Don't call him a Reinhard?"

"He's Felix. He's his own person, and I'm his godmother. I'm not catering to him, or to Savannah. We're friends. She gave me tons of support when I tried the songwriting thing. She paid for lessons, she set up a showcase for me. She's my *best friend*."

"Sorry," he muttered, though it went against the grain. "I guess it's the rest of the family I can't stand. I never liked how they treated you. You're a strong person, Julie, you always have been. Why don't you stand up to them?"

"Well..." She traced a circle in the road with her boot, sending up a little plume of dust. "I did stand up to them, once."

Ben lifted his eyebrows at her. This was news to him. "Before my time?"

"When we first moved into their guesthouse. I was ten, and they told me I couldn't play in the woods. I threw such an epic tantrum that my mother actually gave her notice. They didn't want her to leave so they gave in. But Mom was so mad at me, I never did it again."

He grinned widely, loving the thought of Julie showing her fiery side to the Reinhards. "That's what I like to hear. Epic tantrums. You should do more of that kind of thing."

She swatted his chest lightly. "Easy for you to say, with all your brothers behind you. I was an only child of a single parent. And they were the all-powerful Reinhards. Who was going to have *my* back?"

"Me, which is probably why they didn't like me."

Smiling, she pulled away from him and hoisted herself back onto the passenger seat of his truck. "Well, maybe, but you have to admit that you've been glaring at me since I got back."

"Glaring? No, I haven't." He strode to the driver's side of the truck and slid back behind the wheel.

"Yes, you have. Glaring and flaunting."

"*Flaunting?*"

"Yes. How many women have I seen you with since I got back? All the girls who've been flirting with you? The blond at the 7-Eleven. The jogging girl at your apartment. The girl at the hardware store. The girl at the pizza place—"

"What girl at the pizza place?" Ben started the truck. He was still steamed at the Reinhards, but this line of conversation was a lot more entertaining.

"Dark hair. Purple sweater."

"The girl who asked for the crushed red pepper from our table? She wasn't flirting with me."

"Whatever." She folded her arms across her chest.

A sense of triumph filled him. Julie had been keeping close track of his friendships with other women. There could be only one explanation for that. "You're sounding a little jealous. I didn't even know you were at the hardware store. Why didn't you say hi?"

"So you could glare at me? I think not."

"Oh, so I would have simultaneously glared and flaunted?" This was the most fun he'd had in about...hmmm...two months. Since the day Julie had first shown up.

"Yes. Glared, flaunted, and annoyed." She laughed, finally catching on to the ridiculousness of the conversation. "Seriously, how do you get any work done with so many women flirting with you?"

"That's a trick question and I refuse to answer it. But it does bring up a very important question."

"Exactly when you turned into such a ladies' man?"

"No. The question is, where does all this leave us? You and me?"

She looked over at him cautiously. "In what sense?"

"I mean, here we are. We're both back in Jupiter Point, at least for now. We've both been through all kinds of shit. We've both been thinking bad things about each other for twelve years. So now what? What happens next in the saga of Ben and Julie?"

13

"Well…" Julie looked at him from under her lashes, this playful, handsome man she'd once known so well. His hands were on the wheel, the engine running, the open road ahead. "I suppose you could put the truck in gear. That would be a good next chapter."

"Done," he said promptly. He jammed his foot on the accelerator and they were back in motion. Julie rolled down the window a few inches and felt the cool wind in her hair. Power lines flipped past them in a happy blur. Plenty more issues hung between them, but for now, this felt good.

"Remember when you taught me how to drive?" she asked him.

"Believe me, that's not the kind of thing a guy forgets. I got to be alone with you in an empty parking lot showing off my fishtail spins. Remember when I showed you the proper way to fasten your seat belt?"

"Yes. Honestly, I was surprised there was more than one way to fasten a seatbelt."

"There isn't." He grinned at her. And oh God, that carefree smile that used to light up her world—it was back. She felt its punch right in her heart—where everything about Ben affected her. "It was a completely lame way of getting close to you."

"Oh my God." She thought back to those spine-tinglingly delicious moments, when Ben's hair would brush against her chin and her throat would go dry with desire. "You sneaky boy."

"Pathetic, right?"

"Well, I have news for you. Remember when I taught you the dead man's float at Stargazer Beach? And I made you close your eyes?"

"Yup. Which wasn't easy, because you looked so crazy good in your lifeguard uniform."

"Yeah, well, I lied—there's no need to keep your eyes closed. I just wanted to look at you without being so obvious."

He threw his head back and laughed. She found herself staring at his profile the way she'd stared at his entire body that day at Stargazer. He had new laugh lines fanning from his eyes, and the curve of his lips was firmer, more commanding. But her beloved Ben was still in there, especially when he laughed. "We had the social skills of a couple of hermit crabs," he told her.

"I just couldn't believe you liked me. It took me so long to figure it out. In the meantime, I decided we could be best friends, and occasionally I could let myself lust after you."

Speaking of Stargazer Beach, she realized that he was steering the truck in that direction. He turned onto the winding back road that paralleled the coast. "Are you looking for another dead man's float lesson?" she teased. Then she clapped her hand over her mouth. "Oh my God. That sounded terrible. I don't mean to be insensitive. I'm so sorry."

He snorted, shooting her an amused look. "You need to brush up on your morbid sense of humor. I don't find that insensitive. My father is dead. It's not news. We've been processing that fact for twelve years."

"Still..." She took a breath of the fresh air blowing in from outside, carrying the first hint of ocean. "I cried for days when I got the news. Your father was always nice to me, even though he terrified me."

"I know he did, but I also remember that time you stood up to him. You won major points in the Knight brothers ledger book for that one."

She frowned, not quite remembering.

"You know, when he was pissed because I didn't fix the lawn mower the way I was supposed to?"

"Because you were helping me at the beach. A boy wandered onto the rocks and got stuck, and I couldn't leave the beach. So you went, even though your dad had given you until the end of the day to get it fixed." It was all coming back to her now, the panic of discovering that a boy was missing, the steady way Ben had stepped in to search. He'd found the boy trapped between some rocks, his ankle twisted. He'd freed him and carried him piggy-back style back to the beach.

"You were such a hero that day." She could still remember the image of her tall, strong boyfriend trudging across the beach with that sobbing boy on his back.

"No, you were the hero. My dad came at me like thunder. I thought he was going to pull out the old witch hazel switch he used to use when he was *really* pissed. Then you piped up and stood right in front of him and told him I'd saved a kid's life, and that I should be getting extra dessert, not a scolding."

She laughed. "Did I really say that? It's kind of a blur. I was shaking in my shoes, I really was."

"You did." Her hand lay on the seat between them. He covered it with his own, so much bigger and rougher than she remembered.

A shiver went through her from head to toe. She disguised it with a laugh. "I'm pretty good at standing up for other people. You should see me with Felix's teachers, when they don't understand his issues."

"I bet you're an incredible champion for him," he said softly.

He pulled his hand away so he could downshift as he took the turn toward the beach. "Do you remember how we spent the rest of that night?"

She laughed, even though her hand now felt cold and a little lonely. "I got a crash course in lawn mower mechanics, I remember that."

"Yup. You refused to leave me until it was done. You held the light for me when it got too dark to see. You fetched me tools and oil. You were amazing."

She scoffed. "It was the least I could do. That boy might have died if not for you. Besides, it was fun." She gave him a sunny, innocent smile. "I was with you. Everything was better when I was with you."

He flattened his hand against his chest, as if she'd shot him with an arrow. She knew the feeling.

They pulled into the parking lot that sat above the beach. From here, a little path wound through dune grasses and coarse sand to the ocean shore. To the left, Julie spotted the little lifeguard stand where she'd spent the last two summers of high school. Since it was only staffed during the summer, sheets of plywood now covered its windows. She wondered what lucky crew of teenagers shared that job now.

"I guess that leaves us with the same question I asked before. What's next?" Ben's soft question sent chills along her skin. What did she want to happen next? What did *he* want?

"Well...I suppose we could get out of the truck," she suggested. "Be a shame not to."

"After coming all this way, it would seem like a waste," he agreed. As if they'd rehearsed, they both opened their doors and swung out of the truck, a coordinated movement that reminded Julie of how in sync they'd always been.

He led the way through the dunes to the beach, which had a winter bleakness to it, now that it was exposed by the low tide. Only a few seagulls swooped and cawed overhead, occasionally landing on the heaps of seaweed left behind by the receding tide.

They picked their way past the high-tide mark, causing a sandpiper to skitter away in a rapid-fire blur of brittle legs. Julie wished she'd brought something warmer than a sweater; the wind off the ocean wicked the heat away from her.

Ben noticed, of course. He was always alert to that kind of thing. She used to tease him that she loved him mostly for his body heat. From his conflicted expression, she could tell he was hesitating about whether to put his arm around her to provide some warmth. But he didn't touch her this time. Instead, he shifted his position so he blocked the wind better.

Such a sweet Ben-like gesture. It made her heart ache for what used to be between them.

"What's next? North or south? Or back to the truck and blast the heater?" Ben asked.

What's next...

"One way or another, we need to keep moving." She hopped from one foot to the other, trying to generate some BTUs.

"Wait, is that a metaphor or do you mean it literally?" He must have made up his mind about the body heat issue, because he wrapped his arm around her shoulders in a friendly, bear-like way that made it clear this was only for anti-hypothermia purposes, nothing more.

She laughed at her accidental double entendre. "Both, I guess." She started down the beach in the windward direction, with him pacing at her side. "Let's go this way, so we can do the cold part first, then have the wind behind us on the way back."

"Okay, now, is *that* a metaphor? Are you saying we need to get the tough conversations out of the way first?"

The amusement in his deep voice had her laughing too. "How many tough conversations can we have in one day? I think we've met our quota."

"Thank God. I'm a guy, I can only handle so many of those."

He sidestepped around a pile of kelp. "Then let's get to the good stuff. Here's what I think we should do. Start fresh."

"How do you mean?"

He shrugged. "We've both changed. We're not the same people we were at eighteen. I, for instance, am a hardened military veteran. I can land an A-10 Thunderbolt near the front lines as easily as I used to beat you at Ping-Pong."

"Oh-ho. I see you still exaggerate like a champ. I beat you at least one time out of five."

"Yeah, and that one time out of five you were wearing extra-short shorts."

She shoved him a little. "Don't even try to pull the 'distracted' card. I can play that one too. I remember each and every time you played shirtless."

He laughed. "I barely had any muscles to show off back then. Care for a rematch?"

"Promise to keep your clothes on?"

"Not a chance. I need every edge I can get. You don't need short shorts to be distracting any more. You've been distracting me since you got back."

That confession made her heart do a slow spin of joy. "Not intentionally, believe me. I was trying to avoid you," she admitted.

"I was trying to avoid you too." He grinned down at her. "And see where that got us. Don't you think destiny is trying to tell us something?"

"I gave up trying to interpret destiny a long time ago. Now I just put one foot in front of the other. And try not to trip over my shoelaces."

"Wearing those sexy boots is one way to accomplish that."

At his look of hot appreciation, a spark of excitement kindled inside her. It had been a long time since she'd felt anything along those lines with a man.

A wave swept up the beach, as if trying to reach them with a creamy line of foam. "Tide's coming in," Ben observed. "It's getting late."

"Oh my God." She dug in her pocket for her phone. "I can't be late to pick up Felix. It's the kind of thing that can make him extra anxious." When she saw the time, she relaxed slightly, since she still had an hour of freedom. Still, it was amazing how much time had passed. It had always been that way when she was with Ben. He warped the space-time continuum. A day could pass in a blink when she was with him. "We should get back to the truck. I need to drive back to Will's and get my car."

"No need. I can drive with you to pick up Felix, then take you to Will's. It would save a little time."

"Really?" she asked dubiously. "You must have places you need to be. Like, up in the sky somewhere, in a cockpit?"

"No more flights booked today. Sorry, you're stuck with me. I'll be Felix's chauffeur today."

"Well, if you're sure...it would save a little time, instead of going all the way across town." And Felix would probably like it. Especially if she added an ice cream sundae to the agenda.

"Good. It's decided. So, we're doing this, right?" In sync once again, they turned and headed the other direction down the beach, the wind at their backs now.

"Picking up Felix? Or are we back to 'what's next'?"

"Back to what's next. I'm persistent like that. I'm serious, Julie. There was a time when you were my best friend. You knew me better than my brothers did. And that's saying something, considering that they knew every embarrassing quirk from when I was a baby."

"Like the fact that you refused to wear diapers and would always take them off and leave them on the floor? And that one time Will stepped on one of them and fell on his butt?"

"Yes. One of my finer moments. How did you know that?"

She smiled. "I think I bartered for that information. I believe I offered to set Tobias up with a friend of mine in exchange for blackmail material."

"Well, it's official then, you knew me better than my brothers. And that was incredibly devious, by the way."

He put up his hand for a high-five. Their hands met, then clung together instead of releasing for a proper high-five. He tugged her to a stop. They faced each other just yards from the lifeguard shack, where she'd spent more blissful hours than she could count.

"I feel like there's been a hole in my life for the past twelve years. I didn't like it. Heartbreak aside, I wanted to know where you were, what you were doing. I wanted to know what you were thinking about and laughing about. Did you think about me when you were in LA?"

"Ben! Of course I did. I used to look for mentions of you every time the Air Force was in the news. But now—" She broke off. How could she say this without pushing him away? "I don't know how this is going to work while I have Felix. He requires a lot of consistency, a lot of attention, a least when he's not completely absorbed in something. Then I could do the cha-cha in a banana costume and he wouldn't notice. But he doesn't like Jupiter Point and he doesn't like the Reinhards and Savannah's shoot is going over and he needs me."

"I'm not trying to take you away from Felix. I'm talking about resurrecting our friendship, nothing else."

Oh. Her heart twisted. *Nothing else.* Well. Good to know. "Of course. I mean, I didn't think you were suggesting anything else. I just don't have a lot of time, that's all I meant. I try to book jobs when Felix is at school. That doesn't really leave much time for a social life."

He cocked his head at her. "Be straight with me here. Is that a brush-off?"

"No, it's just reality."

"Well, apparently reality isn't always what it seems. You didn't leave me without a word and I didn't stand you up. I say we make our own reality now."

She stared at him in confusion. "What are you talking about?"

"I have an idea. Your business, Green and Pristine. You mentioned that you started it. You run the business, you own it, you're like the Queen of Green?"

She laughed, even though she still had no idea where he was going with this. "That's me. Next time you see me with a spray bottle, bow down."

"Oh, I will. Believe me. I'm in awe of all your hard work. Now I just want to...borrow you for a while. For Knight and Day. We're a new business too, and we have no idea what we're doing. The flying's one thing, we got that. But the accounting, the filing, the keeping track of receipts, the P&Ls, all that stuff. You set up Green and Pristine, so you know the drill, right?"

"I know enough. I just figure it out as I go."

"Because you're smart and savvy, you always were. We need help, Julie. We're booked all the time and we're getting behind on the organizational shit, the systems. I've been staying late trying to get on top of it, but flying tours on no sleep is a bad idea. Lives are at stake." He pulled a pathetic face.

She wrinkled her forehead at him. "Now that's low. You're trying to guilt me into organizing your life?"

"I'm desperate."

"Desperate for a file clerk?" A smile wanted to spread across her face but she beat it back.

"Desperate for you," he said promptly. Then he shocked her by dropping to one knee. "Julie deGaia, will you please come work for Knight and Day Flight Tours? You can choose your hours, work only when Felix is in school, whatever you want. As an added perk, we give all employees and their children unlimited access to flight tours."

"That seems insanely generous. How many employees do you have?"

"You would be the first." He grinned at her, then hopped back onto his feet.

She laughed and shook her head at his ridiculousness. He brushed damp sand off his knee and they kept going down the beach. A seagull swooped past them with a cry, probably disappointed Ben wasn't spreading out a picnic lunch on the beach.

"By the way, one of your jobs would be to help us hire a few more people. We're severely understaffed."

"So, you need a file clerk and a headhunter?"

"No way. We need a queen."

She laughed, finding him too adorable to resist. He always had been. "Well, it's quite an offer." They reached the path that led back to the parking lot. "There must be a catch."

"There is. You'll probably see a lot of me. Despite rumors and appearances, I have no life. I'm basically always at Knight and Day, or up in a plane. I'm begging you, Julie. Be our savior. Ride to our rescue."

"Ride to the Knight brothers' rescue? That sounds backwards."

"It isn't. Believe me. Oh, you'd also have to answer the phone. You have no idea how much help that would be. The amount of time I spend listening to all the messages that come in while I'm in the air, it's crazy. Then I have to answer all those calls. Seriously, Julie. Whatever you're making as a cleaner, we'll double it."

They'd reached his truck and he dug his hand into his pocket for his keys.

"Don't you want to run this by Tobias?"

"Believe me, he doesn't like paperwork any more than I do. He'll fall at your feet if you take this job. And all you have to do is put up with me being around."

He winked at her, but behind his jaunty manner, she picked up on some anxiety. He was truly concerned that she might not want him around. And that broke her heart a little.

"Ben, you do realize that I didn't leave Jupiter Point because of you? That I assumed I'd be coming back to you?"

"I get that now. But I'm not taking anything for granted."

"Okay then." She stepped closer to him. He was still searching for his keys. When she was a few inches from him, he stopped and gave her his complete attention. She breathed in his familiar smell, happiness flooding through her. Then she raised herself on tiptoe and placed a kiss on his cheek.

"Thank you," she said softly. "I'd be happy to put my green cleaning career temporarily on hold."

A wide grin spread across his face. "Thank *you*. Believe me, you'll be doing us a huge favor."

"There is one potential problem."

"Shoot."

"I'm pretty sure I'm going to get the role I auditioned for this morning. It seemed to be mostly a formality. I'm not sure of the schedule yet, but I'll need some time to learn the part."

"I'll help. I'll run lines with you. Remember how I helped when you were Mary Poppins?" He finally found his keys and unlocked his door, then pressed the button for hers. He strode around to the other side of the truck and opened the door with a bow. "That's what friends do."

She climbed into the passenger seat. "So, we're friends."

"Friends," he said firmly. He got back into his seat and started up the truck. "Let's not let anything else ruin that. Ever again."

She could think of one thing that could ruin their friendship again. Having all the same feelings for him as before—except deeper, because she was older and more experienced now, and knew exactly how precious their teenage connection had been.

But that wouldn't happen, because Ben made a good point. They were two different people now, and they were creating a fresh start.

One that involved a lot of filing, apparently.

"By the way, what's the part? The one you think you got?" he asked her as they hit the road that would take them back to town.

"Sandy."

"Sandy, the main character? Olivia Newton-John?"

"Yes, Gretchen from the hardware store strained her vocal cords. It's a demanding part. I rented the movie last night so I could learn the audition song, and wow. It's a lot to learn."

"You can do it." He smiled over at her. "With my help, of course. Know how I know?"

"How?"

He threw back his head and channeled John Travolta. "Cuz' I got chills, and they're multiplyin'."

14

"YOU HIRED JULIE? ARE YOU NUTS?" IN THE HANGAR, TOBIAS sorted through the drill bits, searching for the right size for the shelf he was putting up. "Last week you were afraid to talk to her. Now she's going to be doing our QuickBooks?"

"I wasn't afraid. I just wasn't ready."

"So what changed?"

"Everything, essentially." Ben filled Tobias in on Julie's story, or at least the parts of it that weren't too private. Tobias listened with a dark frown gathering on his forehead. When he was finished, Tobias pressed the trigger of the drill with an ominous whine.

"So, Dad's murderer scared her off, that's the theory?"

"It's possible. Someone did, and there's a good chance it was the killer. That would really be something if she helps us catch him after all this time."

Tobias fitted the bit into the drill. "After all this time. Key phrase there."

Ben stiffened. "He threatened her. She took a chance even coming back here."

"She could have called someone. The police. Us."

"She did call the police, I told you. She called that night. It went nowhere, and then the guy followed her the next day. The police weren't an option."

"Well, what about us? You? Why didn't she tell *you*?"

A soft voice answered the question for him. "I thought about it a lot, Tobias."

Julie stood just inside the side door of the hangar, holding a big cardboard box.

"I wasn't sure what to do. I didn't have any real evidence. I didn't see the man. It wasn't even the same night that the murder happened. Maybe he had nothing to do with that. And I was dealing with Savannah and getting us set up in LA, and finding work, and then Felix and..." She trailed off, shaking her head ruefully. "I know it sounds like a bunch of excuses. I'm sorry. I really am. Looking back, I could have done so many things differently. But I'm here now and I told everything to Will, and someone just dropped off all these flyers, and what do you guys want me to do with them? Do you have a storeroom somewhere?"

The uncertainty in her eyes ripped at Ben's heart. "Julie, don't worry about Tobias. He's just being an asshole."

Tobias swiveled his head toward him. "I am?"

He strode forward, shouldering Tobias aside on the way to Julie, then took the box from her. "Tobias has that 'don't mess with my family' thing down. He actually pestered poor Aiden at college when he thought an older woman was conning him. Turned out to be Carolyn, the best thing that ever happened to him. So that just shows what *he* knows."

Tobias shrugged his big shoulders and pressed the drill to the piece of wood he was working on. "I look out for my brothers, I know that much."

Julie cut him off before he could start drilling. "Hang on, Tobias. I'm not done."

He glanced back at her with lifted eyebrows.

"I did the best I could. I was *seventeen*. I didn't have anyone to stand up for me except for Ben, and we got sabotaged."

Tobias listened without expression, keeping his thoughts to himself. Ben knew that he'd seen Julie's fiery side when she was young; he'd witnessed the lawn mower incident. But it was even more impressive now that she was a full-grown, confident woman.

"I know you worry about your brothers, but honestly, I think Ben came out of it okay. Look at him. He's a reserve Air Force pilot, which basically means he's a dashing chick magnet in a flight jacket."

Tobias shot Ben an amused look. "She called you 'dashing.'"

"Yeah, I caught that. Julie, listen, we get it. No one's blaming you, including Tobias. We want you to stay and work with us. Tobias wants you to stay." He elbowed his brother in return. "Right, Tobias?"

"Absolutely. I don't even know what QuickBooks is."

She still didn't look convinced. Color burned in her cheeks, her chest rose and fell with her breaths. His body responded to her the way it always had, with an instant and eager erection. He hid it behind the box of flyers.

"Please, Julie. Do you want Tobias to get down on one knee too?"

"Excuse me, what?" Tobias swung his head around with a glare.

"Because this is a concrete floor saturated with motor oil. Whole different experience than the beach."

Slowly, Julie's expression softened. To Ben, it was like watching a flower unfurl. She smiled impishly. "I really would like to see that, but sadly, I don't have my camera with me. So I guess it'll have to wait."

Tobias extracted himself from the workbench and rose to his feet. He stepped toward Julie and put out his hand. "Welcome to

Knight and Day, Julie. I'm glad you're here, I really am. I just have one request."

Even though she took his hand, she looked wary. "What's that?"

"If anything doesn't seem right, if anyone shows up who seems suspicious, if there's any hint of a threat of any kind—you tell us. If Ben isn't here, you tell *me*. If you aren't here, you call one of us. I'll give you my number. You can call at any time, day or night. I'm serious, Julie. If there's a chance whoever threatened you back then is still here, we need to be watchful."

Color flooded her face. "That man might have had nothing to do with your dad's murder, you know. That happened later."

"I know. This isn't about that, it's about you. Someone didn't want you to come back to Jupiter Point, but here you are. That takes guts, and I just want you to know we have your back. All the Knight brothers do, not just your ex-boyfriend."

Julie pressed her lips together in a way that told Ben she was holding back tears.

"That thing you said about not having anyone to stand up for you? That's not true, not anymore. You have all of us." He dropped a kiss on the back of her hand.

That sweet gesture must have put Julie over the edge, because as soon as he released her, she gave them both a misty, confused smile and murmured something about checking on the software she'd been downloading. She hurried out of the hangar; it instantly felt empty and dull without her presence.

"Thanks, T." Ben turned to his over-protective older brother. "That was cool. A lot better than ranting at her."

"I didn't rant. I never rant."

"Okay then, scold. Lecture. Jesus, I don't happen to have my dictionary with me. You know what I'm talking about."

Tobias planted a hand on his shoulder. "Ben, you're going to stay away from her, right? She works for us now. Don't we have rules about dating employees?"

Shit. He hadn't thought of it that way. "I don't know, do we?"

"We should probably make some." Tobias looked like he was trying not to laugh.

"Forget it. We're working on our friendship. That's it."

"Friendship. Gotcha," Tobias said dryly. He squeezed Ben's shoulder, then went back to the workbench.

Crap. Tobias was right. There was a good chance Ben had played this all wrong. Workplace romances were always trouble.

Not that he wanted romance, anyway. Because that would be foolish. They were friends, trying for a fresh start. That was all they were and all they would be. He'd just have to make the most of it. Knowing she was in the reception office right this minute, and that she'd be there every morning for the foreseeable future —that was enough.

For now.

GETTING TO KNOW BEN AGAIN—AS an adult—was both wonderful and torturous. Every morning, he greeted her with a big smile and a mug of hazelnut coffee from the Keurig. And every morning, that smile was made of pure, one-hundred percent friendship. No hint of anything beyond that. Hence the "torturous."

The hazelnut coffee was part of Project Friendship, as he'd named it. On her second morning of work, after she'd settled in, he pulled out a notebook.

"This is a quiz," he told her. "A friendship quiz. To speed up the 'getting to know you again' process." The first question was how she liked her coffee. Hence the morning ritual of hazelnut with about half a cup of cream added.

Every day, he asked her a few more questions on the list, and they compared their answers about everything from whether she still liked butterscotch sundaes to what time they liked to wake up in the morning.

"I usually show up around seven, so I'm used to making the coffee," he told her.

"Seven? What about your late nights partying at Barstow's?"

"They explain why I live on coffee." He grinned. "Black with lots of sugar, by the way. In case it comes up."

The phone rang, and she took a moment to book a reservation for a wildlife tour. She jotted the booking down in the ledger they used to keep track of the schedule—for now. She intended to put all their schedules online as soon as she had a chance.

When she finished, she looked up to see Ben smiling at her nostalgically. "What?"

"I was just remembering how nervous I used to get when I called to see if you wanted to hang out. Cassie used to laugh her ass off at me."

"Cassie! How is she? I miss her. Gosh, she must be, what, twenty-seven or so?"

"Yes, about that." In his usual jeans and cotton shirt, freshly shaven, his gray eyes sparkled. "They're planning to come back at least for a visit, maybe in a couple weeks."

"They? Who do you mean?"

He tilted his head at her quizzically. "You didn't know? Mom and Cassie left right after Dad died and they haven't been back since. Mom couldn't handle being here anymore."

He made that last comment casually—too casually. Obviously, it bothered him that Janine was gone. Her heart went out to him. She knew how close he'd been to his mother, and how much he'd worried about her. "I'm sorry."

"Don't be, it's all good." He shrugged.

Oh yes. It definitely bothered him. "I had no idea they left. No one told me about any of that. I feel like I'm the last to know anything."

"You need to spend more time with Mrs. Murphy so you can catch up."

She laughed. "I'm afraid to. I'll have no secrets left if I do that."

She's the master interrogator, not me." She made a mental note to look up Cassie on Facebook. They'd been pretty good friends when she was dating Ben.

"Okay, so what else is on that list?"

Propped against the wall in a casual but mouthwatering pose, he consulted his notebook again. "What's your favorite TV show from the last ten years?"

"*Grey's Anatomy. Scandal.* Anything involving Shonda Rhimes. You?"

"Don't get much chance to watch TV, but I read a lot. Suzanne Brockmann and George R. R. Martin."

"Wait, I know that name. Doesn't she write romance novels?"

"Yes, but they have a lot of action too. Military action, not the other kind. Well, that too." He winked at her. "Guess I never lost my belief in happy ever afters, at least the fictional kind. In real life, happy for now is about all I can handle." He checked the old-school round-faced watch he wore. "I'm going to get Lancelot ready to go."

"Lancelot? I hope that's a nickname for a plane, not something else," she murmured, hopefully too softly for him to hear. Not exactly an appropriate comment for a workplace. Then again, this wasn't really a *work*place. It was more of a *fun* place where she was temporarily earning a wage and answering questions about coffee and TV.

He straightened, eyes alert and filled with laughter. "What did you just say?"

"I was just commenting on what a great nickname that is for a Knight and Day plane." She blinked at him innocently, folding her lips to hold back the laughter. "Knight. Lancelot. What are you going to call the new one?"

They'd just sold the Piper Matrix to Hunter and Starly, and purchased a second Cessna.

"Haven't decided. Maybe Guinevere. Planes are generally considered female, you know. Like boats."

"That explains why you like them so much, I suppose," she murmured. She turned back to the computer and the fuel receipts she was entering.

He took his flight jacket from the pegboard on the wall and slung it over one shoulder. "It's a good thing to have an employee who relentlessly mocks you, right?"

"I wasn't mocking. I was flattering. You're very popular. I know, because I answer the phone. But if you really want an employee who mocks you, I promise I'll work on that."

"You're perfect as you are. Never change." With that breathtaking comment, he disappeared out the door. She was still trying to get her heartbeat under control when he stuck his head back in the room. "Nearly forgot the next item on the list. Favorite lunch food?"

"Does lunch come with this job?"

"Sometimes, if Tobias remembers to stop at the sandwich place before he comes in. Are you still a grilled cheese fanatic?"

"No, that's kid stuff. Now I like tuna melts."

He smiled at her so warmly it was a good thing she was sitting down. "Let me guess. On gluten-free bread?"

Right, the dreaded gluten-free phase, when Mrs. Reinhard had insisted that the entire kitchen be purged of anything with a speck of gluten. Julie always got stuck with the leftovers, which were basically inedible. Once, she and Ben had taken an entire loaf of gluten-free bread to the duck pond. When even the ducks ignored it, they laughed until they cried.

"If you ever want me to quit for real, bring me a tuna melt on gluten-free bread. I'll get the hint."

Soberly, he pretended to write that down in his notebook, then took off.

She sighed deeply. God, he was so cute. A thousand times cuter than he'd been as a boy. And he'd been the king of her entire world back then. Oh, this was trouble.

15

As time went by, Ben's "friendship" questions got more intimate. Any boyfriends? What about breakups? Any pets? What about her singing? Did she ever write songs anymore?

When she'd had enough of his questions, she shooed him away so she could focus on getting Knight and Day in order. It was fun work, a nice change from cleaning. She organized their paperwork, commissioned a better website, got Knight and Day added to TripAdvisor.

The brothers began trusting her with the check-in process as well. Every passenger had to write down their weight and next of kin, and sign a liability waiver. She educated herself about the regulations governing the remote airstrip, the specs of the planes, the history of the airstrip—because tourists asked about that kind of thing.

In the afternoon, she'd pick up Felix from school. Sometimes she brought him back to Knight and Day, which he loved. He still hadn't gone back in the air, but Tobias was teaching him about plane mechanics. He soaked in every speck of information, and at least it didn't make him throw up.

On the weekends, she took him to the Reinhards'.

She still hadn't completely forgiven them.

The first time she saw them after Ben's revelation, she told Felix to wait in the car while she confronted them inside. She cornered them in the foyer, between the Ming dynasty vase and the Louis Quatorze sideboard.

"I need the truth from you both. That message I gave you to pass to Ben. It was really important to me. But he says you told him something completely different."

"It was a difficult time for all of us, have you forgotten?" Mrs. Reinhard adjusted the Hermes scarf tucked around her neck. She didn't like being challenged by anyone—especially by someone the same age as her daughter.

"Of course not." A wave of anger surfed through her. Were they really going to try to bury the whole thing? "All I want is the truth."

"It was all so long ago, Julie—" Adam began.

Julie cut him off. "I don't care how long ago it was. I stayed with Savannah when you asked, and I brought Felix here when you asked. The least you can do is be honest with me. What did you tell Ben? Why didn't you give him my message?"

The couple shared a long look. Julie made her hands into fists, her fingernails digging into her palms, forcing herself to stand her ground. Ben was right; standing up to them wasn't easy for her. They were so powerful, so used to getting their way.

"We were worried about Savannah. And we were concerned for you as well. You were grieving so intensely, clinging to Ben. We were afraid you were going to sacrifice your future. You had talent and smarts. We didn't want it wasted." Priscilla smoothed her perfectly angled bob.

"You expect me to believe you cared about *me*?" The thought was so ridiculous she snorted.

"We're not monsters," Priscilla said, almost indignantly, reminding Julie of her own comment to Felix. "We cared about you, and still do."

Julie stared at her in disbelief. Did manipulating and deceiving mean "caring," in the Reinhards' world?

Adam turned to his wife with a frown. "Didn't we intend to tell Ben eventually, Priscilla? After Savannah found a place?"

"Yes, we did. And in fact, I tried. I called Janine Knight." She shrugged. "But she was gone and so was Ben. Will Knight told me Ben had joined the Air Force, which I thought was a fine and patriotic thing to do. Good for him."

"Ah, right. There you go." Mr. Reinhard nodded at Julie, as if that solved everything. He checked his phone, which was vibrating. "Excuse me." He stepped away, leaving Julie with Priscilla, who looked as if she'd rather be anywhere else than alone with her.

"Okay, I can maybe almost wrap my mind around the idea that you thought I'd be better off away from Jupiter Point. But why didn't you tell me that you hadn't given Ben my message? All that time, he thought I'd dumped him and never looked back."

"Well, honestly, I thought you two would sort it out eventually, if you wanted to. True love finds a way and all that."

Julie folded her arms across her chest. All this time, had Priscilla been a secret romantic? "You really believe that?"

"What I *believe* is that teenagers shouldn't be making decisions that affect the rest of their lives. Sometimes adults need to step in and guide them in the right direction. Did we really do so wrong? You certainly seemed happy whenever we saw you in Los Angeles. You got a chance to pursue your singing, didn't you?"

Julie shook her head, bewildered. Even after seven years in their home, she'd never understand the Reinhards.

"What do want me to say, Julie? This all happened so long ago."

"Well, how about an apology? Some simple humanity? You messed with our lives. You caused us so much heartache."

"Heartache is character-building. But if you want an apology, then fine. Apology granted." Priscilla offered her hand with a polished smile.

Julie blinked at her. Was that a real apology? Did the words "apology granted" actually fit the description of an apology?

Nevertheless, she took the older woman's hand. *We cared about you, and still do.* Those words echoed through her mind. Were they really true, or more manipulation?

"You should apologize to Ben, too. You lied to him, after all."

"Should the opportunity arise," Priscilla murmured, with an expression that clearly said, 'don't push it.' "I'm glad we've cleared the air. Now where's my grandson? I have a project he can help me with. I want to put his obsessive attention to detail to good use. The Winter Ball is in three weeks and he's going to help me plan."

"You want him to plan the ball?" Julie couldn't imagine anything he'd enjoy less. "That doesn't sound like—"

"It will be character-building. Not everything is meant to be fun."

Julie rolled her eyes as Priscilla glided from the room. The Reinhards were a law unto themselves.

Her cell phone rang; Savannah was calling. Julie had filled her in on everything Ben had told her. "Well, did you talk to my parents? Did they fess up to their disgusting sabotage?"

"I think so. I mean, yes, they did. They gave all their reasons."

"Did they *apologize*?"

"That's open to interpretation. They sort of did, in their own way."

Savannah swore. "Typical. Look, just pull the plug on this visit. Bring Felix back to LA, I'll be done with this shoot soon and we'll get back to normal. If my parents can't act like decent human beings to you, they can go fuck themselves."

Julie stared at her reflection in the antique mirror above the sideboard. Savannah had a point. She could leave Jupiter Point and not look back. Put the impossible Reinhards in the rearview mirror.

Drop out of *Grease.*

Quit working for Knight and Day.

Say goodbye to Ben.

But she didn't want to do any of that. She wanted to be here in Jupiter Point. Now that she was back, she didn't miss the traffic that gave her stress headaches or the dry air that hurt her sinuses. She belonged in Jupiter Point. With Ben.

"Not yet," she told Savannah. "I'm not ready."

In the background, she heard someone yelling about lighting. Savannah swore. "I have to go. But Julie, I'm serious. Don't let my parents mess with you, okay? Love you."

She hung up. Julie looked at her reflection in the mirror again, saw the determination written on her face.

Nope, she was staying.

Even if she and Ben were just friends and co-workers, she was still staying. Even if she had to hide the fact that she dreamed about him at night, and lusted after him during the day, masking her feelings beneath quips and banter and answers to silly get-to-know-you questions.

NOT ALL THE questions were light. They got into other topics, too.

One sunny day, as Ben stood on a small ladder to check the oil level in the Cessna's engine, she asked him about his time in the Air Force. "Do you miss it?"

"I miss the brotherhood, the sense of purpose, like you're a band of superheroes saving the world." He bent over to peer at the dipstick; the pose made her mouth water. "My dad always saw me as the soft one in the family, you know that. Will was going to be a lawyer, Tobias was the fighter. Me, I was the lover." He smiled ruefully at her over his shoulder, since only the two of them knew that they'd done everything in the book except make love.

"Dad didn't have a whole lot of respect for that. When I was on active duty, I kept thinking 'if only Dad could see me now. He'd be so proud.' So I guess I miss that. Feeling like I'm making him proud. But I'm still in the Air Force reserves, so that's something."

"You don't think he'd be proud of all this?" She waved her hand at the tarmac and the helicopter and the brand-new Cessna. "It's amazing, what you guys have done. Starting a business from scratch, that's not easy."

He shrugged. "I wouldn't say it's from scratch. We both used the funds from the insurance company after Dad's death. I think he'd be pretty happy with Knight and Day. We used the Knight name on purpose, to honor him."

That made her smile. "He would love that, I know. Your father was a tough man, but he really loved his family. Even I could tell that...especially when he gave me that frown, like," she lowered her voice to a sterner octave, "what are you doing distracting my son from his schoolwork."

He laughed. "He did. We all knew it. Disappointing Dad was like death. None of us wanted that. Still don't. I'll sell off body parts before I let this business fail."

Her impulse was to ask which body parts, and could she have first bidding rights. But she wrestled her flirtatious urges under control. This was "friendship building." Nothing more.

He jumped off the ladder and walked around the plane. He crouched down to check the left tire. His thighs flexed and she swallowed, wondering why this preflight checklist operation was so darn sexy.

"Why did you decide to leave the military and come back here?"

"Hang on, isn't it my turn for a question?" He glanced over his shoulder at her with a grin.

"Nope. I answered all your TV and coffee questions, so I'm just going to keep going here. You could have stayed in the Air Force much longer, right? Why'd you come home?"

He rose to his feet and walked around to the other tire. "A lot of reasons. You know, I read a quote from a four-star general once that said the longer you stay in the military, the harder it is to have a normal life. It's true. I saw it with my parents. You know me, Julie. I like the ordinary things in life."

"Ordinary?" That wasn't a word she would ever associate with Ben Knight.

"I like watching the sunrise with a thermos of coffee in one hand, a girl tucked under the other. I like lunches that last three hours because you're chatting with everyone who walks through the door, all kinds of people, old, young, accountants, artists, whatever. I like to read. I like stargazing on a winter night. I'd like to travel as a normal person, not a soldier. I wanted to get to know my little brother. Aiden's in college now. That's crazy. I missed half his childhood. I love kids. Guys my age here in Jupiter Point are having their own families. And I was still suiting up at zero-dark-thirty for the next mission. I loved a lot of things about the Air Force, and I'm grateful I had the opportunity to serve. But I needed to come home." He kicked the tire one more time and stood up again.

She stared at him as liquid heat gathered in her lower belly and chills traveled through her body. She loved everything he'd just said, every word of it. All those same things had been true before, but he wouldn't have been able to express it so well. This grownup Ben, a man who knew who he was and who he wasn't, was even more appealing than the boy version.

"Can you go tell the clients that we're ready for them?" he asked as he handed over the checklist clipboard.

Wordlessly, she nodded and hurried back to the office before she did something crazy, like kiss him senseless.

As the days passed, not kissing him got harder and harder.

Every time he walked into the office, a current of desire hummed just under her skin, lifting the hairs on her arms and making her press her legs together under the desk. Oh man, she wanted him. She craved him. And not in the wild, intoxicated way of her youth. Now it was a grown-up, down-and-dirty, nitty-gritty lust. Screw the whole Project Friendship thing. She wanted sex with Ben. Hot, fantastic, mind-melting sex.

Did Ben feel any of those things too? She had no idea. He behaved like a perfect gentleman, a dream boss who treated her with respect and appreciation. But occasionally she caught a certain look from him, a smoldering secret glance. Those moments made her giddy with hope. There were also times when they inadvertently made physical contact. When she handed him paperwork to sign, and their fingertips touched. When she bumped into him coming out of the tiny restroom, and her entire body erupted into flames of yearning.

The sensual tension between them built the more time she spent at Knight and Day. In bed at night, she'd toss and turn and relive every word she and Ben had exchanged that day. He crept into her thoughts at odd moments—during rehearsals of *Grease,* during phone conversations with Savannah, while listening to Felix's explanation of the difference between a crescent wrench and a socket wrench.

Somehow, amazingly, she managed to keep her distance.

Until the day when a call came in from Sean Marcus, leader of the Jupiter Point Hotshots.

"Knight and Day Flight Tours, can I help you?"

"It's Sean, I need to talk to Ben!" he shouted over the background noise—a dull roar she couldn't identify. "His cell isn't answering."

"I'll get him right away. Hold on."

She transferred the call to her own cell and ran with it onto the tarmac, where Ben was busy with the Cessna. "Sean Marcus," she told him, still breathless from hurtling across the tarmac. "Sounds like an emergency."

Quickly, he hopped out of the fuselage and grabbed the phone from her. His face went grim and dead-serious as he listened.

"What's your location?" He nodded. "Be right there. Give me fifteen minutes." He hung up and tossed the phone back to her. "I need your help, Julie. Cancel the rest of the tours for today. Radio Tobias and tell him the Hotshots are in trouble and I'm taking the chopper up." He headed in the direction of the Robinson helicopter.

Julie followed him outside, her stomach tightening in fear. "Is this about that wildfire up north?"

He nodded, then sped up to a jog. "Keep the radio on. Keep your cell handy. Keep all lines open. When you reach Tobias, fill him in."

"Ben!" she called after him. "Be careful!"

He gave her a thumbs up as he opened the door of the helicopter, then swung onboard. He moved with such grace and efficiency that before she knew it, the rotors were slicing through the air and blowing her hair from her face.

She drew in a few deep breaths. Ben was a soldier. He'd be fine. He'd flown missions and faced dangers she had no clue about. Surely flying a helicopter into a fire zone would be...well, not exactly safe...

Focus, Julie.

Inside the cockpit of the Robinson, Ben's head was bent over the gauges. He was doing his job, getting ready to save lives. She sent a prayer in his direction, then ran back to the office to follow his instructions.

Her hands shaking, she radioed Tobias and relayed Ben's message. Then she set to work contacting the rest of the day's clients.

The wildfire had been in the newspaper for the past couple of days. She'd been reading about it every morning, and now it was all too real. A winter hiker had left his campfire burning during high winds in the wilderness about two hundred miles north of Jupiter Point. The fire season hadn't begun yet, but Sean Marcus, Josh Marshall and Finn Abrams, who all lived locally, had headed up the coast to lend a hand.

And now the firefighters were apparently in trouble. She thought about Suzanne, who was married to Josh. And Evie, Sean's wife. *When he sees a crisis, he plunges right in*, Evie had told her. Now Ben was doing the same thing. Were they all used to this kind of terror? Could anyone *ever* get used to it?

When she was done, she checked her watch and saw it was almost time to pick up Felix. But she couldn't leave, not now. Not while Ben was putting himself in danger to rescue the hotshots.

Gritting her teeth, she dialed Mrs. Reinhard and asked if she could pick up Felix just this once, even though it went against the grain to ask her for anything.

"Of course," said Priscilla. "Felix can help me with the invitation list this afternoon."

"He might be anxious because it's a break from our routine," Julie warned her.

"Don't you worry. I have everything under control."

Julie made a face as she hung up. Did Mrs. Reinhard really think she could control everything, even Felix's emotional states? Maybe she could control wildfires. If so, Julie would love her forever.

16

DURING HIS NEXT CONTACT WITH SEAN, BEN GOT A FEW MORE details about how they'd gotten trapped. Before the hotshots had even reached the command post, they'd spotted a new burn, a finger of the forest fire closing in on the highway, near a small settlement.

They called it in, then set about going door to door, letting people know a wildfire had them in its sights. When everyone had been warned, they got back into their crew buggy and hit the road. Except the road hit back. A deer, panicked by the oncoming wildfire, charged onto the highway. Sean swerved to avoid it and the vehicle hit a patch of melted snow and fishtailed into a tree.

No injuries, just a fast-moving fire and a broken-down truck. They didn't want to divert resources from the big wildfire, so Sean had called on Ben.

This was exactly why Sean had sold the airstrip to the Knight brothers, and why they'd purchased the Robinson. Helping out the hotshots with rescues and reconnaissance flights had always been the goal. Of course, Ben hadn't imagined that he'd be rescuing the hotshots *themselves*.

He kept in close communication with them as he buzzed up

the coastline. They'd had to retreat back to the village they'd just warned everyone to evacuate.

"Is there a town square or something where I can land? Or maybe a nice big bank building with a flat roof?"

"There's a gas station, a video store, couple guesthouses, a pub and that's about it. Not a flat roof in sight."

"At least you can check out some videos while you're hanging around."

"Jokes. Awesome. Just what we need."

Ben flipped through his options. A rescue generally required two people, one to pilot the chopper, one to put on a harness and ride a cable to retrieve the victim. The Robinson had been customized with regulation rescue gear. If he could get the door open and the cable lowered, the hotshots could put the harness on themselves. That would bring two up at once, and there were three of them. Two trips up and down.

But as he drew closer to the scene, his strategy changed completely. Wind was pushing the wildfire straight toward the highway and, judging by his gauges, it was picking up speed. Just to confirm, he switched to the nearest AWOS frequency and caught the tail end of the updated forecast. checked in with the nearest air traffic control.

Twenty knots east-southeast and picking up speed.

He switched back to Sean. "I'm going to need you to find the best spot on that highway for me to land. Got any flares with you? That'll tell me more about the wind too."

"Yup, we'll set one off."

"We need to make this as swift as we can. I just got a look at that fire." He didn't want to incite a panic, but he needed them to know.

"Ten-four," said Sean calmly. "We have line gear with us, and that includes shelters. You're plan A, but we have a plan B."

Ben relaxed a tiny bit. The hotshots were pros, they knew what they were doing. Many of them had survived a burnover a couple years ago, when they'd deployed their emergency tents and a wildfire had burned right over their heads.

He followed the curving line of the highway until he spotted the smoke from the flare. He throttled down and maneuvered the chopper down, down, through gusts of smoky air. It was a tricky descent, with treetops whipping back and forth on either side of the highway, and bursts of wind pummeling the Robinson. But the chopper was a big, heavy, mighty beast, not easily buffeted. Operating a rotorcraft wasn't much like flying a million-dollar fighter jet. But as soon as he'd left the Air Force, Ben had gotten his helicopter rating, with this exact kind of crisis in mind.

As he lowered down, the wind created by the rotors made the firefighters' mustard-yellow shirts whip against their bodies. He recognized Sean, Josh Marshall and Finn Abrams. They all wore heavy-looking backpacks and boots, and were grinning at him and waving.

As soon as the helicopter's skids touched the pavement, he put the hand brake on and yanked open the door. He eyed the rugged firefighters and their gear. Three hotshots, plus him, crammed into a helicopter designed for four—they'd just make it if they didn't go over the weight limit, which was eight hundred pounds, give or take. He estimated their combined weight, then gestured at their gear bags. "How much do those weigh?" he shouted over the *thwacking* of the blades.

"'Bout fifty pounds," Sean shouted.

"Feels like a hundred some days," added Josh, who was always the jokester of the group. Ben had spent enough evenings with them at Barstow's to know.

That added up to an extra hundred and fifty pounds. "Easy to replace?" he asked.

Without another word, Finn dumped his bag onto the street. Ben gave him a salute as the others followed his lead. One by one, they ducked under the blades and climbed inside. When they were all aboard, Sean closed the door and gave him a signal.

With a wary eye on the wildfire raging a few hundred yards away, Ben opened the throttle. The rotors sped up into a blur. Murmuring a quick prayer—the Robinson was pretty damn close to its weight capacity—he slowly pulled up on the collective and depressed the left foot pedal, which controlled the tail rotor. The helicopter lightened on its skids and slowly lifted into the air.

Always an incredible feeling. Of course, he'd never flown the copter in conditions like this before.

The Robinson struggled hard against the force of the head-winds created by the fire and the weight of its load. Ben fought the cyclic pitch, which kept wanting to steer the helicopter in the wrong direction. The firefighters stayed quiet and let him battle it out.

"Come on, come on," he muttered under his breath to the overburdened Robinson. "You can do this, baby. Make me proud."

Slowly, painfully, the craft put distance between itself and the ground, and Ben was sure they were going to make it. A hundred feet, two hundred, the highway now a gray, curving line between forests, flames on one side, virgin green on the other.

And then a terrifying jolt made the chopper drop about twenty feet.

Shit. Turbulence? An in-draft created by the fire? He twisted the grip of the collective to get the rotors spinning even faster. He felt the quiver of the engine in the palms of his hands.

Not now, he thought in a sudden, profound panic. *I still have to...Julie.*

Julie. He had to see Julie again. And not in the friend way. In the love way. The way in which two people show their true hearts to each other. He had to show her, tell her how important she was to him. Had always been.

He fought the cross current that had seized them, Julie's smile shimmering in his mind's eye. Right hand gripping the collective, feet on the pedals, he powered through the gusty fire-generated winds. *Go, go*, he chanted. Not silently, as he'd thought. But out loud, and joined by the hotshots. *"Go, go, go,"* they all repeated, until the chopper had enough altitude to level out. Then they changed their chant to "Yeah, Ben!" and pats rained down on his shoulders and back.

He drew in a deep breath and let it out. He tilted his head back and forth to release the tension. "Sorry, guys," he called over the engine noise. "Didn't expect it to be so white-knuckle."

"Dude, you are never paying for a drink at Barstow's again," shouted Josh. "That was fricking amazing!"

Ben grinned, more out of sheer relief than anything else. He'd had some dicey moments in the Air Force, but somehow that was different. These were firefighters, friends, guys whose wives and girlfriends he knew. If something had happened to any of them, the heartbreak of Evie, or Suzanne, or Lisa... God, he didn't want to think about it.

Julie. He wanted to see her, now. He wanted to sweep her into his arms and nuzzle her hair and tell her that he'd never stopped loving her. And never would.

As soon as they approached the Knight and Day landing strip, he started looking for her. She came racing out of the office as the helicopter descended toward the tarmac. Tobias followed at a slower jog, but Ben barely noticed him. *Julie.* He wanted Julie in his arms as soon as humanly possible.

The skids touched down, and he powered down the craft. The firefighters stepped off first, whooping as they landed on solid ground. Tobias veered toward them, but Julie kept going. She darted around the nose of the Robinson, reaching him just as he set foot on the tarmac.

Before he could even say a word, she flung herself into his arms.

"You're okay. You're okay," she kept whispering. "I was so scared."

"Hey, hey." He soothed her by tracing slow circles on her

back. Her heart was racing, rapid heartbeats drumming against his chest. How many missions had he flown without anyone fretting over him? All of them. Until now. "I wasn't the one in danger. All I had to do was swoop in with the chopper. Nice work if you can get it." He kept his tone light and teasing, or at least he thought he did.

She drew back a step, looking at him sternly. "I know you. It wasn't that simple, was it?"

"Not quite," he admitted. He'd liked it more a second ago, when she was pressed up against him. "Hey, if I tell you I cheated death by a whisker, will you hug me again?"

That brought a real smile to her face. She swatted him lightly on the upper arm, then dove into his arms again. "I'm sorry. I know I shouldn't do this. I know we're starting fresh and we're friends and all of that. Can we just...have this moment and then go back to your friend questionnaire?"

"I'm not sure it works that way." He brushed a silky lock of hair away from her face so he could see her. "I'll try, but now that I've had you in my arms..." He gazed into her wide eyes, still dark from the adrenaline that had rushed through her system. "I'm not sure I can forget how good this feels."

And God, did it feel good. She molded her body against him, warm and soft and tempting. He filled his hands with her, drank her in. His cock went hard as steel, but he shifted so she didn't feel it. Maybe she wasn't ready for that yet. Maybe she was still on Project Friendship. He didn't want to screw things up, but God, he wanted her with a throbbing, aching need.

She tilted her head and rested her chin against his chest. "I never forgot how this feels," she whispered. "Never."

Did she mean... God, he hoped so.

"Julie." His voice was rough from smoke and desire. "Would you like to come over tonight? Maybe someone could stay with Felix."

"Come over..." Color rushed into her face. "Like we used to? In the old days? Come over and do homework and make out?"

He grinned widely. "We can skip the homework."

The sound of a throat clearing made them both jump. Ben kept his arms around Julie—no way was he letting her go now—and turned to see the three rescued hotshots, along with Rollo, grinning at them. Rollo must have come to pick them up.

"Just want to say thanks again for the extraction," said Sean.

"You bet," Ben answered. He liked all these guys, he really did, but right now he just wanted them gone so he could settle things with Julie.

"It was a little hairy there for a moment, huh?" Josh said. "My life actually flashed before my eyes. I liked the last part best, everything with Suzanne and Faith in it."

Ben felt Julie stiffen in his arms at Josh's mention of his life flashing.

"Right?" Finn laughed a little. His facial scar was a little redder than usual—irritated by the smoke, maybe? "That was a hell of a ride. You have nerves of steel, Ben Knight. Couldn't ask for a better rescue pilot."

"Jupiter Point's damn lucky you guys are here and geared up the way you are," added Rollo.

"Spread the word. Knight and Day Flight Tours, the experience of a lifetime." He grinned as he shook Rollo's hand.

The hotshots saluted him again, smiled at Julie, then took off across the tarmac toward Rollo's rig, an impressive crew of good-looking, rugged individuals. Solid, good guys. And he'd just saved them.

As soon as they were out of sight, Julie swung around and pushed at his chest. "You made it sound like it was easy! Like you were never in danger!"

"There's always some danger. There was a wildfire. They're dangerous."

"But—" The stormy look on her face dissolved into something else, something deeper, more emotional. "Tonight. What time?"

"Anytime. Just show up. I'll be waiting."

She nodded, and the air between them quivered with electric anticipation. The adrenaline from the rescue still hammered through his veins. He remembered this feeling from the Air Force, when every sense was heightened, and the world appeared sharp and clear and present.

Except now Julie was here, and all his senses were completely attuned to her.

17

Julie left soon afterward to check in on Felix. She shot Ben a text message that read, "Mission still a go for tonight. (Air Force lingo, right?)"

With the rest of the day's tours cancelled, he and Tobias closed up early. Tobias went home to his new family, while Ben decided to surprise Julie with the most romantic meal he could think of. Would flowers be overboard? What about a chocolate hazelnut torte from Pie in the Sky?

What if she couldn't make it after all?

When she finally tapped on his door, he felt a rush of relief so strong, it rivaled a safe landing in an A-10. *She hasn't changed her mind.* He took a breath and opened the door for her.

At the sight of her, his jaw dropped. She wore a silky little clingy dress that hit her mid-thigh, along with some kind of sky-high heels that made her legs look endless. She held a bottle of red wine, about the same shade as her dress. He could drink her up in one gulp.

As he stood gaping at her, she sniffed the air. "Lasagna? Seriously, you made lasagna?"

"I checked my notes. Still your favorite." He shook himself out of his stupor and opened the door farther. She walked in, her dress swirling around her hips, so sexy he couldn't breathe. He nearly groaned out loud at the throbbing in his cock.

How the hell was he going to make it through an entire dinner? And dessert? Maybe he could toss that torte out the window before she even saw it. And why had he bothered with appetizers—crackers and gorgonzola and olives? What a frickin' waste of time! This was going to take forever. What if they didn't have forever? What if Felix needed her? She could get a call and leave at any moment, leaving him with a terminal case of blue balls. Were there any medical consequences to blue balls?

Crazy thoughts like these ran through his head as she stepped into his condo. The space had a simple layout, with the living and dining room separated only by a bookcase, and a pass-through window from kitchen to dining room. He'd only been living here for a few weeks, since Carolyn and Sarah had moved into the farmhouse. But at heart, he was a homebody, and he'd taken care to make the space the way he wanted it. A rug he'd bought in Greece covered the living room floor, and embroidered throw pillows from Turkey added a touch of color to the couch.

Julie walked through the living room to the dining room table, where she set down the bottle of wine. Tall tapers burned in wooden candleholders he'd found at an outdoor market in Afghanistan. They were carved into the shape of horse heads, and had so much personality that he'd paid outrageously for them. She touched one on its flared wooden nostrils and smiled.

Then her gaze traveled to the bouquet of early tulips that he'd acquired from Brianna's greenhouse. They sat in a vase that his mother had found at a vintage store.

"I remember that vase," she said softly. "Milk glass, your mom called it."

He couldn't answer. Right now, he felt so exposed, so laid bare. It was crystal clear how much effort he'd made for this dinner. How much he wanted to impress her. How much she mattered to him. Even down to the music playing on his iPod speaker—Whitney Houston, who had always been Julie's favorite singer as a teenager.

Would his need for her, his desire, scare her away? Should he have played it cool, the way he usually did? Six-pack and an order of takeout, with the highlight being a strip of condoms?

Slowly, she turned to face him. The candlelight made her eyes glisten like dark liquid jewels. "You did all this for me," she whispered.

"Well, the UPS guy couldn't make it, so I guess it's all about you," he quipped. But his joke was off, and they both knew it. There was too much strong emotion coursing between them. "Hey, if it's too much, don't worry about it. We can take those tulips to Knight and Day. And you know how Tobias is with lasagna."

She sniffed. "Don't say that. I love it." With one finger, she blotted the tear about to roll down her face. "I remember when the only thing you knew how to make was beef jerky on crackers. It's just—this is amazing, because no one has cooked a meal specifically for me since Mom died." Her mouth quirked into a smile. "And that was probably vegan and gluten-free."

His heart just about melted away. In two steps, he was at her side, his arms around her. "Aw, man. And I loaded this up with cheese. What was I thinking?"

She laughed, her face lighting up. "I like how you were thinking. I wish I'd brought more than just wine."

"Well, you did bring that killer dress." He slid his finger under the edge of her neckline to the silk of her skin. In the candlelight, she was luminous as a star. "That's worth about a month of lasagnas."

"I made a quick shopping trip. I had nothing that would catch the eye of a dashing pilot."

"Everything you wear catches my eye."

She leaned toward him, lips parting, pupils darkening.

He bent down and did what he'd been wanting to do since the first moment she'd walked back into his life. He touched his lips to hers.

And there it was. The sizzle. The fire. The electric connection he'd never felt with anyone else.

They used to kiss for hours at a time. During the two years they'd been together, they'd probably racked up a couple of months' worth of kissing. And it all came back, like riding a bike. Eyes closed, he moved his mouth against hers, savoring every sensation, every warm puff of breath, every sweet meeting of soft flesh. He loved her lips, and he knew them so well. That plump swell of the lower lip, the little upward curve on the right corner. And then there was the little chip in one of her teeth, a tiny roughness that sometimes caught him short.

That was gone, he realized. She'd seen a dentist in LA. Of course she had. One tiny change among thousands.

Like the curve of muscle along her spine. She had more sumptuous, mouthwatering flesh there now. And the way it flared into her hips, with that bodacious swell, oh my God. She was all woman now. And when she drew away from him, gasping for breath, the woman looking at him had all the heat and passion of an adult, not a tentative girl.

"Would you take it as an insult if I suggest we hold off on dinner?" she said breathlessly. "I want it. Every bit of it. But I want you more."

He growled deep in his chest, filling his hands with the firm globes of her ass. "I was going to say the same thing. I was afraid of coming off like a horny kid."

She cupped the front of his pants, where a hard bulge met her fingers under his black jeans. It was a bold move, one she wouldn't have made as a teenager. "Reminds me of my favorite horny kid," she whispered. "The one named Ben Knight."

"Name sounds familiar. But I can't think right now." His voice sounded raspy, like sandpaper. He pulled away, then took her hand in his, ready to lead her to the bedroom.

"Wait one second." He released her hand so she could bend down and unfasten the ankle straps of her stilettos. "I can't handle one more minute in these torture shoes. The sales clerk made me buy them, said they were guaranteed to get your attention. She didn't warn me that I might be crippled by the end of the night."

"Honey, if you're crippled by the end of the night, it's going to be for an entirely different reason." He winced. "Uh, that didn't really come out right. I meant it in a good way. Like we're going to be at it all night long. Until we're so exhausted, neither of us can walk. That kind of crippled."

She laughed up at him as she slipped off her second shoe. "Ben. Don't worry. This is me. Julie. You can say anything."

"Anything?"

"Absolutely. You know what?" She rose back to her feet, substantially shorter than she had been a minute ago. "I'll start. Where's your bedroom?"

He put his hands on her shoulders and spun her toward his room. "That-away."

18

Julie's stomach felt as if a swarm of nervous bees had invaded it. As Ben shut his bedroom door, enclosing them in his private space, her lustful side warred with her anxious side.

"You realize that this is," she counted on her fingers, "thirteen years in the making. We never actually had sex back then."

"Believe me, I remember." He hadn't stopped touching her since they'd left the living room, and now he tucked one crooked finger under her chin. "We came close, the last time we were together. I always thought we'd be each other's firsts. That was the plan."

"Me too." She managed a smile, even though her heart gave a sad little dip. "I guess we missed the boat on that. But you can still be my third."

His eyes darkened to an intense stormy shade. "Third? You've only been with two men until now?" His hand traveled to the back of her head, where he began massaging lightly. He could probably tell that she was nervous. Maybe he was slowing things down to make her more comfortable.

"I've had my hands full. I've dated my fair share, but mostly I got some funny stories out of it. Savannah and I used to try to top each other's dating nightmares."

Also—though she didn't want to say it-- no one had appealed to her, compared to Ben.

"And then?"

"Well, first Felix's occupational therapist asked me out. I figured it was about time I had sex, and he was a nice guy."

Oh, that hand of his, relaxing the tendons in her neck, spreading sweet honey through her system. She dropped her head back and surrendered to his touch. "So where is he now?"

"I think he might be married now. It ended on a good note, but we didn't really stay in touch. Number two didn't last long either, no details necessary."

Ben pressed a kiss against her neck. "Good to know. I don't want to have to compete with some occupational therapist good guy. Or kick his ass."

She giggled at the thought of Ben having to compete with Simon. No contest there. "What about you? Obviously I'm not your first." She winced as soon as she brought it up. Honestly, she wasn't sure she wanted to know Ben's side of this story. A hot fighter-jet pilot, flying for his country, a guy as sweet and sexy as Ben? She probably had a mile-long list of women to compete with.

"You're the first," Ben said cheerfully.

"Um..." She frowned skeptically. "I'm sorry, but that's impossible to believe. Look at you." She stepped back and swept her gaze up and down his body. "Not buying it."

"The first in all the important ways."

She rolled her eyes. "Okay, nice line. Anyway. Moving on." She tapped a finger against her chin, as if negotiating "How about this? I promise to forget about all those others if you take your shirt off."

"Done." He quickly unbuttoned his light blue cambric shirt,

which he wore over a ribbed undershirt that clung to every mouthwatering muscle.

"Both shirts," she ordered him.

"Bossy. Demanding. I like it." He pulled the undershirt off, but it snagged on his head, giving her an extra moment to appreciate the full spectacle of his perfectly honed torso. She tried to imagine all the crunches and lifts that must have gone into building musculature like that. Looking closer, she noticed a small tattoo over his heart, but she couldn't quite make out what it was.

Finally, he got the shirt all the way off, just in time to catch her peering at his naked chest. His gray-blue eyes laughed at her. "I know you think I'm leering at you, and I am," she admitted. "I'm also trying to figure out what your tattoo is."

"It's a mountain and a star. Jupiter Point. I got it overseas, when I was homesick as a baby. I missed everything...my family, you, the fricking Milky Way ice cream shop. The mountain and star kind of summed it all up."

She traced it, noting the beautiful colors, the deep green of the mountain peaks, the blue of the star. "Right over your heart," she murmured.

"Yup. I'm a sap. I actually balled the entire time I was getting the tattoo. That way I could blame it on the needle gun."

She smiled mistily at the image of big strong Ben weeping on the tattoo table. Ben had never been afraid to show emotion, but maybe things were different in the Air Force. "Those needle guns would make anyone cry. Even a tough girl like me."

His gaze sharpened, and he padded closer to her, until his half naked magnificence was only a step away. "You're talking personal experience?"

"I am. Want to see?" She teased him by inching up the hem of her dress, bit by bit.

"Hell yes." With greedy eyes, he watched every movement she

made. The heat from that look set her on fire. "Let me guess. Lower back?"

"No."

"Inner thigh?" he asked hopefully.

"No."

"Please don't say breasts, because that just sounds painful. And your breasts are so perfect and beautiful, I think that would break my heart."

Her dress had reached the upper edge of her thigh-highs. Not her favorite part of her body; the elastic pressed into her flesh, so it spilled over a little. It didn't seem to bother him. He watched her ravenously, savoring every bit of exposed skin.

Finally, the lower tip of the tattoo could be seen, then the entire thing. It traveled around her rib cage, five little marks, each one no bigger than a thumb, but the flock of them combining into a flight of cranes across her torso.

Over the fabric of her dress, she watched Ben closely. Would he recognize the meaning? Would he remember the pond her mother tended in the hopes that the cranes would alight there during their journey north? Would he remember the time, after Mom had died, when she and Ben had been jogging down the back road and a pair of cranes had swooped by, a few feet above their heads? She'd started crying, right then and there, sure that those cranes had been a message from her mother. That her mother wanted her to be happy, to be in love.

She could tell from his expression that he remembered. Ben was the only person in the world who would understand her tattoo without some kind of explanation. She pulled her dress the rest of the way off her body, until she faced him in nothing but bra, underwear and thigh-highs.

He touched each tattooed crane in turn, gently, the soft caress sending thrills though her. "She would have loved this. I remember when she got really into figuring out everyone's spirit animals."

"Yes, she loved that kind of thing. Whenever I came home crying because Savannah was so much more beautiful than I was, she would say, 'the peacock might draw more eyes, but he cannot fly into the heavens like the crane can.' Which didn't really help at all, but it was a pretty thought. She was kind of magical like that."

"She was." The way he looked at her made her knees quiver. His gaze traveled from the flock of cranes to her breasts, still hidden behind the silk bra she'd purchased just for this very moment. "*God*, you're beautiful."

The worshipful tone of his voice made her lower belly clench. Under his gaze, she couldn't imagine ever *not* feeling beautiful. She held her breath as he touched the pad of his index finger to her right nipple. Slowly he circled it, his entire focus arrowing in on her pebbling flesh.

The pleasure was insane. How could such a light touch have such an intense effect? It made no sense. She swayed on her feet, her eyes drifting half-closed as she drank in every pulse of sensation created by his sure finger.

An iron band behind her back stabilized her. Scratch that. It was his arm, the other one, the one that wasn't attached to the hand currently teasing her nipple until it throbbed. "God, Ben," she whispered. "I missed this so much."

"Me too," he rumbled. "Your breasts were my obsession for all of junior year. I don't know how I've managed to live without them."

She nearly choked on a bubble of laughter. "You're so ridiculous."

"I'm serious. And now they're hiding behind a damn bra. Do you mind?"

She shook her head, relaxing in his arms as he unfastened her bra from behind and slid it off her body. He cupped her breasts in both hands. His exaggerated groan of appreciation made her smile. "They're just breasts," she noted.

"Oh no. These are not just breasts. These babies are an important part of my psyche, I'll have you know." He filled his hands with her flesh, using his thumbs to elicit more delicious sensations from the tips. "If you knew how many fantasies they starred in. Between your swimsuits and your sports bras and those little belly shirts you used to wear...oh my God. I swear, these boobs are like my long-lost BFFs."

She was laughing so hard now that she almost didn't notice he was now reaching for the waistband of her underwear. "I seriously didn't know you had such an intense relationship with the girls."

"I didn't want you to get jealous. I still liked you best."

Her breath caught as he slid a finger under her panties, which were made of a filmy, clingy kind of fabric that teased as much as it covered.

"I gotta say, much as I love your underwear, the thought of you in nothing but those thigh-highs might make me come in my pants."

"Better take them off, then." She flicked him on the arm. "I can't believe you're still wearing them while I'm practically naked."

"They're the only thing keeping my cock from springing out like a fucking jaguar."

Cock. Had the young Ben ever said the word "cock" to her? She didn't think so. "Dick," maybe. Even that had made her blush.

He noticed her reaction. "Sorry, too salty? I've been in the Air Force; my language is rougher than it used to be."

"No no. It's fine. It's actually...I like it." All the saliva had dried up in her mouth, so she passed her tongue over her lips to moisten it. He tracked the motion with hot eyes. "It makes me feel like I can say things like, I don't know, 'clit.'"

His eyes danced. "Yeah, that's a new one from Julie deGaia. I think if you'd ever said 'clit' to me back then my head would have exploded. I barely knew what a clit was. I actually think I looked 'clitoris' up in the encyclopedia. I had to do some research before we took that step, remember?" His hand slid under her panties until it reached the warmth between her legs. "There it is. Right where I remember it."

"Some things don't change." She gasped and held on to his shoulders as he fingered the tiny nub of flesh crying out for attention. She had to hand it to the clitoris—it might be small and soft and hidden, but it was amazingly powerful. It was making her do crazy things, like open her legs farther and beg him not to stop touching her. It took charge of her body, putting the rest of her on notice. *We're doing this. Oh God yes, we're doing this.*

He caressed her until she was slick with wet, juicy desire, until the dampness ran down her thighs. *This* was what she'd missed with the others. This searing, electric pleasure, the powerful connection that caught her up like a rushing river.

Ben had always been a sensitive lover, watching her closely to see how things felt for her. He'd check in with her all the time— does this feel good? Does this hurt? Do you like it when I touch you here? Sometimes his questions had made her blush.

But now, along with the sensitivity, he had a new level of confidence. When he touched her, she saw no trace of doubt or hesitation. He stroked her clit with his long fingers, his expression tender, focused, intent. He slid one finger inside her, and she nearly came right then from the shock of pleasure.

She thought of the first time she'd had an orgasm with Ben. He'd been so amazed that he'd pulled it off that he'd actually howled at the moon in triumph. She'd laughed at his glee, but when the tables were turned and he came in her hand, just from her touch, she'd felt the same way.

Face it—Ben was special to her, special in a way that no one else could ever be. And now they were about to do the one thing they'd held back from.

Was she really ready to have sex with Ben? What if it meant

that he'd be even more cemented into her heart? Sex was the one piece they'd never shared, and maybe that was why they were able to attempt a friendship now. Would they still be able to be "friends" if they slept together? The stakes seemed so insanely high. And Ben was so important to her. Such a part of her life, her history, her being.

So she pulled away from his dizzying touch and took a step back so she could catch her breath and get a grip on her emotions.

Ben's bedroom held a king-size bed with a simple oyster-colored comforter, neatly made up. A night table sat on each side of the bed, with lamps and books and an iPad, all in orderly piles. "You're so much tidier than you used to be."

"The service will do that to you." Ben watched her, eyes still dark with arousal, his chiseled, bare torso covered in a light sheen of sweat, which gave his muscles even more spectacular definition. He looked so downright incredible that she felt dizzy all over again. He folded his arms over his chest. The flex of his biceps made her mouth water. "Are we taking a break to admire my housekeeping skills?"

"Well, I *am* a professional," she pointed out weakly. "And you do an excellent job."

"Thanks. I try. Order is important to me. I like things to be nice and harmonious around me. All the better to mess it up when I have a good reason."

A full-body shiver went through her; his expression made it obvious what that "good reason" would be. "You're still wearing pants," she said. "It didn't seem fair."

"That's why you stopped?" He quirked his eyebrows and put his hands to the fastening of his jeans. "No problem." He shucked off his pants and faced her in nothing but his boxers.

At first, she was so riveted by the long, sleekly powerful muscles of his thighs that she didn't notice the boxers. But eventually her gaze made it to his underwear—and she burst into laughter.

"What?" He faked an innocent, wounded look. "You're not supposed to laugh when a man strips down to his underwear. A guy's ego could get mortally wounded by that."

"Have you been wearing those all these years? There's no way. That's not possible." She put her hand over her mouth to stop the giggles from pouring out. But she couldn't help it.

The very first time she and Ben had taken their clothes off together, he'd been wearing those same boxers as a joke. They were black with flames printed on them, along with the words "Pull Down in Case of Emergency." They'd looked ridiculous back then, but now, with his added muscle and bulk, they were outright hysterically funny.

He grinned at her as she cracked up. "I found them when I was moving my stuff from the farmhouse. It really brought back some memories. Nice, huh?" He struck a muscleman pose, arms above his head, tendons straining. "Sexy, right?" He shifted into a quick comical sequence of bodybuilder poses. By the end of it, she was laughing so hard, she had to sit down.

"Oh my God. Please stop! I can't take it. You know what's the funniest?" She gestured at the stiff mound of his erection straining behind the printed flames. "You can barely fit your erection in there."

"Believe me, I know." He plucked at the fabric, screwing up his face in a look of discomfort. "But I didn't want to take them off until you got the full effect. I thought you'd appreciate the flashback."

"Oh, I do. I haven't laughed so hard..." She wiped a tear away. All her tension, all her anxiety about the stakes involved in sleeping with Ben, it all disappeared. This was *Ben*. The sweetest, most tender soul she'd ever known. They'd be fine. They'd figure it out. Whether or not they slept together.

And damn it all, they'd gotten this far, the two of them nearly naked except for a pair of thigh-highs, panties and boxers covered in flames. It would be practically criminal to back out now. When she was eighty and thinking back on her life, she didn't want to remember that time when her beautiful Ben wore nothing but his ridiculous boxers and she walked away.

She rose from the bed and took two steps, until she was pressed against him. Tucking one finger under the waistband of those boxers, she felt the heat radiating from his penis. "Love the boxers, but I'm even more excited about what's under them, flyboy."

His eyes flared. "They're gone. I'll set the damn things on fire if you want."

"Don't you dare. They're historical relics now. They need to be preserved." She slid her hand against the warm, flat surface of his lower belly, tangling her fingers in the springy hair she found there. He groaned softly as she played with him, barely brushing the large shape of his erection.

He put his hands on her upper arms and looked at her closely. "You sure you want this? You looked a little anxious there for a moment."

"I'm sure. I was freaking out a little, I admit. Sex changes things; it always does."

"We did everything except make love back then. It almost seems like a technicality."

"Maybe. But maybe not. I guess there's only one way to find out." She wrapped her fingers around his hot shaft. No, there was no way she was walking away now.

Urgent hope flared in his eyes. "Julie, you know how bad I want this. But not bad enough to mess things up." He ran his hands down the outside of her arms to her wrists, then back up. She shivered, her nipples rising all on their own, just from the light feathering of his palms along her arms.

"We won't mess things up. We're adults now. All grown up. We're not kids, so consumed with emotion that we can't just enjoy ourselves." She pushed his boxers down his thighs, revealing the iron firmness of his muscles, the light scattering of hair, the thick rise of his newly freed erection. He was so masculine, so strong and sturdy.

He stepped out of them, leaving them on the floor next to the rest of his clothes. Now he was completely naked, her familiar Ben in a new and outrageously sexy form. Heat rushed to her face as she saw the full extent of his arousal—thick and full and hard and desirous.

He wanted her just as much as she wanted him. And she wanted him so much that her thighs were quivering.

He watched her with hot eyes. "I want to taste you again. I've never gotten the flavor of you out of my head." He crowded against her, causing a gasp of pleasure to burst from her mouth. He laid her back on the bed, then braced over her, one knee on either side of her legs. He bent down and licked one erect nipple until it throbbed, then the other. The place between her legs ached for him. She lifted her hips to him, wanting, needing more...and he was there. He tugged down her panties with an impatient hand and claimed her sex. The contact was direct and intimate, and she gave a cry of happiness.

He held her for a moment like that, then lowered himself down so his head came between her thighs. His tongue, that glorious organ that had studied her and learned everything about her in the past, touched her clit. Then swirled and tasted and savored.

She gave herself over to him, letting him spread her legs wider, hook them over his shoulders. At first, she tilted her head to watch him, but the sight of his tousled head planted between her legs, still in thigh-highs, his wide shoulders bunching with muscle, was too much for her.

So she lay back and closed her eyes, letting the sensations play through her, each one taking on a sound in her head, a melody or a rhythm. He trailed his fingers across the tender skin of her inner thighs, adding a high note of pure delight. Then his thumb joined in, its thickness sliding alongside her clit, making her bite back a scream. Then came a finger inside her again, then another, stroking deep, finding a spot inside. She wanted to explode into fireworks.

Nearly delirious with pleasure, she flung her arms wide, digging her fingers into the comforter, as if she might fly off into the ether if she didn't anchor herself.

And then she *was* flying. He sent her there, into the upper atmosphere of bliss. As if riding a magic carpet, she soared high overhead, all hint of gravity gone. All time, all space, vanished. On waves of pleasure, she floated, each convulsion shooting her higher, offering more ecstasy, until the world was entirely hers, and she was entirely his.

She came down in stages. First a long moan, then a touch on his hair, then a tug on his shoulder. "Come here," she whispered. "Up here. With me."

He crawled up her body so his face was level with hers, so he could drop a lingering kiss on her lips. She tasted sex on his mouth. "Come inside me," she urged.

He nodded briefly. The tension on his face made it looked carved from stone. Her orgasms had always been the biggest turn-on for him. Nothing revved him up quite like watching her come apart under his touch. Apparently, the same thing held true now, because when she reached between his powerful legs, she found his penis scalding hot and hard as steel.

"Condom," he said as he reached for the drawer of his nightstand.

Of course. Condoms. They'd never needed those before, but of course he was right. They weren't two virgins experimenting anymore. They'd been out in the world, and the world could have left its mark.

She shoved the thought aside. It didn't matter. That was the whole point—they were adults now, doing adult things like "going all the way." Wearing a condom was part of that. If they'd had sex back then, they probably would have used a condom as the easiest form of birth control.

He sat back on his heels long enough to cover himself with latex. As he did so, she feasted her eyes on his form. Every bit of him was familiar to her, with some new details. A silvery scar on his right rib cage. Whimsical swirls of light brown hair arrowing toward his crotch. And of course, the mountain and star tattoo. But the way he bent his head, the way he smiled crookedly when he was done, the warmth in his eyes—that was all the same. Her beautiful, wonderful Ben.

She smiled back, pouring her entire heart into it. Emotion throbbed between them, so strong it was nearly tangible. He lifted his body over her, bracing himself with arms made of pure corded muscle. She reached down and took him into her hand. Even through the latex, his heat and firmness made her heart sing. She guided him to her entrance, which was already slick and slippery from her climax.

"My sweet Ben," she whispered as she lifted her hips for him. He eased inside her, his eyes wide open and focused on her face. No place to hide. No way to disguise how it felt to be filled by him.

It felt glorious—beyond glorious. As if they'd found paradise, just the two of them. She felt her heart open up to him, along with her body. Nothing stood between them, nothing but a thin layer of latex and the last remnants of her wariness.

When he was fully seated inside her, he whispered in her ear, "This. This is it. You and me."

Whatever he meant, she barely heard him, because her attention was riveted to the hard flesh filling her to overflowing. He drew out, long and slow, and impaled her again. She gasped at the sensation of being *claimed*. That was how it felt as he thrust deep once again, then again, the pace scrambling her brain. She couldn't control her response. She could only release all hesitation, all fear, and abandon herself to the flight he was taking her on.

"Oh baby." He groaned and ran his hands across her skin, the backs of her thighs, her calves, her shoulders, anything he could reach. "God, you feel good. How can anything feel this good? It's impossible."

She gave a broken laugh, wanting to say something but unable to summon words. To be like this with Ben, after all these years, when she'd feared she might never even see him again, let alone go to bed with him—it was overwhelming.

He checked in when she didn't say anything. "You okay?" Typical Ben, thinking of her even when he looked like he was about to detonate in the world's most explosive orgasm.

"Good," she managed. "So good."

"I can't last very long. Sorry."

"No, don't be. It's okay. I want you to come." She wanted him to feel as good as she did. If he could experience even a fraction of the bliss she had, she'd be happy.

But even though she'd already orgasmed, new streams of pleasure were coursing through her system. The feel of his body, the scent of his skin, the sound of the bed creaking, his panting breaths, the sensual slap of flesh against flesh, the glimpses of damp hair, hard, flat nipples, straining muscles...it all added up to a kind of surround-sound extrasensory state. Immersed in sensation, she lost track of herself, of what was her and what was him.

And when his body stilled, rigid as his release seized him, she slipped into a soft, rolling orgasm, almost a sympathy climax triggered by his.

He fell into her arms after that, and they rolled onto their sides, holding each other. Deep tremors vibrated through his frame, like the aftershocks of an earthquake. She stroked his long, muscled back, collecting the dew of his sweat on her fingertips. In a sweet daze of afterglow, words came and went, drifting in and out but not surfacing into actual expression.

Thank you, she wanted to say. *Wow. I love you. I've always loved you.* The sort of thing it wouldn't be wise to say out loud, not now. Maybe not ever.

Sex changes things. She knew it was true. But "change" was a big word that covered a lot of territory. What kind of changes? Good, bad? Heartbreaking? Glorious?

"Oh man." Ben finally stirred. "I'm dead. I think I'm dead." His tone, a combination of humor and sexy appreciation, made her smile. As always, he had a knack for chasing away her worries.

"You'd better not be. Those Cessnas won't fly themselves."

"Heartless. That's what you're worried about? You practically kill me with sex and you're concerned about the flight schedule?" He pulled the condom off his penis and tossed it toward a wastebasket in the corner.

"You hired me for a reason."

He lifted himself up on one elbow. Alarm mingled with satisfaction in his gaze. "Shit, I forgot about that part. You work for Knight and Day. Did we just break an HR rule?"

"Well, since you don't *have* any HR rules, I'd say no. And besides..." She hesitated briefly. "I need to quit."

19

"WHAT ARE YOU TALKING ABOUT?" BEN'S HEART SANK. THIS WAS the last thing he expected to hear after the intensely intimate experience they'd just shared.

"You only hired me to get you organized and get your systems set up. That's all done now. So, I'm quitting." She smiled at his horrified expression. "You'll be fine, I promise. I found a book-keeper who can come in once a week and keep you on track."

"No. I won't be fine." Was Julie disappearing again? Already? No, it wasn't fair to hold her previous disappearance against her like that. *Lighten up.* "I'll be going through Julie withdrawal," he said lightly. "You'll have to let me see you every day to get me through the transition."

"No problem. I have the perfect opportunity. How about I hire *you* this time? I need help running my lines for *Grease.* You mentioned before that you'd be willing to do it."

"Of course I will." Relief flooded through him. She wasn't ditching him. At least not yet.

"It's crunch time now; the first dress rehearsal is in two weeks and I'm still not off-book. That's one of the reasons I need to quit Knight and Day. I don't have time for everything."

He grumbled at her. "I guess that will have to satisfy me. Running lines with you. Naked, of course."

"Yes, didn't you know this is the nude version of *Grease*? I mentioned that the part of Danny is being played by the gospel choir director at the Baptist Church, right?"

"The one with the big belly and the bald head?"

"Yup. He has the best voice in town. And he can really move. You should see him in the 'Greased Lightning' number."

He traced the inner slope of her hip bone, where the texture of her skin became even softer. "Are you sure it's safe to do something so public, Julie? What if that man is still hanging around?"

"That's exactly why I told them no at first. But I've been here over a month now, and it's such a small town. He would know by now. So I think he's gone. I really do."

"I hope so." He spread his fingers across the slight rise of her lower belly.

She shivered. "I don't. I wanted to catch him. I wanted to be the hero who put that bastard behind bars."

With a soft laugh, he nuzzled her hair. This was the fiery side of Julie, the one who'd stood up to his father. "Nice thought, but I'd rather you stay safe. Count me in for whatever rehearsing you need. You know my schedule better than I do by now."

"So true." She turned her head so their lips met in a long kiss. "Thank you. I tried to get Felix to help, but there's just no way to sing 'Summer Lovin'' to a scowling kid in glasses without cracking up. I'm not that good an actress."

He laughed at that. "Speaking of Felix...do you think he'll be okay with us," he wasn't quite sure how to put it, "being together?" There, that seemed vague enough to cover all the bases.

"He knows we're old friends." She looked away, tangling her fingers in the scatter of hair on his chest.

"You don't plan to tell him more than that, huh?"

"Well..." She ran her tongue across her lips, a sure sign she was nervous. "He doesn't really do well with change. Coming to

Jupiter Point has been tough enough, not to mention dealing with the Reinhards. I'd rather keep this quiet, if we can."

Ben's heart sank even further. As teenagers, they'd hid plenty of stuff from their parents. He'd snuck out to meet Julie when he was supposed to be doing homework, that sort of thing. But now they were adults. Did they really have to do this?

But she didn't want to upset Felix, and he couldn't argue with that.

"Okay, I get it. So where is this line rehearsing going to happen?"

Her hand traveled farther down his chest, her soft palm cool against his still-heated skin. She was such a sensual woman. How was it she'd had only two sexual partners in the past twelve years? He should probably thank Felix for scaring off all the men, like a solemn little gargoyle watchdog.

The kid could try to scare him off too, but Ben had a few tricks up his sleeve. His charm, his persistence...but most of all, his Cessnas.

"Here, when I can find someone to stay with Felix. Maybe he could go to Tobias and Carolyn's for an evening and play with Sarah. They really hit it off, though I don't understand why. They're so different."

"Sarah never met a kid she didn't like. She's like a wide-open flower, always soaking in the sunshine."

"Wow, I love that image. That's beautiful."

"She's a great kid. Felix is too," he added quickly. "I'm trying to win him over, but he's tough."

"You already have. He likes you, probably because you answer his ten kajillion questions about flight mechanics."

"He's really something. He already knows more than I did after a year of flight school."

Julie smiled proudly. "We call it 'pulling a Felix.' He absorbs information like a sponge. It's pretty incredible. He's even got the Reinhards impressed, and that's hard to do."

"Speaking of the Reinhards..." Ben caught her hand under his, stilling it before she could get too close to his cock and make him forget everything. "Any chance you could wrangle me some invites to the Winter Ball? I'd ask them myself but I'm still filled with rage about what they did."

She blinked at him in surprise. "You want to go to a *ball*? You always thought it was ridiculous."

"Of course it's ridiculous. But I remember how much my mom always wanted to go. She even switched to the Reinhards' church so they'd consider putting her on the list. But they never did. I was thinking that an invite would give Mom an extra reason to come home. How could she turn down a ticket to the ball?"

"Oh Ben." She rolled over on top of him and plopped a kiss onto his chin. "Has anyone ever told you you're the sweetest, most adorable, most endearing, most wonderful, most—"

He stopped the flow of flattery by claiming her mouth in a rough kiss. Seriously, "sweet and adorable?" He didn't want to be that, not anymore. "You'd think that my years in the Air Force would erase all the 'sweet and adorable' out of me."

"Well, they didn't. Sorry. I think you're stuck with it."

He gripped her bare ass, filling his hands with her flesh. God, those curves, that sweet whiskey-and-cream skin, those dark nipples begging for his touch.

"So, will your mom be in Jupiter Point by then? The ball is only two weeks away." She squeezed her thighs on either side of his hips. The tips of her breasts hardened against his chest.

He groaned. "You expect me to answer questions while your pussy is touching my cock and the rest of you is right in front of my eyes?"

She bit her lip, wicked laughter turning her face pink. "You came," she pointed out. "You're satisfied. We did the deed and now we're just hanging out talking."

"You think I'm satisfied?"

"You sure sounded like it. Moaning and groaning and cursing."

"Well, yeah, I was very satisfied. But that was then and this is now."

"That was about ten minutes ago."

"Exactly my point." He was definitely ready for another trip into the mind-blowing realm of sex with Julie. "Ancient history." He reached for his nightstand again and snagged another condom. He brandished it at her. "Ready?"

In response, she snatched the condom from him and ripped it open. She moved her ass farther down his thighs, giving herself space to work. She rolled the condom onto his shaft. With the clumsy way she worked at it, he knew that sheathing a man with latex wasn't something she'd done with the occupational thera-pist. Ha. Another first.

When he was covered, he pushed his swelling cock into the hot cave between her legs. That felt so good that he had to stop and battle for control. He gripped her hips and lowered her onto his erection. Her channel was still hot and moist from ten minutes ago—had it really only been that long? He had no idea. Time with Julie stretched in weird ways. He rubbed his thumb over the nub of her clit and felt it swell immediately.

Oh yeah, she was just as hot for him as he was for her. That had always been true. She'd promised her mother not to have sex until she was eighteen, and they'd kept that vow. But no one had specified anything about oral sex, kissing, finger-fucking, or anything else they could come up with. They'd let their imagina-tions run wild and enjoyed themselves plenty without losing their technical virginities.

But he'd never stopped wanting it. And now that they'd made love, officially, with full penetration, he was actually glad that they hadn't done it before. His primitive boy-brain would have exploded. He would have spiraled deeper into love with her, like

Alice down the rabbit hole. He never would have gotten over her disappearance.

And maybe, in fact, he never really had.

AFTER ROUND TWO, they took a break to devour the lasagna he'd made. Ben was actually a pretty good cook. He'd cultivated that skill as a way to please Julie's mother, and he still remembered some of the recipes she'd taught him. Not lasagna, of course. Too much cheese and pasta; Mrs. Reinhard would have fired her for a dish like that.

Julie pulled on his overshirt, the blue cambric barely clearing the tops of her thighs. She'd finally taken off the thigh-highs, thank God, or they'd still be back in bed going for round three. She lit the candles while he served up the lasagna, garlic bread and salad that had been sitting while they screwed their brains out.

"Sorry the lettuce is wilted. I blame your nipples," he teased.

"And the butter is congealed on the garlic bread. All my fault, too?"

"If you weren't so sexy, we could have had dinner like normal people. So yes. All your fault."

She made a face at him, then took a bite of lasagna and rolled her eyes in bliss. "Oh my God. This is incredible. I'd say it's better than sex, but, well...it's not, quite."

"I'd say I'm insulted, but I'm not, quite."

He sat down with her and they dove into their food with the appetites of two people who had just burned approximately ten million calories having sex. They fell silent as they ate, completely comfortable with each other, completely attuned. Ben was pretty sure this moment marked the happiest he'd been in many, many years. That piece of him that had been missing— well, it wasn't completely filled. Questions about his father, the need to see his mother and sister, all of those realities still existed. But being with Julie, like this, went a long way toward healing the hole in his heart.

True, they didn't have an official term for what they were doing. Were they getting back together? He wouldn't say that. Renewing their friendship? That didn't take into account the getting-naked part. Which he wanted to keep doing as long as possible.

He cleared his throat, looking for a delicate way to bring up the topic of the future. "Is Felix liking Jupiter Point any better?"

"Hard to say. He doesn't complain as much, and he's started spending time with the Reinhards without me around. That's huge progress."

Better just come out with his question. "How long are you planning to stay?" He tried to make it casual but didn't quite get there.

She put down her fork. "I don't know. Until the semester ends, maybe? I sublet my apartment until June."

Until June. That wasn't enough time. Not nearly.

He cleared his throat. "So you like living in LA?"

"No. Not really. It's overwhelming, especially for someone who grew up in a small town like Jupiter Point. But I'm used to it now, and Green and Pristine is doing great. You'd be amazed how much people are willing to pay to get their houses cleaned."

"We have dirty houses here too." He glanced around his tidy condo. "Not mine, of course. I'm a neat freak."

Smiling, she toasted him with her wine glass. "Another point in the plus column. The very long plus column."

He clinked her glass with his. "But seriously. What does LA have that we don't? Besides more traffic and more dirty houses?"

"Felix. Savannah," she answered promptly. "Savannah has nothing but bad memories from here. And you know how Felix is about change."

He struggled with the follow-up question to that, one which

seemed so obvious to him, he didn't even know why he had to ask it. "Couldn't you stay here when Felix goes back to LA?"

She blinked, her face turning pink, then white. "Excuse me?"

Oh shit. He'd put his foot in it now. "It was just a question."

Now two spots of red were burning in her cheeks. "You want me to abandon Felix? I can't do that. He needs me."

"Okay. Okay. I get it."

But she was on a roll now. "I'm his godmother, and that's so important to me. Savannah and Felix are the only family I have. Not all families are based on blood ties."

"I know that."

"No, you can't really understand, because you have your brothers."

Now they were in familiar territory. "Sweetheart, I do understand. That's why we used to talk about all the kids we wanted to have, remember? You wanted a family of your own. We both did."

"Well, now I have one." Her pulse was pounding in her throat, her chin stubbornly lifted. He knew better than to point out that her dream family, the one they'd talked about as teenagers, involved her own babies, not Savannah's. He'd stumbled into a minefield here and he had to get out.

He knew why, too. He'd skipped ahead to the part where she was happily settled in Jupiter Point and he could see her whenever he wanted. "I'm sorry, Juls. Of course Felix is your family, and so is Savannah. I do understand. I swear I do."

"Okay. Good."

Slowly she relaxed, the tension leaving her shoulders, and she sat back in her chair. She took a swallow of the wine she'd brought. Then another one. She fiddled with the stem of the wine glass—okay, so maybe she hadn't completely relaxed, he realized. Damn, he'd really stepped in it.

"Are we okay?" he asked cautiously.

She nodded, then gave him a careful look. Uh-oh, he remembered that expression. It meant something serious was coming.

"Maybe it's a good thing this came up. Because we should be really super clear about what's going on here."

"Sure. Clear is good. Clear skies, clear sailing. Clear skin." He rubbed his jaw ruefully, a reference to the acne that had plagued him in high school. Also, a blatant ploy to play on their shared history.

She didn't smile. "Felix is my first priority. Everything else comes after him."

Now it was his turn to go for the wine—mostly so he could delay his answer. He had to get this right, or he sensed that she might flee. "I understand," he said eventually.

"I can't imagine making any decisions that don't put him first."

"I get it. Really, I do. I just have one question. Who comes after Felix? Savannah?"

She looked back down at her wine glass, tracing a drop of red liquid down the side. "I don't know. Maybe. After my mom died, she was the only person keeping me from being homeless, remember? The Reinhards didn't seem to care about me one way or the other. They liked feeling charitable but I always knew if I caused them too much trouble, they might change their minds. I used to lie in bed at night and think about what might happen if Savannah decided she didn't like me anymore, or wanted me gone. I figured they would have kicked me out like that." She snapped her fingers. "But she never made me feel that way. Not once. She never held that kind of threat over my head."

"Of course not. Only a really rotten person would do that."

In his eyes, Savannah wasn't nearly as generous as Julie thought. Once, when he'd had too many shots of Jägermeister at a party, he'd asked her why she hadn't been upset when he and Julie had gotten together. She'd just shrugged and said that she *was* upset at first, but then realized that with Julie "off the market," neither of them had to worry about competing anymore. Which was absurd, because Julie had never competed with

Savannah. Her mother used to lecture her about that. Don't make waves. Remember that it's their house. Their world. The deGaias were just "extras" in the Reinhard movie.

"I know Savannah comes across as super-confident, but she's not," Julie was saying. "She's very sensitive. Her parents were so cold to her, always trying to control her. They weren't affectionate like my mother. I always knew that Mom loved me. That was why we moved to Jupiter Point, so that I'd have a decent place to live, good schooling. She wanted me to have stability. If not for me, she would have kept traveling. She put me first."

It finally dawned on Ben. "So you want to do the same thing for Felix. Put him first."

She nodded. "I love Savannah, and I know how much she loves Felix. But he's always been really challenging. She needs support, and so does Felix, especially now that Savannah's gone so much. He needs consistency."

He took a sip of wine to keep himself from asking the logical next question—what did *she* need?

Still, she caught his expression. "Don't start thinking I'm some kind of self-sacrificing saint. I'm not. The truth is, I just really love that kid. He was such a funny baby, like a little newborn owl."

"He still looks like an owl. A curly-haired one."

"He does, doesn't he?" Julie's smile radiated pure affection. Ben actually felt jealous of Felix for a moment. "Look, Ben, I know you think I cater to the Reinhards too much. But it's really not about that. That's actually why I started Green and Pristine, so I wouldn't be on their payroll, like some kind of nanny."

She drained her glass of wine and poured herself some more. He hid a smile, remembering how even their occasional beach-party-Solo-cup-keg-beers used to make her extra chatty.

"I looked around and thought, what job does no one really want to do, that I'm totally used to, that doesn't require a lot of interaction? I didn't want to work for someone else, I wanted my own business. I didn't even have my high school degree until I got my GED later on. I didn't qualify for much."

Talk about a tough situation; but Julie was never one to back down from a challenge. And she'd done it. She'd started her own business and thrived.

Ben leaned back in his chair and stretched out his legs. "I had no idea how hard starting my own business would be. I can't believe you did all that at seventeen. Actually, I can. You were always so on the ball. You were the smartest person I knew, and the kindest."

Her face flamed pink as she gave him an embarrassed smile. "And you were the sweetest."

"*Sweet?* Damn. Not again with the 'sweet'. When are you going to delete that word?"

"Never. You were the sweetest, kindest, most tender, affectionate, loving..." With each word, she inched her chair closer to him, until they were side by side, and then she was slipping onto his lap. "Wonderful, amazing..." Now she was kissing him, little feather touches of her lips along his neck. "Extremely handsome, oh so sexy, sometimes funny..."

"*Sometimes* funny? I used to make you laugh until you peed your pants."

"Sometimes. Other times you cracked the lamest jokes. It's okay," she said quickly. "I liked them anyway. And honestly, it's not good to be too perfect."

He snuggled her against him, a warm bundle of sweet-smelling woman—*his* woman.

No, not his. She'd just finished telling him why she wasn't his. Couldn't be.

Her kisses reached his jaw, where she encountered a layer of stubble. "You're a lot hairier than you used to be," she murmured.

"That's because men are hairy. And I'm a man now." He thumped his chest with the hand that wasn't wrapped around her.

"Yes, I think you are," she said thoughtfully, after dropping a kiss on his earlobe.

"What clued you in? My bulging muscles? My sexy-ass flight jacket? My big hard co—"

She sealed his lips with hers before he could get too down and dirty. They dove into a hot, deep, slow and passionate kiss.

When that kiss finally came to an end, she was breathing fast. She ran her tongue over her lips, a lingering movement that made his cock swell against her leg.

"No, none of those things," she said. "Though they're all true. It's the fact that you're mature enough to understand where I'm coming from, and why we can't be anything more than lovers."

"And friends," he added, through the stab of pain to his heart.

"And friends." Her radiant smile didn't soothe him one bit. In fact, it made things worse. "I was afraid that making love would change things too much. I shouldn't have worried. This whole grown-up thing is great, isn't it? It's like having your cake and eating it, too. We can be friends *and* have sex and no one gets hurt. Maybe this is what they call adulting."

He managed to smile at her even though none of what she said felt right to him. *Have your cake and eat it, too?* The cake she was describing was like the kind her mom used to make. Gluten and dairy free with too much sugar in the frosting to make up for the cardboard consistency. Sex was good. Friendship was good. But underneath it all, his heart yearned for something else. Something only she could give him.

But he would never get it from her. He knew that now.

This was a good thing. Better to know. Because maybe all this time, part of him had been hoping for and dreaming of the day he and Julie found each other again.

Well, they had.

And it was wonderful and terrible and...fuck. Confusing as hell.

He hid his sudden emotion behind a laugh—his tried-and-true method. "How about we skip the cake and feast on something else?"

She narrowed her eyes at him. "Are you saying there actually *is* cake here?"

"Would I invite you over and not include dessert? Would I let all that training from high school go to waste? I got a chocolate hazelnut torte from Pie in the Sky."

"Chocolate hazelnut..." She batted her eyelashes at him adoringly. "I take it back. You *are* perfect."

He smiled modestly. "Told you."

"We'll get to that cake." She swung herself on top of him and began unbuttoning her—his—shirt. "After."

20

Julie was right; sex with Ben did change everything. Just not in the way she'd thought. Maybe that was because they'd made things clear from the start. They weren't trying to "get back together" or resurrect what they used to have. They were simply two adults enjoying each other in a physical way.

Sure, there had been moments that first night when she'd looked into Ben's eyes and seen something deeper, more intense.

But that—whatever it was—had disappeared, and ever since then, he'd been the laughing, carefree, playful, teasing Ben who made everything more fun.

Being with Ben felt like a puzzle piece falling into place. It all clicked, just how it used to. Every day glowed with a happy light because they were together.

Rehearsing the part of Sandy became the highlight of her days. While Felix was in school, she'd rush over to Knight and Day and study her part until Ben got back from flying. Then he'd run lines with her until his next flight. If he had something to do in the hangar, she'd hop onto a stool and hang out with him there. The time would fly by.

And yes, there were those naughty moments when he'd get that certain look on his face, and desire would spark in her belly.

"C'mere," he told her gruffly one day. When he sounded like that, rough with lust, she'd do anything he said. She followed him to the back of the hangar into the little restroom, which smelled like motor oil and hand cleanser. He locked the door and they stared at each other for a long, pulsating moment. A deep flush of desire swept through her. Her pulse pounded, her throat tightened, lips parted, nipples hardened. She waited, waited, until she couldn't take anymore.

"Ben—" she began.

"Turn around and put your hands against the wall."

She did, palms against the smooth plaster. He came behind her and slid a hand between her panties and her warm sex. A jolt of sharp pleasure ripped through her. She ground against his hand, seeking more of his rough palm. There, there, harder, God...

"Lower," he rasped. "I want to get inside you."

Cool air breezed against her skin as he unzipped her pants and pulled them down, just enough to bare her ass. She let his hands position her the way he wanted. She was still throbbing with need, panting, dripping. She heard another zip, the rip of a condom foil, then felt his hot hard flesh against hers. His hand came around her front again, found her sex. Pressed between his body and his hand, she pumped her hips, delirious pleasure making her moan. He entered her in one deep thrust. He took a long panting breath there. She pushed back, wanting more of him, faster.

So he hammered into her, one hand massaging her clit, the other braced against the wall. And she exploded into an orgasm so hard and fierce, she nearly blacked out. A few moments later he groaned deeply, his body going taut behind her.

The experience was so intense that he stumbled backwards

toward the sink. His ass hit the faucet and the sound of streaming water made her jump.

She spun around, jeans at mid-thigh, then burst out laughing. He fumbled with the faucet, still shaky from that crazy climax. "What was that, practice for the mile-high club?"

He finally got the water turned off and slumped against the sink. "Apparently we need a lot of practice. Jesus. I think I bruised my right nut."

She couldn't stop laughing after that. She laughed a lot with Ben. She always had.

One night, they went to the Seaview Inn for dinner, and discovered that the manager remembered them from before.

"You were the kids that got a free meal from the couple at the next table," he told them as he showed them to a table on the terrace. "I never forgot that. And you're still together after all these years?"

Neither of them corrected him. Instead, they sat on the terrace, holding hands as they watched the sun spread golden sparkles across the ocean before sinking out of sight.

It was so beautiful, and yet so ordinary. Just watching the sunset, hand in hand. One of those ordinary things Ben had mentioned. Ordinary, and yet extraordinary because they were together again.

They tried to catch up on everything that had happened during the past twelve years. Ben told stories about the Air Force and life on base. Julie talked about her misadventures in Los Angeles. He laughed until he cried over her story of getting lost on the freeways and ending up in the desert instead of the beach. Or her one day as a barista, when the milk steamer had exploded.

"So what about your singing career? What happened with that?"

"What singing career?" She laughed it off, though it was a sore point. "Do you know how many girls go to LA hoping for a performing career? It would be easier to run for president. Better odds. I tried hard, and Savannah did everything she could, but I'm not really ambitious enough. I'd rather just write my songs and sing in the shower."

"Well, if you need help rehearsing those shower songs, you know I'm there for you," he offered with a wink.

She took him up on that. The things that man could do with a removable showerhead...

One day, Evie dropped off the framed photo she'd put on hold, the one that showed Ben at the controls of his plane. Thrilled, she hung it in the living room, where it was the only personal photo in their temporary apartment. When Ben came over, she showed it off proudly.

"I'm calling it 'Ben in His Happy Place.'"

"Maybe the G-rated version," he growled, walking her back toward the bedroom. "In here, that's the X-rated one."

She giggled as he tossed her over his shoulder and marched toward the bed.

After a while, she noticed there was one thing Ben didn't talk much about at all. His mother. He told her about the night of the murder, about Tobias waking him up and asking him to tell Janine while Tobias dealt with the police. After that, he changed the subject. Every time.

Now, when she looked at that photo, she saw something different. It didn't show all of Ben, just the back of his head. He was keeping parts of himself hidden. Not the sexy parts, but the vulnerable parts.

Ben definitely had scars that hadn't been there before. Then again, so did she. But would those scars come between them? Maybe not, as long as they kept things light.

FELIX WAS GROWING MORE comfortable with Jupiter Point. He liked the school and hardly ever asked for a sick day anymore.

He'd made friends with another kid, a large boy who'd been held back for a year. The boy—Tanaka, from Samoa—stepped in to protect Felix from being bullied during recess. After that, they became buddies and Felix helped him with his schoolwork. It turned out he was struggling because of language issues, because no one would talk to him. They were afraid of his intimidating size.

But Felix never had any trouble talking. He'd rattle on about his current obsessions, airplanes and engines and the Alex Rider series. Sometimes Sarah joined in. She was a talker, too. Julie would take them all to the Milky Way after school and they'd work on teaching Tanaka the words "ice cream" and "fudge."

The three of them were the oddest group of friends—the adorable blond pixie, the overly serious kid in glasses, and the large boy towering over them both. But it worked. Before long, Tanaka's language skills reached grade level, and he was bumped back up to his own class.

Felix also started to warm up to his grandparents—or at least he didn't complain so much about spending time with them.

"He sounds pretty happy there," Savannah told Julie, after Felix got bored and handed the phone to her, then wandered into his room to work on his homework. He loved homework.

"It's working out. Your parents are adapting. I have to give them credit. At first they were expecting Felix to be a regular kid, but now they appreciate him the way he is. They like thinking there's a genius in the family."

Savannah gave a bitter snort. "Are we really using the word 'family' when it comes to them?"

Julie's heart twisted. Savannah had no idea what it really felt like to have no family. Hopefully she never would. "You should give them a chance. People mellow, you know. They're in their sixties now."

"I know my parents. Mellow is not in their vocabulary. Anyway, I don't want to talk about them. What else is happening in Jupiter Point? Just the good stuff, nothing with the word Reinhard."

Julie filled her in on rehearsals for *Grease*, and the birthday party for Suzanne's little daughter, and the new owner of the radio station, and the high school making the state basketball finals, and all the new clients requesting her Green and Pristine services. There was a lot of Jupiter Point news to catch her up on.

"And Ben? You haven't been saying much and I've been discreetly not asking. It's been killing me, quite frankly."

Just hearing the name Ben, Julie felt her face relax into a smile. She searched for a neutral response that wouldn't give too much away. "Ben is Ben."

"Oh my God. You're sleeping with him."

Julie's face flamed, and she double-checked to make sure Felix couldn't hear. "How the heck?"

"*Oh my God!* Tell me everything. I have to live vicariously through you, all the men on this set are impossible."

Julie had to give her something, otherwise Savannah would never let her be. "We're having an adult relationship. In all senses of the word."

"Triple-X rated? You go! You deserve some fun. Are you having fun? Have you finally discovered the joys of casual sex?"

"Um..." Was it casual? That wasn't quite the word she'd use.

"Oh no. Oh no! You aren't falling for him again, are you? Sweetie, be very careful."

"Why? What are you talking about?"

"I remember how devastated you were when you thought he'd stood you up. Of course that was my horrid parents' fault, but the point is," Savannah's voice softened, "I've never seen anyone love another person the way you loved Ben. I'm so glad you're back with him, you deserve to be happy. But I'd hate to see you get crushed all over again."

"I'm a different person now. I'm not a naive girl anymore. Anyway, it's not like that."

Savannah didn't need to say anything to convey her skepticism. Her soft snort said it all. "I'm one hundred percent in your corner, you know that. Let's just hope my parents don't fuck it up again. Okay, speaking of my parents...I've been getting emails from Mom about the Winter Ball. I just can't do it, Juls. This shoot is already over budget and if I ask for time off, I'll get fucking sued."

"Did you tell her?"

"Yes, and I called her. Always a joy."

No doubt. Conversations between the Reinhards and Savannah were more like turf battles between rhinos. Locked horns, bloody wounds and all.

"But Felix seems excited about it, now that he stopped complaining about organizing the invitations," Savannah continued. "I think it's kind of sweet, in a way. You're going, right?"

"Well, yes. Ben and I are going together."

"Uh-oh. I know how romantic those Winter Balls can be. I got lucky with a bartender at the last one I went to. Watch out, girlie! Don't let all that fake moonlight and winter roses get to you."

"Don't worry about me. I'm a big girl."

"You have a big heart, and that's why I worry. And what about the other thing? The man who attacked you? You told Will, right? God, he was always so sexy."

"He's taken," Julie told her. "Madly in love. As is Tobias."

"Must be a Knight brother thing," Savannah said impishly. "Watch out, you. So, has Will figured anything out about the mystery man?"

"Not really, but he's trying. He dug up a recording of my 9-1-1 call. He located the dispatcher on duty that night, and spoke to every officer involved in following up on it. That went nowhere."

He also drove out to the hotel where she and Savannah had stayed that fateful night. The entire staff had turned over in the past twelve years, so that was a dead end too. He even went to the junkyard where she'd left her VW. It had long ago been crushed and was probably part of a soda can somewhere by now.

"Well, I'm glad he's on top of it. It's a good thing all those sexy, handsome brothers are looking out for you. You deserve this, Juls. Just don't fall too hard, baby girl."

Sometimes, Julie thought that warning came too late.

She thought about Ben all the time. Every floor she mopped, every window she washed, his face was in her mind's eye. His laughter, his kind eyes, his crooked smile. During rehearsals, she wasn't singing about "Danny," she was singing about Ben. Even while helping Felix with his homework—always an interesting process, trying to keep ahead of him—she felt Ben's arms around her, Ben's intimate whispers in her ear. Sometimes she thought of him as her own private sun, always surrounding her in warmth and life.

She'd almost forgotten this feeling—happiness. Joy bubbled inside her, spilling over into melodies and words. She got in the habit of throwing her guitar in the backseat of her Jetta, so that if she had a few minutes to spare, she could transfer the wisps of song appearing in her head into real notes.

Her strumming was rusty, her fingertips soft from lack of practice. But God, she'd forgotten the sheer, aimless joy of following the notes wherever they would lead. She knew her musical skills weren't enough to make a career. Maybe once she'd hoped they were, but living in LA had killed that delusion. That wasn't even the point. Working on a song was like stepping into a timeless bubble, where nothing existed but music and joy and truth.

If nothing else, being with Ben brought that piece of herself back to life.

But there was so much more. There was midnight stargazing on the night of the new moon, when viewing conditions were at their best. Fleece blankets, warm arms around her, a husky voice in her ear talking about the Pleiades and Sirius, the brightest star in the sky. There were banana walnut pancakes at the Milky Way —her then-and-forever favorite. There were afternoon quickies at her apartment, and long, passionate nights at his.

There was the day they went together to the cemetery, arms overflowing with flowers from Brianna. She knelt at Robert Knight's tombstone and unburdened her soul of all her regret and sadness. "I'm so sorry, Mr. Knight," she whispered to the gray stone with its simple lettering. "I'm so sorry I didn't stop that man, if he's the one who did it. I'm so sorry I hurt your son. And I'm so sorry I never got to see you again. May the angels hold you close."

Meanwhile, Ben placed his huge bouquet of daffodils on her mother's grave and bowed his head in silent prayer. Julie had no idea what he was saying—asking for recipes, perhaps?—but it warmed her heart anyway. None of the Reinhards ever mentioned her mother, not even Savannah. With Ben, her free-spirited gypsy mom felt real again.

And of course, there were those moments when it was all they could do to make it to bed before they tore each other's clothes off. Often they *didn't* make it. Ben's living room couch got a real workout. So did his shower. And his kitchen. And his living room rug. No surface was safe.

She wanted him all the time. Sex with Ben was addictive. She couldn't get enough of him in her body, her mouth, her hands. Anywhere and everywhere.

But she wasn't falling back in love with him. No. Absolutely not. Definitely, positively, certainly not.

She was quite proud of herself, really. It was a feat of strength, not falling for Ben. The Saga of Ben and Julie, Part Two: The Casual Years.

And then came the night of the Reinhards' Winter Ball.

21

"Don't be surprised if Mom and Cassie don't make it," Will warned Ben. "If they were going to show up, they would have before now."

"Have you heard from Cassie? What did she say?" he asked over the burning anxiety in his gut. They were all gathering at the farmhouse before heading to the Winter Ball. Even Aiden, home for the weekend, was coming.

"She said she's trying, and not to pester her. The more phone calls, the more pressure Mom feels. This is hard for her, Ben. She has a lot of guilt built up."

Ben bit back the words he wanted to say, which were—one good way to make up for everything would be to *show up*.

"She'll be there," he said confidently.

"Why would she come to a party instead of meeting us here?" Will squeezed his shoulder in a gesture meant to comfort, but Ben shrugged it off. He didn't want comfort. He wanted to see Mom.

"It's not just any party, it's the Winter Ball. Remember how obsessed Mom used to get about it? How could she pass up the chance to see it for herself?" He tweaked Will's tie, a gray silk number that made his brother's eyes look extra silvery. "Why are you so negative? Have a little faith."

"I have faith that she'll come back when the time is right. I just don't know if that time is now."

"Right for what?" Tobias strolled into the living room, hands in the pockets of his black tuxedo pants. Trust Tobias to totally ruin the cut of his fancy tailored suit. Aiden was a couple steps behind him, messing with the Miami Vice-style white jacket Daisy had found for him at a thrift store.

"Mom and Cassie."

Tobias lifted one eyebrow. "Yeah, I'm not seeing it."

"Cassie said Mom was excited. She said they were coming," Ben said stubbornly.

"*Might*," Will reminded him. "She said they *might* come. With emphasis."

Ben frowned at his older brothers. "You just don't want to be hopeful. I get it. Hope hurts. But I feel it. They're going to be there. Right, Aiden?" Surely he could count on his little brother for support in this. Aiden was still young and optimistic.

Aiden shrugged. "I hope so. But only if Mom's ready. You know how she is."

They all fell silent, thinking of their fragile, fascinating mother. Even before the murder of her husband, Janine Knight had struggled to keep her head above water emotionally. They were all used to tiptoeing around her, careful not to upset her.

Will cocked his head at Ben. "Why is it so important to you?"

"I want to see her, of course. Don't you?"

"Yes, but why now? Why tonight?"

Ben didn't answer, mostly because the reasons were all jumbled up in his head. Because there was a big hole in his heart. Because he wanted to move on, especially now that Julie was back in his life. Because he needed to know she was okay...

Tobias stepped into the uncomfortable silence. "Nothing

wrong with Ben wanting to see her. He went through a lot that night."

Don't. Shut up, Ben wanted to say to his brother. *Don't go there. Not now. Not ever.* But he froze, unable to say a word.

Will glanced at him with more sympathy this time. "You never really talk about that."

"She hit him," Tobias explained gruffly. "It was rough."

But that wasn't the worst part. He never talked about the worst part, not even to Julie.

"I never knew that." Will frowned at him. "Sorry, man."

"Wasn't Mom's fault," he managed. It was all *his* fault. He hadn't found the right words. He should have given her a Xanax first. Or waited for someone else to tell her, someone who wasn't barely eighteen and in shock himself.

"Forget all that. Jesus." He ran a hand through his hair. "We all got through it. I'm just thinking of Aiden here. He's never seen Mom as an adult. The rest of us have."

Aiden leaned his head against Ben's arm. It was a gesture only the baby of the family could have gotten away with. "Yeah, but you were her favorite. You were the one she talked to, right, guys?"

Tobias shoved his hands in his pockets again. "I was a lot closer to Dad, it's true. As much as we fought, Dad and I understood each other."

Will nodded his agreement. "I'd been gone for so long, between college and law school, I really didn't know what was going on with her anymore. You were the one, Ben. Mom's shoulder to lean on."

"I should have gone with her instead of Cassie." He sounded like an iron band had tightened around his throat. "I could have gotten her help. I had no idea she wasn't coming back. She said she needed some time, I figured she meant a few days. If only I'd known..."

Will squeezed his shoulder. "Hey, you can't blame yourself for anything Mom did. She was the adult. It wasn't your job."

"So it was Cassie's?"

"Cassie *wanted* to go," said Aiden. "She needed Mom more than anyone. Remember how she was having so much trouble in school? Some girls were bullying her and her crush dumped her. She couldn't wait to get out of Jupiter Point."

Tobias and Will exchanged a puzzled look. "I don't remember that," Will said. Tobias shook his head too.

"I do," came Julie's soft voice.

Ben startled and spun around. Julie and Felix stood just inside the door.

"She talked to me about it a few times. The worst part was that the ringleader was her former best friend, who apparently liked a boy who had a crush on Cassie."

Ben stared at her, momentarily short-circuited by how incredible she looked. She wore a simple ivory shift dress with crystals embedded in the fabric. Her hair was swept up into a twist, and she wore a choker adorned with a sparkling snowflake.

She smiled apologetically at the brothers. "Sorry, I knocked but no one heard me." She gave Felix a little tap on the shoulder. "Why don't you go find Sarah, Kiddo?"

He ran off, after one more curious look at the brothers. Ben wondered how they looked to him, four brothers in their party best, talking so seriously.

"He's not going to the ball?" Ben asked.

"No. He was planning to, but we were over there earlier helping to set up, and he got overwhelmed. He asked to come here and hang out with Sarah and the babysitter, if that's okay."

"More the merrier," said Tobias. "But how come I didn't know about the bullying? I would have kicked some Mean Girl ass."

"I'm pretty sure that's why she didn't tell you," Julie explained dryly. ""She had it tough, one girl in the midst of all that testosterone. The last thing she wanted was for you guys to go ballistic.

She swore me to secrecy. I told her I'd keep her secret as long as things weren't getting too out of control. But then—well, everything changed."

Sarah and Felix came racing into the living room. Well... Sarah raced, while Felix maintained his usual upright posture. "I want to see Miss Julie's dress!" She stopped dead, her mouth falling open. "You look like Cinderella," she said in awe.

They all laughed. "Well, you know what they say about pumpkins," Julie said. "We'd better get going before all the ice sculptures melt. Even Mrs. Reinhard can't control the weather."

22

THE THEME OF THIS YEAR'S WINTER BALL WAS "LET IT SNOW," even though it rarely snowed in Jupiter Point, and the town was experiencing a warm spell. Of course, none of that mattered to the Reinhards, whose motto came down to "money can fix everything."

Julie had to admit it was magical. Sparkling fake snow was piled around the front entrance. A hidden fog machine created swirls of mist around the guests' feet as they stepped into the portico. Inside, bare-branched potted birch trees transformed the great room into a winter forest. Filmy white fabric draped from the ceiling, lit by strings of twinkle lights, looked like floating clouds of snow. Huge bouquets of creamy flowers—calla lilies, white hydrangea, jasmine—filled every available corner. And then there were the ice sculptures melting on either side of the front entrance.

Even the security guards hired for the event matched the theme. They wore stocking caps along with their uniforms.

Most of the guests had flown in from out of town. Business connections, extended family, people the Reinhards wanted to impress. As a venture capitalist, Mr. Reinhard had a rolodex full of powerful and wealthy people. An invitation to the Reinhards' Winter Ball was considered an honor, and no one turned down the opportunity to attend.

It was—no contest—the fanciest event in Jupiter Point every winter, but it didn't benefit the town at all. The Reinhards flew in flowers from South America, bypassing everyone else's favorite florist—Brianna Gallagher. Likewise with the caterer, and the decorator, both of whom came from San Francisco. The family only invited a few Jupiter Pointers—the mayor, the heads of the Chamber of Commerce and the Historic Downtown Business Association, the director of the Jupiter Point Observatory, and a few of the wealthiest residents.

Even though Julie and Savannah used to lobby hard for more of a local presence, Mrs. Reinhard had always refused. The only jobs she farmed out to locals were servers and cleanup. In the past, Julie had helped with both. She'd never been a "guest" at the party. She'd always worked the entire time, circulating with platters of appetizers, then cleaning up afterward.

This time, she'd refused to do either of those chores. She didn't live with the Reinhards anymore, she didn't need to work for her supper the way she used to. She could damn well dress up in a spangled, shoulder-baring dress for one night and drink champagne and enjoy herself.

Not only were the decorations breathtaking, but so were the guests. The men wore dress jackets and white tie, the women ball gowns and diamonds. Lots of diamonds. Apparently the rich-person interpretation of "let it snow" involved diamonds.

Julie felt underdressed in her simple vintage dress with its cheap crystal adornments. Not to mention her silver sandals, which barely had a heel. But at least she had the best-looking date, in her opinion.

Ben had his own offbeat interpretation of "Let it Snow." He wore a cream cable-knit ski sweater, which showed off his wide shoulders and broad chest. A pair of ski goggles sat on his head, giving him a sort of winter steampunk look. His gray eyes sparkled every time someone gave him a thumb's up and a smile for his outfit.

Sure, most of those smiling at him were women. Julie couldn't blame them. He looked so much more handsome than any of the investment bankers in the crowd.

Of course, those same women barely gave her a glance, and if they did, she could read their disdain loud and clear.

"I don't think I'm wearing enough diamonds for this party," she told Ben ruefully.

He turned to her with a look of such heat, it would have melted whatever snow was in the neighborhood. "You look unbelievable. I'm not exaggerating. My heart nearly stopped when I first saw you."

The best part was, he really meant it. Only Ben, her sweet man, could look at her with that much devout appreciation. She interlaced her hand with his. "Something tells me I could be here naked and you'd be just as happy."

"Obviously. Well, not *here* here. In a bedroom here."

"I happen to know where all the bedrooms are, by the way. Just for future reference."

His eyes sparkled down at her. They looked so endlessly kind, so full of heart. "You know it was always one of my fantasies to get you alone here. We always hung out at my house, or at the beach, or in your car. Or my car. Never here. This was like the forbidden palace."

"Oh ho, so you want to break the old no-boys-in-the-bedroom-or-anywhere-else rule?"

"Absolutely. Doesn't even have to be a bedroom. Isn't there a walk-in closet we could mess up? Or a library where we could shake some books off their shelves?"

His naughty grin had her inner thighs clenching with desire. Really, it took only one sexy look from those playful eyes of his to make her want him. Right now, she wouldn't mind sneaking behind a fake birch tree piled with fake snow and kissing the breath out of him.

Luckily, they were interrupted by a group of Jupiter Point Hotshots. "How did you get invited to this thing?" Ben teased them. "It's supposed to be power players only."

Sean Marcus jerked his thumb at Rollo, whose big, bear-like form was stuffed into a tuxedo. "Rollington Wareham the Third here made us come."

"I wasn't coming in here without backup," Rollo muttered. "And Brianna refused because they don't buy her flowers. She told me to take pictures of every different kind of arrangement they have here. I feel like a spy."

"I'll do it." Julie smiled at the man, who she knew only slightly. Rollo came from a family of East Coast billionaires, so it made sense that the Reinhards would invite him. Of course, they didn't know that he preferred hanging out with his firefighter buddies and camping and hiking—not to mention the love of his life, Brianna. "I'll be your inside man."

Finn was the only one of the crew who looked comfortable in this atmosphere, with his crisp white dinner jacket. Not even the scar that ravaged the left side of his face detracted from his smooth, sophisticated style. He'd grown up in Hollywood, so this was probably old hat. "Rollo promised us all burgers and beer if we came and held his hand." He grinned at Rollo, who shrugged off his teasing. They were probably all used to it, since they were as close as brothers, at least according to Suzanne.

"Aren't you all tough, strong firefighters?" Julie asked innocently. "What's a party compared to a wildfire?"

Rollo ticked off reasons on his fingers. "A, the dress code's a lot more comfortable at a wildfire. B, the trees are real." He glared at the closest fake birch. "That thing just ain't right."

Sean picked up the thread. "C, it's easier to make conversation when all you need to talk about is wind direction."

"You guys are big whiny babies," Finn said. "Are you saying you'd rather be in the black somewhere eating MREs instead of a portobello goat cheese puff?" He popped an appetizer into his mouth.

"Yes," said Rollo promptly. "Do they have any MREs here?"

Ben and Julie shared a glance of amusement, the way they always used to when they witnessed something that tickled their sense of the absurd. "You guys are breaking my heart," Ben told them. "At least I have my girl with me." He hugged Julie with one arm.

She melted against him. His girl? She could never get enough of hearing that.

"Lisa's here, but she had to help one of the catering crew. First-aid emergency." Finn's face lit up at the mention of his fiancée.

"Evie's here too. She offered to take photos for Mrs. Reinhard," Sean explained. "She's focusing on candid shots, so don't even think about relaxing. You might get caught on camera picking your nose or something."

Everyone else chuckled, but Ben's expression sharpened to hyper-alertness. "Any idea where Evie is?"

"No, but I can find out." Sean dug in the pocket of his black trousers for his cell, then fired off a text. "She's by the bar," he said after an answer pinged. "She says the official cocktail of the ball is called a 'Snowcone,' basically a Slurpee with vodka."

"Thanks, man. Julie, I think there's a Snowcone with our name on it. See you guys around. Don't burn anything down." Ben tugged her in the direction of the bar.

"Ben, what are you doing?"

"If Evie's running around taking pictures, maybe she's seen my mother. It's too crowded here, I'm afraid I'll miss her."

But when they found Evie at the bar, she said she hadn't seen either Janine or Cassie. It broke Julie's heart to see the disappointment wipe the smile off Ben's face.

"You would recognize my mother, right?" he asked Evie as he ordered two Snowcones from the bartender.

"I think so. What I remember most about her was her eyes, a lot like yours. Can I take a picture of your costume?" Evie lifted her camera and snapped a photo.

Ben blinked, and Julie wished she could delete that one. It probably looked too much like a shot of someone in the process of getting his heart broken.

Evie must have thought the same thing, because she lowered the camera, her lovely face more serious now. "I'm sorry, I don't mean to make light of anything. Was your mother planning to be here tonight? I didn't realize she was back."

"It's fine," Ben said in answer. "She probably just hasn't arrived yet. Come on, Juls, let's dance."

Julie barely managed a sip of her Snowcone before he tugged her toward the dance floor. The ballroom—yes, the Reinhards actually had a ballroom—had been transformed into an enchanted fairyland, with shimmering streamers dangling overhead. They were cleverly constructed so the lights made them look like a sparkling snowstorm in motion. An a cappella group dressed in stocking caps and winter scarves were currently singing a peppy rendition of "Winter Wonderland."

Ben swung her into the kaleidoscope of dancers. She didn't have much experience with waltzing, or whatever this was. So she just held on to Ben and let him guide her movements. It should have been romantic and breathtaking, and it was, except for the anxious way Ben checked out every new arrival, every entrance and exit.

Maybe they should have just stationed themselves at the front gate and skipped the party.

They danced, then went back for more Snowcones. They chatted with Merry, who was taking notes for a story in the newspaper. No Janine Knight. They danced again. They ate dainty crepes filled with cream. Still no Janine. They had more Snowcones.

And the clock ticked toward midnight with no sign of the Knight women.

Julie sensed the hope leaking out of Ben's heart. His pace on the dance floor slowed, his shoulders sagged. Every time someone walked into the ballroom, his eyes darted in their direction, but less eagerly, ready for disappointment.

Maybe Mrs. Knight had changed her mind. Maybe she'd tried to come, but discovered it was too difficult. Maybe her car had broken down.

She wasn't coming. Julie knew it in her bones. And she couldn't bear to see Ben get crushed all over again.

The a cappella group shifted to a slower song, "Baby It's Cold Outside," and she and Ben slowed until they were simply swaying in place. "How about we blow this Snowcone stand?" she whispered. "We could go somewhere and share some body heat."

He looked down at her blankly. Beneath his goofy ski goggles, his gray eyes held such a bereft look that her heart tumbled end over end, down a rabbit hole.

And she knew, with a weird sense of homecoming, that she'd do anything for this man. That she loved him. That she'd never stopped loving him.

And that now, she had a chance to be there for Ben the way she should have been twelve years ago.

"I don't...think she's coming," he said numbly.

"Come on." She took his hand and threaded a path through the guests. "Let's go."

Outside, the sound of the party faded away as they ran across the lawn toward the makeshift parking area. She stopped to slip off her sandals, then raced barefoot the rest of the way.

"Toss me your keys," she called to him. "I'm going to drive."

"Why?"

"Because you're toasted. How many Snowcones did you

have?" She didn't give him a chance to answer. "Besides, it's easier to talk when you're not driving. And you're going to talk."

He staggered a little on his way to the truck. She practically manhandled him into the passenger seat, then took the keys and slipped into the driver's seat. She steered down the long cypress-lined drive, away from the twinkle lights and almost-melted ice sculptures.

When they reached the main street, a two-lane country road with no streetlights, she finally spoke. "Okay, Ben. What's going on? I've never seen you like this."

"There's a lot you've never seen," he muttered. "Because you left."

She tightened her hands on the steering wheel. "Yeah, I left. But this isn't about me, is it? I wasn't the only one who left. You're angry with your mother, aren't you?"

"No."

Julie didn't believe that for a minute. "She left you guys behind. She left Aiden, she left you. Of course you're angry."

"I'm not fucking angry."

"Then why do you sound so angry?"

"Because you're holding me hostage in my own truck."

She jerked the wheel to the side so the truck veered onto the shoulder. She leaned over him and opened the passenger-side door. "Fine. Then get out. You might as well, because if you're not going to tell me what's really on your mind, what's the point of all this?"

He gave her a burning look, then flung himself out of the truck. He interlaced his hands behind his neck and tilted his head back. The night sky was so clear it seemed to be showering stars on him.

Right now, he was probably wishing he was up there, in the sky, where he was happiest.

And she was wishing she'd kept her mouth shut. What right did she have to demand that he talk? None. They were casual lovers and old friends. *Former* sweethearts. That didn't mean he owed her anything, any explanation or baring of his soul.

She dropped her forehead onto the steering wheel. A black sadness filled her. What was left for her and Ben? She had no idea.

She felt a brush of air against her side, then his low voice sent a current of awareness through her. "It was that night. When Dad died. I let Mom down...and I hate myself for it."

23

It took Ben a good five minutes to continue. Through his Snowcone buzz, the feeling of that night—raw and surreal, oppressive and wild, like an electrical storm during a summer heat wave—came back to him. The vision of his father's bloodied body on the kitchen floor, the weight of knowing that the police were coming, and that someone needed to tell Mom before they did. And knowing that person had to be him, because Tobias was downstairs securing the house and talking to the police, and Aiden was only eight, and Cassie was only sixteen, and Will was away at law school. And even though his skin felt raw and flayed, as if it didn't even belong to him, and his gorge rose every time he thought of what he'd seen in the kitchen, he'd trudged upstairs, stomach churning, the walls wavering as if they were in a Steven King movie. *Red rum, red rum.*

Stop it. Just get to Mom. Hold Mom. I need Mom.

And then those terrible, stumbling words. "Someone killed Dad. He's dead, Mom. He's really dead."

God, what a stupid way to break something like that to your own mother. He was crying, feeling stupid, like a little kid because he couldn't stop blubbering and he wanted to be strong for her. He wanted to take care of her because that was what she needed, and what he always did. He was the one who could lighten her darkest moods.

Not this time.

He heard the sound of that slap before he felt it. It echoed through his parents' bedroom like an endless church bell. Then she'd covered her face with her hands.

"You hit me, Mom," he'd said, in complete shock, not even thinking. Stating a fact.

"She hit me," he told Julie now. "After I told her about Dad. Then she tried to throw herself out the window."

"Oh God. What did you do?"

"I dove after her. I grabbed onto her foot and wouldn't let her go. It was crazy, like a tug of war. Her hands were on the windowsill and she was trying to pull herself away from me."

"Was the window open?"

"No, she never got that far. The police showed up, their lights were flashing into the room. She kind of slumped onto the floor then and wouldn't talk to me. I think she passed out. I was scared to leave her, but I ran out and found a female police officer. I told her what had happened, so she took Mom into custody for the night. They said it was for her safety. But the next time I saw Mom, she barely looked at me. It was like she didn't remember any of that."

A warm hand covered his. "Maybe she didn't. They probably gave her tranquilizers and who knows what."

Ben clenched his hand tighter, unwilling to take the comfort she was offering.

"I just want to know that she's okay. I want to see for myself. I really just want to see her with my own eyes and make sure I didn't damage her for life with my clumsy-ass teenage words. I screwed up, right when she needed me most."

Gently, she untucked his fist so she could lace her fingers with his. "Ben, do you really think anything you said at that moment would have made a difference? Her husband had just been murdered. I remember when the police came to tell me about Mom's accident. I'll never forget it. They were nice, and they said all the right things, but it was horrible because I didn't know them. At least the news came from *you*, someone she loved."

"But I should have done more," he croaked. "I knew she was close to the edge. Maybe if I'd gotten more help for her, she wouldn't have left. Maybe she would have stayed and Aiden would have grown up with his mother and Cassie wouldn't have to be Mom's full-time caretaker and you and me wouldn't have lost twelve years."

Julie pulled her hand from his—maybe he was hurting her—and started the truck.

"Are you in or out?" she asked him, indicating the passenger-side door.

Confused, he pulled it shut. He didn't know what she had in mind, but whatever it was, he was with her.

She pulled onto the road. "First, your mother is alive. You were afraid she might harm herself that night, right? Well, she didn't, so I say you did pretty well that night. You probably saved her life by telling the police."

"But she left. She didn't jump out the window, but she left."

"But that's not your fault. She's responsible, not you. I knew your mom, Ben. I know how much she loved her kids. She must have been really desperate."

He stared out the window at the dark hills slipping past, the intense starry glow from overhead. The wind was picking up, causing the roadside trees to sway and the truck to vibrate. A storm was coming up, according to the latest marine forecast.

"As for Aiden, he seems pretty good to me. He's a gem. He's in college, he's got a girlfriend. And Cassie? You're thinking the worst, but I know Cassie, and I can promise you, she doesn't do things she doesn't want to. Remember when your mom wanted to give her bangs? It was practically a nuclear standoff."

That was true. Cassie could be the most stubborn goddamn kid in the world. He actually smiled a tiny bit, remembering that.

They reached a fork in the road, and she turned the truck toward the ocean. "Where are we going?"

"I have a surprise for you. I got a text from Carolyn, she said Felix fell asleep on the couch. So, I think this is a good time to address your last worry. That we lost twelve years, you and me."

"How do we do that?"

"Simple. We make up for lost time."

24

"THE LIFEGUARD SHACK? HOW'D YOU MANAGE THAT?" GOD, IT WAS just like old times. How many hours had he spent with Julie in or near this tower? It was essentially a one-room lookout post on stilts, almost like a tree fort.

With a big grin, Julie led the way up the ladder-like steps and unlocked the padlock. They ducked through the entrance and into the cozy nest. It smelled like ocean air and tar, with a trace of coconut suntan lotion. That smell brought so many hot memories rushing back.

Julie lit a hurricane lantern and hung it from a hook in the ceiling. Its dancing flame revealed a pile of blankets nested on the floor. The wind blowing off Stargazer Beach whistled through the gaps in the plywood boards. The ocean was likely a froth of whitecaps by now. Pretty soon storm clouds would be rolling in, and all the stars would be blocked out.

But that wouldn't matter, because he'd be snuggled inside with Julie where nothing could hurt them.

"How long have you been planning this?" he asked her.

She glanced his way, her eyes huge in the light from the

lantern. "I happened to run into the firefighter in charge of the lifeguards here. I begged him to let me use it just for one night. I even told him why. He's kind of a romantic, and he remembered how inseparable we used to be." She smiled at him impishly. "I also told him I'd clean his house for free."

"I'll help. I'm great at windows."

She laughed. "Don't you worry your handsome ski-goggle head about it. I can clean houses in my sleep. Sometimes I do."

God, was he still wearing those silly things? Had he bared his heart, told Julie all about that night with his mom, while wearing *ski goggles*? He ripped them off his head and glared at them. "You're dead to me," he told the goggles, while Julie laughed again, then kneeled on the blankets.

"So. Before we get to the...ahem...good stuff," she gave him an elaborate wink, "I have a song to play you." She reached into the shadows in the corner and came out with a guitar. "I've been working on it for a while and I think it's finally ready for other human beings' ears. Well, yours. No one else's."

"You left your guitar here?" He lowered himself next to her and stretched out on the blankets. As soon as he lay flat, his head started to spin, and he realized those Snowcones had been stronger than they seemed.

"All part of the plan."

"If you're trying to seduce me, you should know I'm already a sure thing. Besides, I'm a little buzzed."

"Nah, this isn't seduction. This is...well, I guess you'd call it an apology."

She strummed, humming a pretty, wistful melody, then softly added words. "If you only knew, how I knew it was you, the one for me then, the one for me true. If only I knew, how close we flew, how long we'd be gone, when I knew it was you."

The song was both plaintive and quirky, an upbeat rhythm married to a minor-key tune. And as he listened to her sing, watched her head bent over the guitar, her fingers press the frets, he thought of his mother, the last glimpse of her face before she'd driven off in their SUV. The desperate look in her eyes, the determination, the *conviction* that she was doing the right thing.

She left because she had to. Because Ben couldn't help her. None of them could.

He couldn't help any of it—couldn't keep Julie from being scared away from Jupiter Point, couldn't stop his father from being murdered, couldn't make time go backwards, couldn't fix that night or anything about it.

Julie finished playing and glanced up to see his reaction. Her eyes went wide. "Are you okay?"

Startled, he realized his face was soaked with tears. More were coming, streaming from his eyes, and he hadn't even realized it. "Yeah, yeah. Fine. I just…"

He tried to swipe them away, but they just kept coming.

"Your mother. It made you think of your mother." She scrambled over the blankets toward him. "Oh Ben! I'm so sorry. So sorry about everything. I should have been there to help you through it."

Her arms came around him. Warmth and softness surrounded him—the fleece of the blankets, the heat of her body, the sweet silk of her skin. He felt so lightheaded, as if he was floating in the upper atmosphere instead of rolling around on the floor of a lifeguard shack. He closed his eyes, and when he opened them again, her clothes were gone, his hands cupped her bare breasts, her naked thighs wrapped around his hips.

Despite her nakedness, she wore a solemn look. "I need you to know something, Ben. Even though we lost those twelve years, I never stopped loving you. I still do."

He wanted to speak, to tell her that of course he still loved her too, but his mouth just wasn't working right. His head was still spinning and he couldn't get that last image of his mother out of his head—the way she'd turned to look back one more time. He felt the burn of her hand against his face, and the terror of watching her nightgown billow on her way to the window. That visceral fear slithered through him like a black fog. He couldn't see, couldn't hear anything but the desperate beating of his own heart.

But this time, Julie was with him. Her warmth surrounded him, her soft breaths whispered in his ear. He held on to her for dear life, his fingers clutching at her bare skin, needing her closer, closer.

They were both naked now—how? He wasn't quite sure. God, he'd had too much Snowcone, or too much emotional crap, or both. He shook his head, desperate to get back some clarity. He was naked with Julie in the lifeguard shack, and fuck, he didn't want to miss a second.

Now she was spread out under him like some kind of center-fold, the curls between her thighs glistening with moisture. He dragged a hand across her sex, wanting to feel her intimate heat with every inch of his palm. She moaned and arched her back, which drew his attention to her erect nipples, made perfectly for his mouth. He rasped the flat of his tongue across one tip, savoring the softness of her areola and the pebbling hardness at the center.

She clutched at his shoulders and ran her heels up and down his calves. His hand explored the glory of her pussy, found the pulsating core of her pleasure, then searched inside her muscular channel. It gripped at him in tight little spasms. She wasn't coming yet, he knew the signs. But she was close. Her body was grabbing at him, working against his knuckle, seeking that satisfaction she craved.

"I want you inside, please," she begged. The light from the hurricane lamp swayed in a sudden gust from outside. Shadows chased across Julie's face, lit golden sparks in her half-closed eyes.

Inside was where he belonged. Inside her, inside this lifeguard shack, this blast from their past. Inside the circle of Julie's love.

And so inside he went, sinking into infinity with her. It wasn't until he was deep within her, sliding into heat and bliss and oblivion, exploding at the same time that she did, her legs tight around him, his body rigid with the most complete and total release he'd ever experienced...that he realized they hadn't used a condom.

Shit.

He lowered himself next to her, rolling onto his back and shoving his hair out of his face. He wasn't worried about catching something, or giving something to her. She'd only been with one man other than him, and he was always careful to use a condom. He'd never tested positive for anything. But unprotected sex...pregnancy...

Huh.

A gust of wind shook the little shack, like a wake-up call. He was definitely awake now, and his head was finally clearing.

Julie swatted him on the arm. "We forgot the condom." He heard the panic in her voice. "I stashed some in my guitar case and totally forgot about them."

"I know, I just realized it myself. Don't worry, you're in no danger. I got tested right before I left the Air Force. Totally clean. I always wear a condom."

"I'm not worried about that." She put her hand on her belly. "Maybe I should get that morning-after pill."

He rolled onto his side to watch her. Hadn't she said she loved him? Would getting pregnant be so bad? "Where are you in your cycle?"

He used to be pretty attuned to her cycles, because every month like clockwork, he became the most irritating thing in her life—for about half a day. They used to have an agreement that he wouldn't get upset if she bitched at him during one twelve-hour period.

Julie counted on her fingers, then smiled in relief. "We should be safe. I forgot that you used to know all about my periods. God, we really told each other everything back then, didn't we?"

"We did. We even used to talk about what to name our kids, remember? We wanted three, and we were going to name them after stars. Andromeda, Castor, Vega."

"And we were going to put aside funds for the poor kids' therapy, too," she said dryly. "Which they would have needed with names like that."

"My point is, you just told me that you still love me."

She lifted herself onto her elbow. Her hair fell across the curves of her shoulder and breast with the grace of an artist's brush marks. "I do. But that doesn't mean I'm ready for three kids and a therapy fund."

He glanced away from her, watching the sway of the lantern's shadows against the wall. He wasn't ready, either. Or was he? What was he waiting for? Wasn't that really why he'd come back to Jupiter Point?

His brothers were right. He didn't want to play the field. He wanted love. A family. He wanted Julie.

She was still talking. "I don't even know where I'm going to be in a month. I might be back in LA. I definitely can't rush into anything. Condoms from now on, buster."

Right. Of course. That was the smart thing.

Or was it?

"But you could decide to stay here," he said slowly. "Especially if you were pregnant."

She sat all the way up. "Wait a second. Didn't we already settle this? I can't just abandon Felix."

"So, you're saying that you can't have your own child because Felix needs you?"

She stared at him, the lantern's shadows sweeping back and forth across her face. Her hair caught glints of bronze from its light. The wind whistled and moaned through the cracks in the wood. "No. I'm just not ready. That's all I said."

"When would you be ready? When Felix is in middle school? High school?"

"What's your point?" she snapped.

"My point is, you always put everyone else first. I know you always wanted children. So when are you going to go after what *you* want?"

"I am!" She nudged him with her knee. "What do you think *this* is all about? I lured you here and played you my song and told you I loved you. That's me going after what I want."

"And that's it? That's where it ends? You got me." He spread his arms wide, one hand hitting the side of the shack. "Ben Knight, at your service. What do you want to do with me? And don't say anything with sex in it, because I know you, Julie deGaia. It was never just about sex for us. I want you in my life. I want the same things we always talked about. I want them more than ever, because I'm older and wiser and I know what it's like being apart from you."

Her face glowed. "Really?"

He picked up her hand and kissed it. "Yes. Really. Though we might want to rethink 'Andromeda.' It's a little heavy for a girl. The rest of it, yes. One thousand percent. I want you, I want our children. All of it. Now I'm asking what *you* want."

Her eyes filled with tears and her throat worked with emotion. "Oh Ben. This. I want *this*. You. Children of my own. Jupiter Point. It's everything I've *always* wanted. I just don't know what that means for Felix."

His heart swelled until he thought it might break in a million pieces of light. They were together. They loved each other. Everything else was just details.

"We'll figure it out," he said softly. "Maybe Savannah has some ideas. I don't want to hurt Felix either. As long as we know where we stand with each other, we'll be fine." The wind knocked against the shack again, making them both laugh. "As long as we don't get blown away, of course. Come here."

He tugged her back down against him and wrapped his arms around her. Snuggled together, they listened to the wailing of the wind. He couldn't imagine anything more perfect than this moment in time.

A phone buzzed and Julie stirred. "Oh crap, I thought I turned my phone off." She felt around for it in the mussed pile of their blankets, then squinted at the screen. "It's Savannah."

"Maybe she knew we were talking about her."

"I think she generally assumes that everyone is talking about her." Julie's affectionate tone took the sting from her words. "Hey lady," she said into the phone. "Are your ears burning? Ben and I were just—"

She broke off, her face going dead serious. Ben heard rapid talking on the other end of the phone.

"*What?*" Then, "Are you kidding? When? Oh my God. No, I had no idea. No hint. Nothing. Believe me, I would have warned you. Or gotten the hell out of town... And me? They really said that?"

Another pause, during which Julie rubbed her forehead and listened. All the lovely afterglow ambiance of the lifeguard shack was shattered now. Ben sat up and pulled on his undershirt, then wrapped a blanket around Julie's bare shoulders. She was chewing at her thumbnail while Savannah ranted on. Rack his brain as he might, Ben couldn't imagine what the crisis could be —but the fact that she'd mentioned getting out of town put him on edge. Hadn't they just decided she was going to stay?

Finally, she ended the call and buried her hands in her face.

"What happened?" He put his hands on her shoulders, pressing the tension from her muscles. "Some kind of movie-set emergency?"

"No. It's the Reinhards."

He paused, taken aback. "What about them? We just saw them at the Winter Ball. Did something happen since then?"

"No, *they're* perfectly fine. And completely insane." She lifted her face from her hands, and he saw color burning in her cheeks. She wasn't upset. She was furious. "Savannah just got notice of a lawsuit. They're filing for custody of Felix."

25

THE OUTRAGE ON BEN'S FACE LOOKED EXACTLY HOW SHE FELT.
"How the fuck can they do that? He *has* a mother."

"Yes, but they say Savannah's an absent mother. Which, okay,
she sometimes is, but only when she's on location. And she
makes sure Felix is taken care of. He's always either with me or at
school or with a tutor." She cast around for her clothes, which
had gotten tangled up with Ben's and the blankets.

Cold waves of fury kept coursing through her. She'd never felt
anything quite like it before. *How could they?* How could they do
this to Savannah, to her, to *Felix*? And why?

Ben helped her locate her underwear. Her hands were
shaking so hard she had trouble putting her panties on, so he
helped her with that, too. Right now, she was so glad he was with
her that she could have cried. Except that she refused to cry. She
was too damn pissed.

"What did Savannah say, exactly? Is she getting a lawyer?"

"Yes, of course, but her parents totally blindsided her. She's
freaking out."

Poor Savannah. Julie had never heard her so shaken up.
Despite her bravado, Julie knew how much Savannah doubted

herself when it came to mothering. But Julie didn't doubt her. Savannah was the only person in the world Felix would allow to cuddle with him in the usual way. They shared jokes no one else understood, not even Julie. Felix needed his mother and adored her.

Who were the Reinhards to say otherwise?

"They say we're spoiling him," Savannah had cried. And by "we," Julie assumed they meant her, since they hadn't even seen Savannah with Felix. "Spoiling him by letting him indulge all his obsessions and allowing him to be weird. They say he should have a more stable life and that I can't provide it since I'm working so much."

"And me?" she'd asked, almost afraid to hear the answer.

"They say you're too soft with him because you're not a real family member. And that I'm leaving too much in your hands now that Felix is older. They said if I can't be his main parent, then a blood relative should be, not you."

"They really said that?" After everything she'd done for the Savannah and Felix, to be dismissed like that—"not a real family member"—it was so cruel it took her breath away.

"A lot of it's lawyer-talk, hon. Don't take it too personally." Savannah's voice grew bitter. "I know how they roll. They'd probably say they're just doing it for the good of the Reinhard bloodline or some shit. I knew it was a bad idea for you to go back there. I never should have trusted them! Jesus, is Dad even sick or was it all a ruse?"

A headache hammered at her temples, like piano keys on the inside of her skull. Everything she and Ben had just talked about flew out of her head, and all that mattered was Felix.

She squirmed into her dress, which no longer felt like Cinderella's dream ball gown. It may as well have been made from ashes, for all the appeal it had now. This was the dress she'd worn to the Reinhards' the night they tried to steal Felix—that was how she would remember it forevermore.

"I need to clear my head." The lifeguard shack felt as if it was closing in on her. She crawled toward the door. "A call from her lawyer came in, then she's going to call me right back."

"Hang on. You can't go out there alone, you'll get blown away. Wait for me."

Ben yanked on his pants and rolled the blankets up in the corner, all except one, which stayed wrapped around her shoulders. He blew out the lantern, causing a whiff of acrid smoke to drift through the air. She barely saw what he was doing, her mind so occupied with this shocking news.

Her first impulse was to grab Felix and hit the road for LA. But Savannah had made her promise not to do anything until she'd talked to the lawyer.

She stood barefoot on the dark beach, the wind pummeling her body. Storm clouds streamed across the sky, the moon peeking in and out of view. She should have been cold, but the blanket kept the chill off. The wind whipped her hair against her face, but she didn't mind the sting. It clarified her thoughts.

Ben stepped next to her and put his arm around her shoulder. She leaned against him and spoke over the rush of the wind. "Remember when Savannah talked about joining the Peace Corps after graduation?"

"Yeah, it always seemed out of character."

"Actually, it wasn't. She's much more generous than you think. But anyway, she wasn't really serious. It was a negotiating tactic to freak her parents out. It was right after my mom died and I was afraid I'd have to go into foster care or something. Savannah told her parents she'd drop the Peace Corps thing as long as I could stay in the guesthouse."

"Are you serious?"

"Yes. Savannah used to say her whole life was a series of chess moves, of her trying to claim power from her parents. Whenever she wanted something, she had to give something up. They always want to be in control. Savannah knew how to fight them, but Felix doesn't. This would be such a disaster for him."

Ben squeezed her closer against his side. "I don't think they stand a chance. Who's going to take a child away from a mother who wants him? Don't the judges always go by what's in the child's best interests?"

"I don't know. I'm totally clueless about this stuff. I'm afraid it could depend on who has the best lawyer. Which will be the Reinhards. I mean, Savannah's an actress. Her lawyer negotiates contracts and stuff like that. This is completely different. What if she loses custody?"

She felt everything falling away from her, like sand sloughing with the tide. She had no legal standing in Felix's life. She could lose him tomorrow. Maybe the Reinhards wouldn't want her around anymore if they thought she was too easy on him.

Her phone rang again. She snatched it to her ear. "Savannah?"

"Where is Felix right now? My lawyer wants to make sure he isn't with my parents. He was going to go to the ball, right? Is he still there?"

"No, he never went." At least that was a lucky break. "It was too much for him, I took him to Ben's brother's house."

"Can you go get him? Just to be on the safe side."

"Absolutely."

The thought of *doing* something instead of waiting for a call sent energy rushing through her. She hung up and turned to Ben. "Let's go back to the farmhouse."

"It's three in the morning."

She looked at her phone in amazement. Sure enough, they'd been snuggled in the lifeguard stand for three hours. In some ways, it felt like days, as if they'd traveled a long way in that time.

She hesitated, debating. Felix was safe at the farmhouse, sound asleep. The Reinhards probably didn't even know where he was. "My car's still there. I need to pick it up, and be ready to pick up Felix first thing in the morning."

"I'm staying with you," he told her, taking her hand and heading for the truck. "I'm not leaving you alone tonight."

"That's sweet, but Ben—everything I said before, it doesn't matter now. I can't think about anything besides Felix. He comes first."

His face tightened, but he didn't answer. They got into the truck, with Ben at the wheel this time. He turned on the heat, and even though she still had the blanket wrapped around her, she shivered. From cold or shock, she wasn't sure which.

Ben started the truck and roared out of the lot. "First of all, I'm going to stand by you no matter what. I care about Felix, too, you know."

"I know. I just don't want you to think—"

He cut her off. "Second, I know a good lawyer. She helped Carolyn adopt Sarah, and she really knows the Jupiter Point family court system. She could be helpful. Do you want me to call her?"

She shot him a curious sidelong look. Something in the tone of his voice indicated more than a business acquaintance. "When you say 'know'..."

He snorted. "Don't worry, we barely made it through coffee."

So, he had gone out with the lawyer. And why not? Ben was a catch, the sexiest man in Jupiter Point. And she loved him, but she had to put the brakes on. She had to deal with this situation with Felix, and if that meant going back to LA, she'd do it. And Ben would still be here in Jupiter Point. Just as cute and sexy and wonderful as ever.

God, her timing was the *worst*. Then and now.

When they reached the farmhouse, all the lights were blazing and a vehicle idled in the driveway. Horrified, Julie recognized Priscilla's Rolls. Brooks, the driver, was waiting at the wheel while

Priscilla hurried toward it, Felix in tow. Poor Felix had his glasses on crooked and looked as if he'd dressed in the dark.

Carolyn and Tobias followed behind. They were both on their phones, and in the next second, Julie's buzzed in her jacket pocket.

She ignored it and opened the door of the truck. She jumped out before Ben had even brought it to a stop. "Mrs. Reinhard!" she yelled as she ran toward the Rolls. It felt like a nightmare in which she ran and ran, but got nowhere. She'd never reach the Rolls in time. "Stop this!"

"We'll talk in the morning, Julie," Mrs. Reinhard called. "We don't want to upset Felix."

"You're *already* upsetting him!"

"If he'd come to the ball like he was supposed to, this wouldn't be necessary," she snapped as she manhandled Felix into the Rolls.

He barely had time for a plaintive, "Julie?" before the door closed behind him. The Rolls veered around Ben's truck and took off down the driveway, its taillights winking like evil red dragons' eyes.

"What on earth is going on?" Panting, Carolyn ran up to Julie. "She showed up in the middle of the night with her lawyer on the phone. She refused to wait until I called you."

Tobias closed his phone. "Will's on his way over."

Julie stared after the departing Rolls. Why was she so shocked? This was how the Reinhards did things. They steam-rolled over everyone else to get what they wanted.

She turned to Ben, who'd swung out of the truck to join them. "I need that lawyer's number. Right away."

"You got it. But Julie, you'd better call Savannah and tell her to get her ass to Jupiter Point."

She nodded, already digging for her phone. Only one person had ever really stood up to the Reinhards and all their money. That was Savannah. "I'll call her right now."

Will arrived in his Jeep and Tobias and Carolyn crossed the driveway to talk to him. Julie understood why they'd called him. As a former deputy sheriff, he was the most familiar with California law. But what if the law was on the Reinhards' side? What if they never had to give Felix back?

She shivered as she waited for Savannah to pick up. Ben's hand cupped her neck, a comforting, warm weight. It seemed like a year ago that he'd told her about his mother, and the night of the murder. He must be exhausted.

"You can go home," she mouthed.

He shook his head firmly. "Not happening. I'm going to follow you home. You're upset, it's late, and I want to make sure you're safe."

Savannah's voice mail answered. *Damn it.* "Savannah, call me the second you get this message. It's urgent. Beyond urgent. Are you there?"

Which was ridiculous, because no one had answering machines that you could listen to anymore. She hung up, exasperated and furious.

Carolyn's soft voice floated through the air. "How about you guys stay here tonight? It's so late to be driving around and you both look exhausted. Also, Sarah's planning to make waffles in the morning."

Julie's heart twisted hard. She knew why Sarah wanted to make waffles. *For Felix.* That idyllic morning scene at the farmhouse with waffles and the Knight family, and Ben and Julie and Felix, all filled with sunshine and warmth and laughter, might never come to pass.

Because once the Reinhards got involved, they always got their way.

26

BEN WOULD HAVE CANCELED ALL THE NEXT DAY'S FLIGHTS AND stayed with Julie, but she refused to allow that. She left the farm-house first thing in the morning to meet with the lawyer, while he gushed over Sarah's waffles. Then he drove to Knight and Day to begin work for the day. The familiar smells of the hangar, the sight of the two Cessnas with their sleek curves, even the hand-painted sign that usually brought him so much joy—none of it had its usual effect.

Julie had said she loved him. He ought to be the happiest man in Jupiter Point right now—maybe excepting his brothers. But instead it felt like a huge, cruel tease. She loved him and he loved her, but it might not matter at all. It all depended on Felix and Savannah and the Reinhards—and damn it, why did the Rein-hards keep screwing things up between him and Julie?

He went through his preflight checklist in a foul mood.

His first passengers showed up fifteen minutes ahead of schedule. He wasn't sure what was worse, their campfire aroma or their sappy newlywed smiles. They were a young couple from Montana, Barb and Pete, who were spending their honeymoon backpacking through California. Now they wanted to get airborne for another view of the territory they'd hiked.

He tried to smile back, he really did. But he was pretty sure he saw the girl flinch away from his crabby attempt.

"You'll have to enter your weight and next of kin here," he told them, swinging the logbook across the desk toward them.

"But we're each other's next of kin," said Pete. "If we go down, we go down together."

"Romantic. I'm touched, truly I am," Ben grumbled. "Doesn't change the law. FAA regulations."

"Of course." With a wary look at him, Pete bent over the book to fill out the information.

"How'd you two meet?"

"High school sweethearts." Barb took her turn at the logbook. "Our parents wanted us to wait, but we thought, what's the point when we know exactly what we want?"

Ben ground his teeth. "Sounds like smooth sailing for you two. That's just peachy keen."

"Excuse me?"

"Nothing. Come on out when you're ready." Ben left them with the logbook and went onto the tarmac to undo the tie-downs on the 206. He kicked the right rear tire to check its air pressure. And because he felt like kicking something.

"Hey, mister." Ben swung around to see the Pete had followed him out. "If you don't mind, we'd like to request a different pilot."

"What are you talking about?"

"Dude, it's our honeymoon. You're scaring my wife. I don't know what's going on with you, but I don't think you should be taking anyone up in a plane."

Ben kicked the right rear tire again, then shifted to the next tire. "Planes are not the problem. Up there, that's my happy place."

Pete scuffed his foot on the tarmac, making him look even younger than his twenty-something years. "Uh, I get it, I think.

Sounds like you have some issues. But this is about us, not your happy place."

"I don't have *issues*. Jesus. I'm ready to fly. I'm always ready to—"

"Excuse me."

A heavy hand landed on his shoulder. Ben turned to see Tobias giving him a strange look.

"Hey, where'd you come from?"

"I work here, remember?" Tobias wasn't usually the smiling sort, but he directed a wide grin at Pete and shook his hand. "Tobias Knight, pilot. Hope you don't mind if we switch things around and I take you up."

"Nope, that's awesome. I'll go tell Barb." With a look of sheer relief, Pete dashed across the tarmac toward the office.

Ben scowled at Tobias. "What are you doing? I got this."

"Saving the company. I came in to finish up those bookshelves and overheard you about to ruin some poor kid's honeymoon."

"Me? I wasn't going to ruin anything. Reality will do that all on its own." Ben undid the tie-down and tossed it to Tobias.

"Reality, huh? Here's reality: no newlywed wants to hear your sad story. Here's more reality: those honeymooners pay our bills."

Ben thought of his comment to Julie—*let's make our own reality*. Well, they'd given it a shot. Hadn't worked out the way he'd imagined.

He walked away from his brother, then tackled the next tie-down. "What's the point, T? Why are we doing this? You didn't even want this business. You're in it for me."

"So? It was a good idea. I like it now. What does it matter who thought of it?"

"It matters because I'm an idiot. I should have stayed in the Air Force. Things were simpler there. You get your orders, you go where they tell you. They plan, you execute. I don't know what I was trying to prove with this Knight and Day thing. Who cares?"

"You want a list of who cares? Because it's a long one. Look, if you're having some kind of emotional crisis, I get it. Julie, Mom, Felix, it's a lot. But could you do me a favor and leave Knight and Day out of it?" Tobias took the second tie-down from him. "I've gotten attached to this place. And Sarah loves it. So does Felix. So do you, last I heard. Did something change?"

"No. Nothing. It's just..." Ben ran a hand through his hair, struggling to put his wild emotions into words. "I'm an idiot, that's all. That whole happy-ending shit. It's a fantasy. Know why I wanted to start Knight and Day?"

"So you could still fly?"

"Not just that. It was for *Mom*. I kept thinking, what does she even have to come back to? The house is gone, Aiden's all grown up, we're scattered all over the world. I wanted her to have a reason to come home."

He had to look away from Tobias at that point, because his older brother always saw so much with that intense gaze of his. Instead, he focused on the windsock hanging limp from its pole, perfectly still after the crazy blow from last night.

"Stupid-ass idiot, that's what I am. Like this is something to draw her back." He spread his arms to include the tarmac, their tiny fleet of planes, the office building, even the windsock. "You should have told me to go pound rocks when I suggested a flight-tour business."

Tobias growled at him—actually growled. "Fuck that. Think about it, Ben. What about the hotshots? They could be dead right now if not for you. What about the kids at the Light Keepers? What about all the fricking joy and happiness we've given everyone who goes on one of our tours?"

"Fricking joy and happiness?"

"Yeah. You heard me. Fricking joy and happiness. Who says happy endings aren't real? Did you ever think I'd get married and be this happy? A few months ago, wasn't I the one scaring the customers? Now look at me."

He clasped his hands and batted his eyelashes like a cartoon Snow White. He even kicked up one heel, looking so ridiculous that Ben burst out laughing.

"Laughter. That's better," Tobias said with satisfaction.

Ben felt something in his heart shift. His gruff older brother was trying to cheer him up. That was worth something. That was worth a whole lot of something.

"Aren't I supposed to be the one getting *you* to lighten up?" That was usually how it went. Ben was supposed to be the charmer, the smiler, the lighthearted one.

"I guess we're in the upside-down now." Tobias shot him a rueful smile. "Don't get used to it, because you're still the guy on the flyers. And that ain't changing." All playfulness gone, Tobias came closer and planted a hand on Ben's shoulder. "You know, Ben, our family is never going to be the same. It can't be. But we're still pretty fucking lucky. We got the Knight brothers all in one place. And that's not all."

"What do you mean?"

"Besides being worried you were about to take that poor kid's head off, I came out here because I got a call from Julie. She's been trying to reach you, says your phone must be off."

Ben snapped to attention and dug in his pocket for his phone. It must be something urgent if Julie had reached out to Tobias. "Something about Felix? Did she meet with the lawyer yet? Is Savannah on her way?"

"Nope. None of the above." Tobias showed him the screen of his phone, where an address flashed. "Julie found Mom and Cassie."

"*What?*"

"Yeah. I don't know the details, but she saw them, and now they're waiting for you. This is the address where they are. I'll handle the rest of the flights today. With a smile, I promise."

He bared his teeth in a classic Tobias expression that qualified more as a grimace than a smile—unless you knew the amazing person underneath it.

Ben reached out and hugged his brother. Not a shoulder-bump hug, either. The real deal. "Thank you, T."

Tobias was right. He was pretty fucking lucky.

THE ADDRESS WAS that of a hotel on the outskirts of town. On his way there, he called Julie back. "My ringer was off, sorry. What happened? How'd you find Mom? I thought you were busy dealing with the Reinhards today."

"I'm outside the Reinhards' right now, waiting for them to see me, so I don't have long. I was going crazy this morning, there really wasn't anything to do after I met with the lawyer. So I logged onto Facebook and sent Cassie a message. She happened to be online, so I just laid it all out for her. I said you were really hurt that they didn't come to the ball last night, and that she needed to make it right. She asked me to come out and help her persuade your mom. So I did."

"Jesus, Julie. What did you tell her?"

"She was afraid you hated her for leaving. She feels really guilty. It's eating her up. I told her it was hard for me to come back, too, and that I was afraid you hated me at first. And you kind of tried to hate me, but you couldn't pull it off." Laughter ran through her voice. "Because you're a sweet and loving person. Yup, I used the S word. Sweet."

Ben shook his head in amazement. "Just this once, I forgive you. I can't believe you did all that, today of all days."

"I didn't know how long your mom would stick around. It's a good thing I did, too, because Cassie said they were considering leaving today. But she promised they wouldn't. Okay, Ben, I have to go. Priscilla just came out and she's glaring at me like some kind of guard dragon." Tension threaded her voice. He heard her car door open and close again. "Wish me luck."

"Good luck, and I—"

She hung up before he managed to spit out the rest.

"Love you," he said to a dead phone connection.

Why did their timing always suck?

27

"WHAT DO YOU MEAN, I CAN'T COME IN?"

"Just what I said." Priscilla's crossed arms and forbidding frown didn't leave much doubt what she meant, but Julie could still barely believe it. "This is a family matter. We're grateful for all you've done for Felix, we really are, Julie. But this needs to be sorted out between us and Savannah."

"Savannah's coming. She's already on her way. Why can't we talk in the meantime? The way you're doing this is hurting Felix. He needs consistency and familiarity. Sudden change is really hard on him. Forget how you feel about me. This is about *him*."

Priscilla raised an eyebrow. She wore pearls and a tight cashmere sweater and showed no trace of a party hangover. "We have no problem with you, Julie. We just don't see why you should be raising our grandson. I'm sure the courts will agree. Now until this is litigated properly, I think it's best you don't confuse Felix further. You should keep your distance. In fact, it might be best for you to go back to LA for now. I promise we'll keep you in the loop."

"Keep me in the *loop*? Are you serious?" Julie gripped her fists so tightly she might have cut into her skin. "Felix needs me."

"Felix is just fine. He has his family around him. He doesn't need a nanny. He's been doing his homework and reading a book. You don't need to worry. Go now, Julie. This doesn't concern you."

The word "nanny" burned almost as much as Priscilla's dismissive tone, but Julie tried to hold on to her cool. "I promise I'll go, I won't make trouble, but I want to see him first. I want him to know I'm not abandoning him. I promised him that I never would."

"I'll pass it along." Priscilla turned to go back inside.

"Like you passed along my other message?" Julie snapped before she could think better of it.

Priscilla's chin lifted to an imperious angle. "Careful, Julie. I'm being patient because of your loyalty to our family. But you have no standing in this situation. Felix isn't your child. Beyond that..." she hesitated, then steamrolled forward. "Isn't it time you made your own life? I say that in the most sincere way, with your best interests in mind."

Julie swallowed hard.

Her stomach churned as Priscilla's words ripped through her. *Family matter. Nanny. No standing in this situation. Your own life.* Mrs. Reinhard was right. Felix wasn't her child. Fairy godmother wasn't a legal position. Her only claim on Felix was that she loved him.

Numbly, she turned to go, barely seeing the stairs under her feet.

And yet, Mrs. Reinhard was wrong, too. She didn't understand love, or people, or children. Or teenagers, for that matter. All she understood was the law.

All these years, Julie had been so careful not to cross the Reinhards. And where had it gotten her?

Halfway down the stairs, she turned back. "I demand to see Felix."

"Demand?" Priscilla's spine went straight, as if an iron rod had just snapped into place. "You're in no position to demand anything."

"Are you so sure about that?" Julie's control broke, and a lifetime of diplomacy slipped away from her. "You want to talk about the courts? Any judge who hears the case is going to want to talk to *me*. I've been Felix's primary caretaker, aside from Savannah, his entire life. They'll be asking me plenty of questions. And do you know how long I've known *you*, Mrs. Reinhard? I was ten when we came here. I have years' worth of material I could share with a judge. I know you, I know Felix, and I know Savannah. Are you sure you want to alienate me? When all I'm asking is to see Felix and let him know I'm not abandoning him?"

The shock on Mrs. Reinhard's face was priceless, but Julie couldn't even enjoy the moment. She just wanted her threat to work.

"In case you think I'm not serious, I just hired a lawyer. She's very experienced with custody cases in Jupiter Point."

Priscilla snorted scornfully. "You can't afford a lawyer. I heard you were cleaning houses to make ends meet."

"Indeed. As it turns out, the green-cleaning business is booming. And my mom left me a little money, too. So yes, I can." Technically, she hadn't hired Eileen yet. But the lawyer had said she'd do anything for a friend of Ben Knight. Close enough, Julie figured. "Come on, Mrs. Reinhard. I only want to see him for a few minutes. I'm not going to snatch him away from you. You can be there the entire time."

Finally, the woman relented. Julie nearly threw up from the stress of standing her ground like that. In all these years, she'd never, not once, gotten her way with the Reinhards. How did Savannah stand it?

"Stay here," Priscilla commanded, then disappeared inside. Julie drew in a deep breath and turned around to survey the front lawn. She'd been so focused when she drove up that she hadn't realized the place was full of people breaking down last night's party. Two vans belonged to the decorators, based on the swooping decal logo on the side. A young woman who must be the florist was collecting her vases; she carried two, one in each arm, toward her SUV.

Well, at least Julie had been spared her old task of cleaning the kitchen after a party. That was one advantage of being *persona non grata* at the Reinhards.

"Julie." Mrs. Reinhard cleared her throat. Julie turned back to her—and saw that her face had turned as gray as her sweater. "Felix is gone."

"What? What are you talking about?"

"I think he ran away. His window is open."

"Ran *away*? To where? No. It's not possible. Where would he go, if not to me?"

Mrs. Reinhard narrowed her eyes at her. "Did you take him? Is this all some kind of smoke screen?"

"Are you insane? I can't even conceive of something like that. Savannah! She must have him." Quickly, she pulled out her phone and dialed Savannah. When her friend answered, she could tell from the road noise that she was on speaker. "Is Felix with you, Savannah?"

"With me? Does he have magical teleporting abilities?"

"Don't joke. He's not here."

"Right, because my evil parents took him."

Mrs. Reinhard's face twisted, but Julie didn't have time to worry about her feelings right now.

"No, I'm with your mom right now. She just came from his room and said he's gone and his window's open. She's telling the truth."

"Jesus!" Savannah's voice lifted in panic. "Tell Mom to search the grounds. Call the police. Call the sheriff, call *everyone*! I'll be there in an hour or so. And Julie..."

"What?" Her throat closed up in fear. This was real. This was happening. Felix was missing.

"I'm sorry. I should have come to Jupiter Point from the start. This is all falling on your shoulders, and it's not fair."

When had anything ever been fair? Nothing in her life had been *fair*, but she didn't care about that. All that mattered was Felix. "Just get here as fast as you can."

28

BEN HADN'T FELT THIS NERVOUS SINCE HIS FIRST SOLO RUN IN flight school. As he knocked on the door of Room 121 at the West Wind Hotel, his phone buzzed, but he reached into his pocket to turn it off. He was about to see his mother and sister for the first time in twelve years. Everything else could wait.

The door opened—and there she was. His mother, the same but different. Same expressive gray-blue eyes, both vulnerable and hopeful. Same tentative smile. The years and all their emotional toll showed in the form of new wrinkles and a streak of white through her sandy hair. Even though she was thinner than before, the flesh around her neck and face was looser. She wore a blue cardigan over a loose tunic and wide-legged harem pants.

The outfit made him nervous. It reminded him of the "bag lady" clothes she used to wear when she was heading into one of her dark spells. If she dressed like a homeless person, her kids knew to be extra well-behaved around her.

But when she spoke, she sounded perfectly lucid. "Ben. My goodness, you're a man now. So tall and strong, and handsome.

Cassie, come here. He's so handsome! Are you really my little Benny?"

"No one calls me that anymore," he muttered. Then winced. That wasn't exactly the most welcoming thing to say. "It's good to see you, Mom."

That wasn't especially warm either. God, he didn't know what to say. This was a freaking out-of-body experience.

Her eyes clouded. "I'm so sorry about the Winter Ball. It sounded wonderful in theory, but then I thought about all the people there and what they must be thinking of me. And really, I just want to see you and your brothers. If..." She hesitated, looking so uncertain that the ice around his heart broke open.

"If we want to see you? Yeah, we want to."

He opened his arms, leaving the next step up to her. Yes, he'd been hurt by her leaving. He was still hurt, still wanting to understand. But he couldn't find one corner of his heart that didn't ache for her.

With an exclamation, she stepped into his arms and he closed them around her.

Her scent flooded his senses. All these years, and she still smelled like his mother—how did she do that? He couldn't even put a name to it, though it had a touch of rose, a hint of patchouli. But he'd know it anywhere, whether he was blindfolded or staring right at her.

They didn't say anything else for a long moment, just held each other close. A tremor kept running through her body, maybe from emotion, or release of tension, he didn't know what.

Over her shoulder, Cassie stepped into view.

Ben had to blink a few times to clear the tears from his eyes. Also, he barely recognized her at first. The gawky teenager was gone, replaced by a vibrant young woman with a smile as big as California.

"Holy shit. Cassie?"

"Ben!" She stepped toward them and flung her arms around the two of them in a big group hug. Moisture still prickled his eyes, but he fought them back. Any sign of tears and they'd all be balling in a few minutes.

Finally, they unwound themselves from the hug.

"You look good, Mom. Healthy."

"So do you, my sweet boy. I'm so proud of you." Her forehead crinkled. "It feels so odd to be called 'Mom' again. Cassie often calls me Janine now."

He glanced at Cassie, who nodded. "Is that weird? I can go back to 'Mom.'"

Their mother smiled ruefully. "I haven't been much of a mom to anyone in a long time."

He tried the name out. "Janine. Yeah, it's a little weird."

Mom—Janine—laughed, then took his hand and drew him farther into the room. "You call me whatever you want. I'm just so happy to see you. I admit, I was hoping you'd show up in your uniform. Julie told me you were an Air Force pilot. And now you're running a flight-tour business? That's so impressive, Benny! I remember how much you used to love airplanes, ever since you were little."

The hotel room had a microscopic seating area containing a loveseat and an armchair. She sat down on the loveseat and curled her legs under her. Ben took the armchair, while Cassie perched on its arm and ruffled her fingers through his hair.

"You used to have a buzz cut, didn't you?"

"How can you tell?"

"One of my many random jobs was haircutting. I recognize the signs." She wore denim shorts over patterned leggings, and radiated the same kind of freewheeling zest for life she'd always had.

"I thought you got your mechanic's license?"

Janine jumped up from the loveseat. "You two catch up for a

minute. Benny, you want a soda? You still like cherry vanilla?" She headed toward the mini fridge on the other side of the room.

Cassie bent down and whispered in his ear. "She's really trying. This is a lot harder than she's letting on."

"At first, I thought she seemed better," he whispered back. "But now she seems so anxious."

"She's definitely better. Believe me. And she really wanted to come here and see you all. Especially you, Ben. This is huge for her, it really is."

It was huge for him, too. So huge it felt surreal. So huge, he didn't think he'd be able to process it until after he left.

Janine came back with three sodas, and handed him a can of cherry vanilla. He cracked it open. It tasted like his childhood. Like innocence and hope.

And a little like Julie.

Julie had made this happen. He knew it. Not just by making contact with Cassie, but by easing the way. By coming out here and talking to his mother, by sharing her own story.

He took a big gulp, letting the harsh, prickling carbonation fill his sinuses. "Mom, I mean Janine—I'm sorry," he said abruptly.

"Sorry?"

"That night. I said everything wrong. I didn't know what I was doing or how to deliver bad news or anything. I screwed it up. I'm really sorry."

Her expression turned shadowed. "You shouldn't apologize. That's my job. That's why I'm here, to make things right. It shouldn't have taken this long, but..." she drew in a breath, as if inhaling strength along with the oxygen. "I wanted to make sure I wouldn't do more harm by coming back."

"Harm?" His hand tightened around the soda can, drops of cool condensation tickling his hand. That was the last thing he'd expected her to say.

"I wanted to be good for you, not hurtful. Especially Aiden, since the rest of you were grown. And that night..." Her eyes swam with tears. "I remember it all in flashes, you know. I remember waking up because weird lights were flashing on the ceiling. I went toward the window to see what they were, but I couldn't get there. It was like one of those dreams when you're running and running but staying in the same place. I think maybe I wasn't really awake yet. Half asleep, half dreaming. Then I saw the police cars and I knew. I just knew. After that, I don't really remember anything."

Ben frowned down at the floor, at the vague geometric patterns in the hotel carpet. It was like static, meaningless background noise. It helped him focus, to block out the emotions of that night.

"And I remember...I remember slapping you. And how terrified I was. Of everything. Of myself." She rubbed at her forehead, between her eyes. "I should probably stop talking about this now."

Cassie sat on the couch next to her, a hand on her shoulder. "I was just about to say the same thing," she said in a voice pitched to lighten the mood. "I want to hear what's up with you, Ben. Are you back together with Julie? I tried to pin her down, but she didn't really answer that question."

Ben rolled his neck to release the tension that had built up. "It's complicated."

"Isn't it always," Cassie said wisely. "That's why I have a strict policy of no attachments. We're always picking up and moving anyway. It works out well because that way, there's no chance of getting too involved."

"I've been there. More than I want to admit."

She grinned and clicked her soda can against his. "To meaningless relationships. But don't tell Mom, she'll give us both a lecture about true love."

They both looked over at Janine, who was fiddling with the

hem of her sleeve. It was a habit he remembered from his child-hood, when she would unravel entire sweaters one thread at a time. At least now she wasn't actually picking it apart.

"No lectures from me. I think I've lost that right." She smiled sadly at them. "But look at Tobias and Will. Julie said they're both very happy."

"Yeah, who would have ever thought old Tobias would be walking around with a sappy grin on his face all the time. It's pathetic. He's all about his family now, which is Caro and Sarah, her half-sister, who she adopted. It's a crazy story, I'm sure they'll tell you all about it. When are you going to see them?"

Janine hesitated, then bit her lip, giving Cassie an uncertain glance.

Ben's stomach sank into his shoes. "Are you kidding me? You aren't going to see everyone else?"

She tugged at her sleeve again. "I want to. I really do. I just…"

Ben found himself rising to his feet. "No. Not okay. Not okay, Mom. Janine. You can't leave without seeing them. What about Aiden? You haven't seen him since he was *eight*, and you wouldn't believe what a great kid he is. Will did such a phenomenal job raising him…and you haven't even seen Will, have you? He's been searching for Dad's killer, and he's going to want to interview you, see if you remember anything. And Tobias, what about—"

He snapped his mouth shut, appalled at himself. All those years of tiptoeing around his mother, and now he was just letting it all hang out? But he couldn't stop. "You owe us, Mom. You *owe* us." The words ripped from his heart.

His mother looked stricken. She didn't shy away from his fierceness, but she couldn't seem to find her tongue to answer.

Cassie spoke up. "Mom gets it, Ben. I promise you she does. She's been on the phone with her therapist twice a day for the past month. And I already told her I'm staying for a while no matter what."

"I'm sorry," he muttered.

"No. No sorries. Just give me a moment." Janine got up and took her soda can to the kitchenette, where she dropped it in the trash, then headed for the bathroom. Ben resisted the urge to run after her and grab her by the ankle the way he had that night. *Don't leave. Don't disappear out the window.*

He stared down at the carpet, his anger draining away. Why had he thought seeing Mom would fill some kind of hole in his heart and transform his life? That apologizing for his clumsiness would change everything? He was just as clumsy now. *You owe us.* What kind of thing was that to say, even if it was true? Maybe their runaway mother did owe them, no matter the reasons that drove her away. But that argument wouldn't work. If it did, she never would have left.

Suddenly he wished passionately for Julie, for her soft arms and sympathetic smile.

"You said Will is looking for Dad's killer?" Cassie asked. Her big blue eyes were fixed on him with a clear message—*I know how you feel. Don't give up yet.*

"Yes, since the police basically dropped the case a few weeks after it happened. Will left the sheriff's department and now he's working as a private investigator. He has a new office and everything; you guys should come see it."

But his voice held no conviction that it would actually happen. His dream of a happy family reunion felt so silly now. The reality was that his mother was struggling, and probably always would be.

"I want to find Dad's murderer too, but I don't know how much help I can be. I was asleep and didn't hear or see a thing."

"I get it. But Will's a really good investigator, so you never know. He managed to pry a memory out of Tobias when they went back to our old house."

"Really, they went back there?" She shivered and tucked a

long strand of strawberry-blond hair behind her ear. "You couldn't pay me to go back. Life already sucked for me even before the murder. So what was the memory?"

"Something about the hutch. Remember that old pistachio-avocado vintage piece Mom kept in the kitchen? With all of Grandma's china? Tobias remembered that Dad was gesturing toward it."

Cassie screwed up her face. Ben remembered how she used to make them roll on the floor laughing with her expressions and voices straight out of a cartoon. "The hutch? That's a weird clue."

"Yeah, but then Will and Tobias put it together that Dad kept his medals in the bottom shelf. So he's been tracking down all the guys who were part of his last mission. The one he didn't like talking about because they came under fire while he was being carried on a gurney."

Janine came back into the room, wiping her hands on a towel. Her eyes were red, but she looked stronger. She smiled at him apologetically, sending relief rushing through him.

"Hey Mom, do you remember anything about the hutch that used to live in our kitchen?" Cassie asked.

"The hutch that used to belong to the Reinhards?"

Ben froze. "The Reinhards?"

"Yes. When they first moved to town, they bought that big mansion fully furnished. It was a foreclosure situation, I believe. Or a short sale, something along those lines. Anyway, they sold off most of the furnishings so they could start fresh with all those fancy antiques of theirs. I bought a few things from the sale. The hutch, that little oil painting of Stargazer Beach, a set of wonderful cut-glass tumblers. I never understood why they didn't want to keep some of that stuff. No sense of history, you know?"

"The Reinhards," Ben repeated. "The same place where Julie lived?"

"Well, yes, but long before she and her mother arrived. I wish I remember who owned the house before them, but I'd have to think about it. You could probably check the property-tax records if you really want to know where that hutch originally came from. I'm sure Will knows all about that sort of thing."

Ben and Cassie exchanged a glance. Nothing fired up Mom like rehashing Jupiter Point history. She'd always been fascinated by local lore.

"That's a great idea, Mom. I'll let Will know. Maybe our idea about his Army buddies was all wrong."

"His Army buddies?" Janine exclaimed. "Absolutely not. I don't believe that's possible. He stayed close to a few of the other soldiers in his unit, but there's no bad blood that I remember. I think he would have mentioned it."

"But one of them is going by a different name now." Ben couldn't come up with the name of the man Will was trying to trace.

"Oh sure. That's different. He became a woman." Janine's face turned impish. "Now didn't *that* throw your dad for a loop. Good old Hawkeye turning into Ladyhawke, that's how he used to put it."

Ben blinked at her, then at Cassie, who was busy cracking up. "Well, that clue sure went in an unexpected direction."

"Right?" Cassie jumped to her feet and impulsively threw her arms around him. "God, Ben, it's so good to see you."

"It sure is." Having his little sister in his arms might not fill that hole in his heart completely, but it helped. "I'm glad you're sticking around a little longer. I can't wait for you to see Knight and Day."

"Promise to take me up in a plane?"

"Absolutely."

She drew back, rocking on her heels and tucking her thumbs in her belt loop like some kind of cowgirl.

It was time for him to go, he realized, while he could still do so on a good note. He stepped toward the door.

Cassie followed. "It's weird, seeing Jupiter Point again."

"Not much has changed, really. Stargazing, butterscotch sundaes, and honeymooners everywhere you turn." The door handle felt cool against his hand, an escape route awaiting him.

"Good old Jupiter Point. I missed it, even though I'm such a rolling stone now."

"Personally, I don't enjoy traveling," said Janine, joining them at the door.

"You don't?" Cassie gave a double take.

"It would never be my first choice. But it seems to be the best way to keep my head."

How should he say goodbye, Ben wondered? With hugs? Another apology?

Saving him from the decision, she came close and reached up to give him a soft kiss on the cheek. "Goodbye, Benny. My beautiful boy. I've thought about you so often. If you only knew."

And then he was out the door, the touch of his mother's kiss still on his cheek.

If you only knew... as he jogged down the staircase, Julie's plaintive song ran through his mind, as if he could hear her voice, see her lips crooning the words, smell the warm skin in the crook of her neck.

With sudden fierceness, he craved her presence. He glanced at the old-school watch on his wrist. Amazingly, he'd been here for an hour. How was it going with Julie? Had she made any progress with the Reinhards?

The Reinhards, from whom his mother had bought their hutch. The hutch that Dad might or might not have been pointing out. Was it a lead? He needed to call Will right away.

After he called Julie.

Even if seeing Mom hadn't filled that empty place in his heart, the fact that Julie had given him this moment—that was everything.

As soon as he slid into the driver's seat of his truck, he dug out his phone and turned it back on.

An explosion of texts and notifications scrolled across the screen. Will, Tobias, Carolyn had all called. Julie had texted twice and called once. What the hell?

Then he started reading her texts—and his heart nearly stopped. *Felix.*

29

THE SEARCH OF THE GROUNDS TURNED UP NO SIGN OF FELIX. IT made no sense. He had a phone. He was meticulous about keeping it charged. He had several research apps he liked to consult, as well as a few games that soothed him during stressful moments. He *always* kept his phone with him. They turned his bedroom upside down, but it was nowhere to be found. The logical conclusion was that he'd taken it with him. So why wasn't he using it? He hadn't called Julie, Savannah, Sarah, or anyone else she could think to ask.

A horrible thought kept nagging at Julie. That fateful night outside Ben's house, her attacker had taken her phone. Had the same thing happened to Felix? Had someone snatched him? He was the son of a movie star and the grandson of the richest family in town. Was someone planning to hold him for ransom?

The terrible scenarios that ran through her brain were driving her nuts.

The Reinhards' property swarmed with people. The household staff, Will Knight and his intern, Chase. Tobias and Carolyn, along with Sarah. But the person she longed for most, Ben, still hadn't called her back. Of course, she knew he was still busy with his mother, but my God, all of the crappy timing. She'd never needed him more.

Finally, he arrived, pulling up in a rooster tail of gravel. He ran across the lawn to her and swooped her into his arms. She clutched at him, burying her face in his chest, his familiar scent flooding her with comfort.

"Any news?" he murmured.

"No. He's gone, his phone is gone, no one's heard from him." Panic bubbled close to the surface, but his strong arms around her kept Julie grounded.

"Looks like the whole town is here to help."

"I know." She drew back and wiped her eyes. "Mrs. Reinhard thinks he ran away, but I'm not so sure. Felix isn't the type to run away. He's too cautious."

He gazed down at her with sober eyes. "So, what do you think happened?"

"I just...I have this horrible feeling that it's something even worse."

A jaunty voice interrupted them. "I can see that I've arrived in the nick of time. Things are getting entirely too dire around here."

They both turned.

In dark sunglasses and a white swing coat, Savannah Reinhard—Savannah St. James to her fans—aimed her famous megawatt smile at them. Even Julie felt the impact, and she was used to Savannah's presence.

They exchanged a quick hug, then Savannah focused her attention on Ben.

"Well. If I'd known you'd grow up this nicely, I would have fought a little harder for you."

"Savannah!" Julie frowned at her friend. "You can't flirt with Ben when Felix is missing."

"I doubt it."

"*Excuse me?*" Julie glanced toward Ben, who looked just as mystified.

"It's a Reinhard thing. Do you think I don't know my parents and the lengths they'll go to? I worked it all out while I was driving down here. I think my parents have him stashed somewhere. I'd bet my Austin-Healey on it. This is a negotiation tactic, like everything they do. And it worked, didn't it? I'm here. And I guarantee that nothing else would have gotten me to Jupiter Point, so it's fucking brilliant."

"That's insane," Ben said. "Even for your family."

"Yeah, I think I've finally managed to push them over the edge." Savannah shoved her sunglasses on top of her head, turning her wild black hair into a rich waterfall down her back. She had an old-Hollywood curvaceousness that somehow managed to make everyone else look thin and washed out. Even Julie, who wasn't exactly a lightweight. "Only took twenty-nine years."

Julie finally broke out of her temporary state of shock at Savannah's suggestion. "I don't think so, Savannah. Your mom seemed really shocked when she told me he was gone. I can't believe she'd make us go through all this."

"That's because you're a kind person and always think the best of people. I don't. Look at what my parents did to you and Ben. They lied to you. We can't trust anything they say or do."

Julie and Ben exchanged a wary look. Savannah made a good point. The Reinhards could be manipulative, but would they go this far? On the other hand, if they had Felix, at least that meant he hadn't been kidnapped.

"Let's go talk to them," Ben said grimly. "It's time they answered for some of the shit they've pulled."

"Agreed," said Savannah. Together, they all headed for the portico, where Priscilla was talking on her cell phone. "Finally, I have company for this sort of conversation. I never had that before."

Julie's phone buzzed with a text and she stopped to check it. The message came from Felix's phone, and said in big capital letters—SAY NOTHING AND ANSWER THE PHONE ALONE.

Oh my God, oh my God.

She was right, someone had Felix's phone. Did they have Felix, too?

She scanned the surrounding area in a panic. *Answer the phone alone.* How was she supposed to manage that in this crowd of searchers? Especially around Ben and Savannah, both of whom knew her far too well?

Luckily, they were a few steps ahead of her.

"I thought of somewhere else to check," she called to them. "I'll be right back. Two seconds."

Ben looked over his shoulder at her. "Want me to come?"

"No, no. Go ahead." She waved him away, while Savannah tugged on his arm. He nodded and continued across the lawn toward the portico.

Julie swallowed hard as she watched him walk away from her, so tall and strong.

She had the terrible sense that this could be it for them, the end of their second chance.

Alone, the message had said. Whatever was coming, she had to handle it by herself, for Felix's sake.

She withdrew behind a flower delivery van. A moment later, her phone rang. Did that mean the caller could see her? That Felix was somewhere nearby? Or at least his phone was?

"Hello," she answered in a low voice. *Please be Felix on the line. Please.*

"Hello." It wasn't Felix. It was a strange voice, deep, probably distorted. "I have the little boy. If you want him back, you have to do exactly what I say."

"Who are you? What do you want with him?"

"He's leverage, that's all. He won't get hurt. But I need you to follow my instructions. No negotiating."

"Put Felix on the phone. I want to make sure he's okay."

"That's negotiating."

"No, it isn't. I'm not going to argue with anything you tell me to do. I'll do it. I want to know you're not lying, that's all." There was an expression for it, they'd even made a movie out of it. "Proof of life," she burst out. "That's the phrase. I need proof that Felix is alive."

"I have no interest in killing him. Jesus."

Who was he? His voice wasn't familiar, but something in his intonation *was*. Her singer's ear caught it, a certain downturn at the end of the sentence. Where had she heard it before?

"You weren't supposed to come back. I warned you. If anything bad happens to this kid, it's on you."

Julie froze, the world spinning around her.

That was why he sounded familiar. He was the man who'd grabbed her outside the Knights' house. "You."

"Me," he said smugly.

She thought quickly. If his goal was to get rid of her, no problem. "Listen. This is a big misunderstanding. I came back only so Felix could meet his grandparents, but it's not a permanent thing. I don't intend to stay."

"Then why have you been talking to Will Knight? You've been digging up the past, haven't you? You should have stayed in LA."

"I'll stop. I'll leave. Right away. Just let Felix go. I'll leave and never come back."

"I don't believe you. I've seen you with your old boyfriend. I can't be sure you'll stay away."

"Yes, you can. You can be absolutely sure. If that's the price of Felix's safety, I can guarantee no one will see me in Jupiter Point ever again. Let me talk to him. That's all I ask."

"No specifics, no questions about where we are or anything like that."

"Understood."

The man disappeared from the phone, while Julie's blood

hammered in her ears. After what felt like forever, Felix came on the line. "Hi Julie."

"Hey, buddy boy. Are you okay?"

"Are we going back to LA? I heard what that man said."

"Yes. We're absolutely going back to LA. Tell him I said so, that I'm really looking forward to it."

"But what about Ben, and Sarah, and everyone else?"

Julie could tell from his voice that the thought of leaving Jupiter Point actually made him sad. Unfortunately, she didn't have time to savor the irony. "I'm sure we'll see them all again. LA isn't that far. Everything's going to be fine...especially if you pull a Felix. Okay, Kiddo? Hand your phone back to the man and I'll see you really soon."

A pause while he absorbed her words. Would he pick up on her "pull a Felix" request? If he could focus his mind on accumulating information, he'd stay calm. "Okay. Bye Julie."

The man came back on the phone and directed her to a gas station just outside of town. As she listened to him, she realized something else. His intonation was familiar, yes—because she'd heard his voice *recently*.

"Not a word to anyone until you're a hundred miles out. Then you can call off the search. Tell everyone you found the kid and you're taking him home to Los Angeles. And then you *stay there*. You got it?"

"I got it."

Yup, she got it. History was about to repeat itself. Once again, she had to leave Ben behind with no word.

And this time, she had to stay away, for good.

BEN HAD MANAGED to catch a couple of Savannah's movies over the years, but her confrontation with her mother had to be her best performance of all time. She tore into her, flinging accusations of kidnapping and worse. But no matter what tactics she used, Priscilla held firm that she hadn't hidden Felix anywhere. She'd given him the best guest room in the house, and when she went up to find him, the room was empty.

Mr. Reinhard, who'd been at a doctor's appointment most of the morning, backed her up. He even apologized to Ben for their deception all those years ago. "We went too far. We shouldn't have lied, no matter what our reasons. But faking a kidnapping? That's over the line. We're not criminals." He turned to Savannah. "Come on, Savannah. Please. *Kidnapping*? Look at all the law enforcement crawling all over this place. Does that seem like a smart move?"

"Then why did you file for custody of Felix? Why are you pulling all this crap?"

"We can talk about that later. Right now, we just need to find him."

Slowly but surely, Savannah's face registered the horrifying reality. "Oh my God. You guys are telling the truth. He's really missing."

"Yes. On my watch!" Priscilla burst into tears, something so uncharacteristic, it had to be real. "I can't believe this happened! With security guards here, and so many people. I'm so sorry, Savannah. I feel terrible. I never wanted *this* to happen. Everything's so awful...first Adam getting sick, now Felix is missing. I just—"

Adam put one arm around her, and Savannah took her hand. It was probably the closest the Reinhards would ever come to a group hug.

Ben stepped away to give them a moment of privacy. He looked around for Julie and realized she was nowhere to be seen.

He called her and got no answer. Had she joined a search party? She wouldn't just disappear without telling him, would she? He scanned all the cars and delivery vans parked on the property. No red VW Jetta.

He called Will, who was searching the woods adjacent to the Reinhard property. "Something's wrong. Julie wouldn't just leave like that."

"Any chance she found Felix and decided to get him away from the Reinhards?"

"Maybe, but why wouldn't she answer my call? Something's wrong, Will. I feel it. This is going to sound crazy but...can you track her car? Put a call in to your buddies at the sheriff's department?" He scanned the busy crowds of searchers, caterers, and staff members. With so many people on the property, anyone could have snuck in here.

"I don't know if that's a good idea," Will was saying. "Remember Julie's suspicions about the police?"

"Is there a channel that just the sheriff uses? A private one that no one else can access?"

"I'll see what I can do. In the meantime, keep trying to call her."

They hung up. Ben stood for a moment, feeling utterly lost and useless. Will's suggestion made a certain amount of sense. If Julie had found Felix, her first priority would be getting him to safety. And if she thought the Reinhards weren't safe, she could very well take off without a word.

Not even to him.

Felix came first, after all. He had to accept that. Julie wouldn't be Julie if she didn't give her all for someone she loved.

He nearly jumped out of his skin when Will called him back. "We're in luck, sort of. Deputy Jernigan spotted Julie in her Jetta on Highway 29, heading out of town."

Heading out of town.

"Does she have Felix with her?"

"No, she's alone."

"Okay. Thanks, Will."

"Sorry, man."

Ben clicked off. So Julie was leaving Jupiter Point. But she wouldn't leave while Felix was missing. She must know something. Why was she cutting him out? Why wouldn't she tell him, let him help?

Didn't matter.

This time, he wasn't a kid anymore. He was a grown man who could handle a fucking setback. And he wasn't about to give up on Julie, not until she looked him in his face and told him to go away. *This* time, he was going to trust their relationship. He was going to keep the faith that Julie loved him, and she was shutting him out because she had to.

But that didn't mean he couldn't provide backup.

He strode toward his truck. Savannah spotted him and tried to wave him over, but he gestured toward his phone, as if it was an important call he couldn't get out of. Until he knew what was going on, he didn't want any reinforcements—at least any that weren't named Knight.

His brothers—that was another matter.

He called Tobias, who was circling in the chopper above the property looking for anything that might help. "T, I need you to make a little flyby over Highway 29."

"What am I looking for?"

"Red Jetta. Julie's car. Last spotted heading east on 29."

"Ten-four. Stand by."

God, he loved it that in a time of crisis, he could ask his brothers for anything and they didn't argue. He got into his truck and started it up, ready for whatever Tobias might find.

"Yup, got her. She's pulling into that gas station outside of town. What do you want me to do?"

Ben thought fast as he started up his truck. He was a good fifteen minutes out, but he could shave some time off that. In the meantime, he didn't want to freak Julie out. "Can you hover *discreetly*? I don't want to set off any alarms, but I want to know what's going on."

"Okay, I might need a few more details here. This isn't more of your Ben-and-Julie relationship drama, is it?"

He let out a snort of laughter, then felt guilty for finding any kind of amusement in this situation. "Yeah, I'm using up our precious fuel stalking my ex-girlfriend. Totally normal. Honestly, I don't know what's going on but I have a bad feeling. Can you just trust me?"

"Yeah, I can trust you, but discreet hovering ain't a thing, pal. Oh, hang on. She's out of her car. Looking around, like she's meeting someone. Shit."

"What?" Ben nearly drove into one of the cypress trees lining the drive. "What's going on?"

"It's Felix. Some man has him. He's wearing a hat and scarf and sunglasses, hard to tell who he is. Looks like a disguise. But he's definitely got a tight grip on the kid. Damn. I can't tell if he has a weapon, but I don't think so. Okay, what now, Ben?"

Shit. Ben slammed his foot on the accelerator. He needed to be there, *now*.

"Gain altitude. I don't want them to suspect anything. Let me know what happens."

"Got it. Gaining altitude." The background noise shifted as Tobias pulled up on the collective.

Ben reached the highway and floored the accelerator. The pine trees whipped past, punctuated by telephone poles passing at a rate that felt like the beating of his pulse. *Get to her. Keep them safe. Please, Lord.*

"Julie has Felix now," said Tobias. "The bad guy is walking away, back into the gas station."

The gas station must have a security camera. They could find out who the guy was—maybe. He'd call it in to Will as soon as he got off the phone.

"Now Julie's hugging Felix. They're getting in her car. Driving away. Heading out of town. What's going on, Ben? Why are they leaving?"

"I don't know."

"We need to call the cops. Call 9-1-1, call the state troopers. Call everyone!"

"And tell them what? That Julie now has her kid back? Tobias, something is going on but we *have to trust her*. If she isn't communicating, there's a good reason. Promise me. Give me an hour, that's all I ask."

The drone of the chopper filled the silence that followed. "One hour," Tobias finally said. "Want me to keep on her tail? Or stick with the man at the gas station?"

"Gas station. I'll go after Julie. The dude is probably going to ditch his clothes for something else, so keep a sharp eye out."

The gas station was up ahead. He was tempted to pull over and see if he could spot anyone who matched the description Tobias had given, but it didn't seem as important as finding Julie. What if she was being threatened or coerced in some way? What if she thought she was safe, but she wasn't?

Tobias came back on the line. "Another car just drove away from the gas station, going in the same direction as Julie. I don't know, Ben. Could be nothing. But something about the way he's driving looks fishy. Keep an eye on a gray Taurus, okay? Just to ease my mind."

"Got it. Thanks, T."

Shortly after Ben passed the gas station, he spotted the gray Taurus. He wanted to get a look at the guy, but without giving himself away. He rummaged for his gym bag, which he kept in the backseat. He had a sweatshirt in there, one with a hood. Once his head was covered, he waited for a convoy of semis to catch up with him. As they passed on the left, he picked up speed and slipped between two of the big trucks.

He risked only a quick glance at the driver as he passed the Taurus. The man, probably in his fifties, now wore a cowboy hat and big aviator glasses, with a hefty growth of beard. Definitely not recognizable, at least to Ben. Maybe it wasn't the same man who'd taken Felix. He certainly didn't pay any attention to Ben. He stayed in the right-hand lane, keeping a sharp focus on the road ahead...and the splotch of red that Ben quickly realized was Julie's car.

The semi slowed down, forcing Ben to do the same. The Taurus slipped past him. He changed to the right lane, keeping far enough behind not to draw attention.

It was getting close to evening now. How far was Julie planning to drive? Assuming she'd filled up at the gas station, she could go for a while. But Felix was a kid, and he'd get hungry before long or have to pee, or something. Other worries multiplied like rabbits. What if the man in the Taurus had noticed him? What if he was the wrong guy?

Thirty minutes later, Julie pulled into a rest stop.

The Taurus followed.

30

JUST GET OUT OF TOWN, JULIE KEPT CHANTING TO HERSELF. *FIGURE out the rest later.* It wasn't much of a plan. She had to let everyone know that Felix was safe. She had to come up with some kind of explanation that made sense to everyone. *Felix had a meltdown, he wanted to go home. Sorry for all the trouble.*

She still couldn't pin down where she knew the man from. Either her musician's ear was failing her or she didn't know the man very well. Maybe she'd just heard him in passing around town.

But most importantly, Felix was okay.

"Did he hurt you, kiddo?" Julie was trying to keep her cool, she really was. But her hands were shaking so hard it was difficult to steer.

"No. He just surprised me, that's all. I climbed out the window because I didn't like it there. As soon as I got to the ground, he grabbed me. I tried to scream but I couldn't make any noise with his big hand over my mouth." Felix made a face of disgust. "I can still taste his glove."

"I'm so sorry that happened. Jeez, Felix, I was scared out of my wits. Everyone's searching for you back at the Reinhards', even your mom."

"Mom came?" Felix's pale little face brightened as he adjusted his glasses. "She really came?"

"Of course she did. No one knew where you were. We were terrified. I'm *still* a little terrified." She touched his arm lightly, not enough to bother him. "I will be until we get home."

"One hundred percent rayon with leather strips, size twelve, made in China," Felix said. "Do you think he'll ever give me my phone back?"

"I wouldn't count on it. We'll get you a new one. What's that about China?"

"The man's gloves. Remember when you said I should pull a Felix? Right after that I saw the tag on his gloves."

She grinned at him, delighted. "Good work. Maybe you'll actually crack this case. I want that man off the streets."

"Do you think he's on the streets?" Felix asked seriously. "Right now?"

"Figure of speech. I don't know where he is, and I don't care, as long as he's nowhere close."

"When we left, he was going back inside the gas station, but maybe he was buying gas. Or going to the bathroom. I have to pee."

Julie's heart sank. Of course he did. He was a kid, and kids always had to pee at the most inconvenient moments. The man's instructions had been to drive straight to LA and not stop for a hundred miles. But did that pertain to bathroom breaks? Exactly how would he enforce that? She checked the odometer. They'd only driven sixty-two miles since they'd left the gas station.

But when you had to go, you had to go. Felix wiggled back and forth in his seat. With a sigh, Julie gave in and took the next exit, which led to a rest stop. She grabbed the parking spot closest to the men's bathroom, which wasn't difficult because the parking lot was empty. Tourist season was still a month away.

"Make it as quick as you can, Felix. And I know you won't like this, but I'm coming in with you."

"What? That's stupid."

"I'm not letting you out of my sight, buddy boy, not unless you can hold it until we get to LA. You can have all the privacy you want back home."

"I can't hold it that long," he grumbled. He hopped out of the car and stalked to the men's room.

"Wait. Let me check it first." She peered under the doors of each stall while he hopped from one foot to the other. When she was sure it was safe, he marched inside a stall and banged the door shut. She leaned her back against the main door and scanned the space. Rest-stop bland, with two screened-in ventilation windows too high to reach. Perfectly safe. God, she was paranoid.

Felix emerged from the stall and went to the sink. He always took a long time washing his hands. Julie suppressed the urge to ask him to hurry. He'd been through enough today; if washing his hands soothed him, she'd give him all the time he needed.

"I want to go back to Jupiter Point," he said as he squirted soap on his hands. "I don't want to leave."

Trust Felix to be contrary.

"I know it's sudden, but we didn't have a choice. Don't worry, we'll call everyone as soon as it's safe. You can say goodbye properly."

"No, I mean I want to go back *now*. I want to see Mom. And Tanaka is having a birthday party tomorrow at the bowling alley. I've never bowled but I think I'd be good at it. I already have a present for him. I'm going to give him my old calculator."

Julie stared at the back of her young godson's head. His neck looked so thin and vulnerable as he bent over the sink, obsessively washing his hands. "It's not safe, Felix. You heard what the man said. We can't go back."

"But what about Ben?"

"Ben will understand. He wouldn't want either of us to get hurt."

Felix squished the soap between his fingers, carefully coating each finger with slimy bubbles. "That's not what I mean. Ben is strong and tough, and so are his brothers. They'll watch out for us."

"Yes, but as long as that man is running around free, we'd never be completely safe. They can't watch us all the time."

"So we should catch him. You said to pull a Felix, and I did. Not just with the gloves. I figured out a lot of other things, too, about his clothes and his car and his disguise. He doesn't really need glasses, that's one thing. Julie, I really want to go back. I want to catch him and put him in jail so he can't hurt anyone. What if he tried to scare Sarah or Tanaka or one of the other kids? I *hate him!*"

That fierce statement gave her a shock. Felix might be an undersized, unusual kid, but he was a lot tougher than he appeared.

"I know how you feel. I swear I do. I don't want to leave Jupiter Point either. I love it there. I always have. But I love you more, and we can't risk it."

Felix swung around and stomped his foot. "I'm not getting back in your car. I want to see my mom. I want to go back!"

Oh God, just what she needed right now, an epic Felix emotional breakdown. "Sweetie, we'll call Savannah as soon as we can and she'll come to us. I promise. I'm just trying to keep us safe."

Felix didn't answer, just crossed his arms over his chest and set his face into the mulish lines that meant "no deal."

God, was she going to have to overpower him? Lie to him? Physically drag him into the car? Then he'd have an even bigger meltdown *and* they'd be in a moving vehicle.

She dug her fingernails into her palms, fighting for calm.

This situation was her and the Reinhards in a nutshell. *All* the Reinhards. They decided what they wanted, and she went along.

What must it feel like to fight for what you wanted, even when everything seemed lined up against you? What must it feel like to claim your own power? Like Ben said...*when are you going to go after what you want?*

What did she want?

She wanted to stay in Jupiter Point. With Ben.

Of course, she also wanted Felix to be safe. But damn it, Felix was making some good points. Between Ben and Will and Tobias, and even the Reinhards, they had a lot of backup. And if Felix really had learned everything he could about his kidnapper, why not try to find the man and get him arrested?

This time, maybe running was not the answer.

She whooshed out a deep breath, hoping she was doing the right thing here.

"You know something, you're right, Felix. I mean, you're also wrong. It's not cool what you're doing right now. I'm really unhappy with you. Except that I'm also extremely happy you're okay, so I can't even be mad. And I'm starting to think you have a good point."

"I do have a good point."

God, the confidence of a Reinhard. Maybe some of it would rub off on her.

"Let's go back to Jupiter Point. I'll take you to your mom, we'll go see Will, and you can tell him every detail you picked up about the bad guy."

Slowly, Felix's stiff form and clenched fists relaxed. He pushed his glasses farther up his nose and took in deep breaths, the way he'd learned when he needed to calm himself.

In typical Felix way, he didn't apologize or gloat, but simply said, "Let's go then."

She laughed ruefully, then opened the door and led the way outside.

As soon as she set foot on the pavement, something hit her from the side. Rough arms grabbed her, and a hand came over her mouth.

A man. Not just a man...*the* man. She remembered everything about how this felt—the powerlessness, the meaty push of his chest against her, the heavy weight of his arms digging into her sides.

Not just his arms—something sharp as well, pricking at her ribs. A knife?

"Why won't you ever fucking listen to me?" he growled in her ear. "Why can't you just go away and *stay* away? I didn't want to hurt you. But now I have to."

31

SHE KICKED AT HIM, BUT HIS LEGS WERE AS SOLID AS TREE TRUNKS. She squeaked again, hoping to keep his attention on her instead of on Felix, who was hopefully still in the bathroom.

"You know what your problem is? You're weak. You were a scared little girl back then, and you're not much better now. You let a *kid* tell you what to do and where to go? Jesus!"

Where did she know him from? She couldn't pin it down, but she knew his voice from somewhere. Not well. But enough.

He dragged her away from the restroom. The world tilted like a funhouse ride—she saw the restroom, the vents that must have enabled him to eavesdrop, cars in the parking lot.

Cars. One of them must belong to this man. But the others...if she could just make a sound loud enough to be heard...

She tried to scream, but his hand was so tight over her mouth that only a squeaky breath came out.

"Give it up, little girl. I'm done with you. I didn't want to hurt you, I just wanted you gone. But you know what happens to people who get in my way."

Horror seized her. Was he talking about the murder of Robert

Knight? Oh my God...this man *was* the killer. A killer who *really* didn't want her in Jupiter Point.

If she could just get her mouth free, not to scream but to ask him some questions...he was probably dying to tell his story. Wasn't that what they did on TV shows, goad the suspect into boasting about their evil deeds? But how were you supposed to goad when you could barely squawk?

He dragged her toward the wooded area behind the rest stop, where the leaves of birch and aspen trees fluttered in the breeze. To make matters worse, it was almost sunset. Felix was all alone back at the rest stop. He didn't have a phone or the keys to the car. Please let someone at the rest stop be a Good Samaritan type. *Please be smart, Felix.* If only she'd given him her phone.

If only...if only...if only she could have seen Ben one more time. Just one more chance to feast her eyes on him, to soak in the bliss of his presence. Okay, might as well be greedy...one more time to get naked with him, to travel to that intimate place where they were the only two people who existed.

The man grunted harshly in her ear and his grip loosened, just a bit—enough for her to break away. She lost her balance and stumbled to the ground. She heard the *thump* of flesh on flesh, along with a vicious curse. She scrambled to her knees to see what was happening.

Ben.

Ben was happening. His fury made him seem ten feet tall as he loomed over the man and slammed a vicious blow into his kidney region.

"Who are you?" Ben demanded. "What do you want with Julie? Why'd you take Felix?"

The man cowered away from him, shielding his head with his arm. He was wearing a cowboy hat that by some miracle hadn't flown off yet. Julie wondered crazily if he'd glued it to his head somehow. He'd planned everything—the change of disguise, Plan B in case she didn't follow instructions, a weapon—

"Ben!" she shouted. "He has a knife, watch out!"

"I don't fucking care! I just want answers." Ben moved on the man like some relentless force of nature, while the guy ducked away, just out reach. The man was probably in his early fifties, no match for Ben's strength and power—except for that weapon. "Do you know who he is?"

"No, but he's the same one who grabbed me before. He admitted it!"

Where was that knife? Julie tried to spot it, but saw no sign of anything sharp or shiny on the man's person. Maybe she'd imagined it.

Ben kept after him. "Why'd you scare Julie away? What were you so afraid of? Did you kill my father? Where do you think you're going, asshole? You're not leaving here without fucking handcuffs! The police are on their way. The only question is whether you'll be conscious when they get here so you'd better start answering. What's your name?"

The mention of police spurred the man into action. With a desperate growl, he reached for his hip.

The knife! Julie knew it was coming. She scrambled to her feet and dashed toward Ben and the man, who were only separated by a few feet. She fixed her gaze on the hand going for the knife.

It flew out of the man's hand, its blade glinting orange in the sunset light, bright and terrible, sailing toward Ben's chest, his beautiful heart.

Before Julie even made a conscious decision to do it, she was off her feet and airborne.

She hurled herself through the air at Ben. She rammed into him with the force of a linebacker and toppled him to the ground. She felt a quick, burning sting on her arm, but barely noticed compared to the bone-jarring impact of colliding with Ben and then the ground.

Everything went momentarily dark and confusing, as Ben's elbow hit her jaw and she saw stars. Someone was shouting—

actually she thought it was her, warning Ben about the knife. A feral growl sounded near them. Someone was kicking her in the stomach, or maybe kicking Ben—no, both. She felt pain, though Ben's body absorbed most of the impact.

Ben grabbed the man's leg and twisted hard. The attacker spun through the air and landed on his ass. Then he saw something in the direction of the parking lot, and scrambled to his knees.

At a flat run, he took off into the woods, thrashing past trees and through thickets of branches until he'd disappeared from sight.

Julie turned her attention to Ben, who lay underneath her, warm and alive. Sweaty and panting. Beautiful and *there*. "Are you okay?"

"Yeah. Are you?"

"How did you find me?"

"Friends in high places." He winced, lifting his eyes toward the sky.

Way up there, she saw the Knight and Day chopper hovering.

"Oh." God, her head was spinning. "Felix! We have to get Felix!"

"Already did. I put him in my truck and locked the door. I didn't want him getting near all this. Will and Savannah are on their way."

Relief had her slumping against him. He wrapped his arm around her, and even though it hurt, because her arm was sore from all the battling, it made her so happy she wanted to cry. "God, I was so scared. I was thinking about you, right before you appeared out of nowhere."

"You were?"

"I was afraid I might never see you again. And what if you thought I'd abandoned you again, and I kind of did, because that creep said I had to leave and never come back. I was terrified you'd never forgive me if I did the same thing all over again."

"Julie." He cupped her face, two big hands cradling her. "I love you. That's not changing. Not ever."

Tears started in her eyes.

"I figured you had a good reason for taking off. I only followed in case you needed backup."

"Thank God you did." Feeling dizzy again, she buried her face in his neck. "I don't want to be without you, Ben, not ever again."

"I'm here, my love. For good."

Her vision blurred around the edges. Her eyes were starting to close and she felt so, so tired. All she wanted to do was sleep. Well, and be with Ben. While she was sleeping. Sleeping with Ben, that was the definition of bliss in her world. Sleeping with Ben, waking up with Ben, making love with Ben, laughing with Ben...

"Goddamn it." His profanity jolted her back awake. Ben had pulled his arm away from her. A terrible frown creased his face. She wanted to smooth out all those lines, bring back his happy smile. But she couldn't seem to lift her hand.

"Why didn't you tell me you were injured?" he said harshly. "Jesus, you're bleeding! He hit you. That knife he tossed at me—it hit you! I thought it missed both of us."

"Oh." That did make sense. Her arm throbbed as if a vicious little ice skater was racing back and forth across it. That image made her smile dreamily. At least the knife hadn't hit Ben. It couldn't have, because now Ben was scooping her up off the ground and carrying her toward his truck. No, toward police lights and cars and paramedics rushing toward her. It was a terrifying sight.

She spotted Ben's truck in the middle of the madness, and Felix's bespectacled face pressed against the window.

She tried to smile at him and wave, but it hurt so much she winced. Ben saw where she was looking. "Don't worry, I'll take care of Felix."

"It's okay. I see Savannah." Her friend was racing across the pavement, her black hair flying behind her. Ben called Savannah's name as he dug through his pocket, somehow managing to hold her with one arm. She clung tight to his neck, aware that she was soaking him with her blood.

"Savannah, here are my truck keys," Ben yelled. "Felix is in there."

She nodded, but hesitated before heading that way. "Julie? Is she okay?"

"Just a scratch," Julie piped up. "A really really really bad scratch."

"She still has her sense of humor, I think she'll be okay." Ben adjusted her in his arms again. He veered toward the paramedic van, where a crew was getting a gurney ready for her. A gurney. For *her*. She felt like a star in a medical show, and giggled at the thought.

"Who cast this show?" she asked, thinking it was perhaps the most hilarious thing anyone had ever said. "They got it all wrong. I'm not the star, I'm the comic relief. Or maybe the best friend."

"Baby, *you* have it all wrong. You've always been the star. You always will be." Ben's deep voice resonated through her, bringing peace and comfort.

A paramedic ran toward them with some equipment. He was going to take her away, she knew. She clutched at Ben. "Will you stay with me, Ben? Promise?"

"Always. I guarantee."

"Word of a..." She was falling into a deep pit as sleep engulfed her.

"Word of a Knight brother. I love you, Julie. I'm not leaving." And that was the last thing she was aware of for a long time.

WHEN SHE WOKE UP, her shoulder burned under a swaddling of bandages. She was in a hospital room, and it was night. The room was lit only by the blinking green indicators on the medical machines, and the washed out light from the street lamps outside the building. The remnants of her dream still lingered—the voices, the singing.

She was alone.

She panicked. Where was everyone? Where was Ben? Felix? Where was *she*? A machine beeped in response to her rising heart rate.

"Hey, hey." A door opened, spilling warm yellow light into the room. Ben's familiar figure was silhouetted against the bathroom light. "It's okay, I'm right here." He hurried to her side and knelt next to her. "How are you feeling?"

"Pretty good, considering. How's Felix?"

"He's all right. Pretty amazing kid. He's been giving Will all kinds of information about the kidnapper. You should see Will's face. It's obvious he's trying to think of legal ways to hire him. He's a phenom."

"Yes, that he is." Images from her dream still danced through her mind. "I have some information, too. I finally put it together... or at least my subconscious did. I knew there was something about his voice that was familiar, but I could never place it. I finally did, while I was knocked out."

"Honey, are you sure you should be thinking about this right now? You just focus on resting and recovering. We'll find the jackass. Tobias was tracking him in the chopper until it got too dark and he lost him. But we know what direction he was heading. Between him and Will and Felix, I'm not a bit worried."

"Ben, I'm fine."

"You got stabbed." His eyes smoldered with anger. "That fucking dipshit stabbed you. He's going to pay for that."

"Not exactly stabbed. More like...flicked."

"No. Not flicked. Sorry, that wasn't a flick. That was a goddamn heart attack in action. I should sue him for nearly killing me." He pulled her hand to his chest, where his heart beat a steady rhythm. "I've just barely recovered. Finally. Only once the doctor said you're going to be fine."

"Just a scratch, right? Told you." She grinned at him, then licked her lips, which were dry and cracking. "Any water around here?"

"Hang on." He brought her a plastic cup with a straw embedded in it. She took a long, grateful sip. "Okay, go ahead and tell me what your subconscious came up with. But just so you know, the only thing that truly matters to me is that you're not hurt. As soon as they release you, we have to have a serious talk about this."

"This?"

"Us." He pressed her hand against his ribs. "The future. *Our* future. But not yet. I know it's a complicated topic, so let's wait until you're out of here."

To be honest, it no longer seemed so complicated to her. She belonged with Ben. Her life had taken a strange detour twelve years ago, and for all that time, she'd lived without him. She had no intention of doing that ever again.

But first, she really had to tell him what she'd remembered. "He sings. That's how I remembered him. I know him from the performance of 'Messiah' that the Community College puts on every year. I sang in it once, that year when your mother talked me into it. Remember, we used to go together? At first, I felt awkward because it was your *mother*. But it ended up being cool. He was in the baritone section. But I don't remember his name or anything else about him. I'm not even sure I ever knew. But that must be why he didn't want me in Jupiter Point. He knew I'd recognize him eventually, after I caught him snooping around the house. And I'm pretty sure I've heard his voice more recently too —maybe from *Grease*, or maybe just around town."

Ben soothed her by rubbing her hand gently. Her tension eased, and she fell back against the pillows. He was frowning thoughtfully at her hand. "So, you think he's the killer."

"He basically admitted it."

"How did he know my dad? Probably not from the Army, huh?"

"I don't know how he did, or even *if* he did. I have a feeling he was there because of your mother."

"My *mother*?"

"I think he was in love with her. She mentioned to me once that one of the singers had tried to flirt with her, and she shut him down. Well…what if he didn't get completely shut down? What if he still wanted her? And your dad was in the way?"

32

BEN LEFT THE HOSPITAL, REELING FROM THE NEWS JULIE HAD shared. She'd finally gone back to sleep, right after ordering him to go home and grab a shower. He figured when someone insisted you take a shower, you should do as they asked. Before he got under the hot water, he called his brothers.

"Emergency meeting. My place, stat."

When he came out, in a clean t-shirt and cotton sweats, his brothers were sprawled around the living room. Even Aiden was there, having just flown home after midterms.

"We have a problem." Ben got right to the point. "I think Mom knows more than she let on back then. I think she has a suspicion about the killer, and that's why she left, and that's why she's been such a rolling stone."

He filled them in on what Julie had remembered.

"Are you sure it's not the blood loss talking?" Tobias asked in his blunt way. "I remember some strange dreams when I got shot by those Light Keepers."

"I don't think so. I mean, he grabbed her, he was dragging her off into the woods and—" He broke off, passing his hand across his face. He still couldn't think about it without losing his shit.

"Point being, she was close to him. Close enough to remember the last time."

Will leaned forward and squeezed his knee, while Tobias shot him a sympathetic look. But it was Aiden, the youngest but in some ways the wisest, who came to his side and hugged him. "You're a hero, Ben. You saved Felix, you saved Julie. And by the way, it's totally okay with me if I'm the last single Knight brother standing. Just so you know."

"I'm definitely going to take you up on that, if Julie's game." He hurried past the personal stuff, which was between him and Julie. And Felix. And Savannah. And...crap. He still didn't know how all that was going to work out. With a pit in his stomach, he changed back to the original topic. "We need to get Mom to talk to us. Mom's the key."

"Agreed," said Will. "How about we all head out there and surprise them? Family style. We'll lay it all out there. Now that we're hot on the trail of this guy, I bet she'll be right there with us. She was probably scared all these years, scared he'd find her." Suddenly he swore. "Damn, it just occurred to me. I wonder if he thought Mom was coming to the Winter Ball. Maybe that's why he was at the Reinhards' property."

"How would he know that?" Tobias asked.

Will and Ben's eyes met, a possible answer striking at the same moment. "Maybe he was one of the security guards. They probably had the guest list."

"Damn, you are one good investigator." Ben offered his big brother a high-five.

"Oh, that's just the start. I have a notebook of clues to put together based on what Felix told me. I'll probably be up all night putting everything on a whiteboard. If anyone wants to come by tomorrow and stare at it with me, you're more than welcome."

"Count me out," said Ben right away. "Right now, it's all about Julie. I'll be back at the hospital until they release her."

"And then what?" Tobias asked. All the brothers stared at him expectantly.

He had no real answer to give them. Because he'd never forget the fear of knowing Felix was missing. He didn't want to do something that might hurt Felix. He and Julie were on the same page now. The problem was, that page was blank.

JULIE WAS RELEASED the next day. He drove her to the pharmacy to pick up some pain pills.

"I hate those things," she grumbled as they walked back to his truck, her arm gingerly cradled in a sling. The pharmacy was located in a little strip mall next to the old two-screen movie theater, where they'd made out during countless double features. They strolled slowly, since Julie was still a little wobbly. "They make my head feel like cotton."

"Pass them over, then," he said dryly. "I have a feeling I might need them."

She gave him a puzzled look. "What are you talking about? Are you injured and haven't told me yet?"

"Not exactly. Not from a knife. It's just..." He stopped and turned toward her. "Julie, I love you. I want to be with you. I never want to be away from you again. But I can't leave Jupiter Point, not now. Now when the business is just starting to fly, and we're so close to solving Dad's murder. Mom and Cassie are going to stay for a while, hopefully a long while if things go well. I just have too much happening."

"Of course you can't leave! I never even gave that a thought."

"But you can't leave Felix, either. I didn't quite get that until he went missing. So I've been thinking...I have my own plane, you know. Two of them. And I can fly to see you whenever—" He only stopped because she put her hand over his mouth and made him. Otherwise he probably would have kept on babbling forever, hoping to find the perfect combination of words that added up to a future.

"It's okay," she whispered. "I have it all figured out already."

"You do?"

"Yes. Do you trust me?"

"Completely."

The speed of his reply seemed to startle her. She took his hand and tenderly held it to her cheek. "Thank you. Then let's go."

"Where?"

"Knight and Day. I'm calling a family meeting."

33

The meeting didn't involve his family, but the Reinhards. And it was held in Ben's happy place—onboard the 206, flying at five thousand feet. In the right seat, Felix showed off his knowledge—and lack of throwing up—to Savannah. Julie sat in the back with the Reinhards. Even though they'd ended their custody bid after Felix was retrieved, Ben still wished he could do a Dutch roll and scare the crap out of them.

But this was Julie's show, so he stuck to flying the plane straight and level like the professional he was.

After Felix had sufficiently wowed Savannah, Julie got down to business.

"I asked you all up here because I have something to say. Ben has promised to find some turbulence if anyone interrupts me."

Ben gave her a thumbs up.

"Okay, members of the Reinhard family. If there's one thing I know for sure, it's how horrible it is to lose your family. I don't want that to happen to any of you...or to me. And you guys, despite everything, are like my family. Priscilla, I know I'm not technically a family member—"

"Take that back," said Savannah. "Either you're family, or we don't have one."

The Reinhards shared a glance. Priscilla took Adam's hand and spoke for them both. "Savannah's right. Felix's kidnapping scared the life out of me, and you're the one who got him back. We'll never forget that."

"With a knife wound to boot," added Adam. "I'd say that makes you family."

"Damn right," Savannah agreed. "About time you two showed some appreciation."

"Honestly, Sav—"

Julie interrupted firmly. "I'm not done yet. Remember the turbulence."

All the Reinhards shut up. Ben grinned proudly. Gotta love Julie and her fiery side, when she chose to show it.

"I asked Ben to take us up in this plane because it's a lot *like* a family. We're all stuck together inside a small space with forces of nature pressing in on all sides. But we can't just walk away from each other."

"Please don't try," Ben added. "Knight and Day has an unbroken safety record."

Julie smiled and rolled her eyes a little, but carried on. "I love all of you, even when you're being difficult. I love Felix as if he was my own child. Savannah, you're my sister. But Ben—Ben is my heart. He's my everything. Past, present, future. Everything."

Gaze fixed on the path ahead, Ben tilted one wing to reveal the stretch of coastline below, with the pretty pastel houses of Jupiter Point scattered like confetti. He didn't want to lose it before Julie got through her speech.

"I love Ben. I always have. And I want to live with him and marry him and maybe have a baby or two. That means I need to be here, in Jupiter Point. This is where I want to be. This is where I want to raise my family."

Ben stole a cautious glance at Felix. How was the kid reacting? Would he understand the implications?

"That's why I requested this meeting. I'm speaking up for what *I* want. I want Ben—and I want my Reinhards, too. That's what I want. Maybe if I say it clearly enough, it'll happen. I'll make my own reality." Ben glanced in the mirror and caught the wink she sent him.

Julie settled back in her seat. The others shared a glance, then Savannah cleared her throat.

"Thank you, Julie. I'm really glad you said all this. But for the safety of all concerned, it's probably best if we don't stay airborne together too long, right? So, I think I can hurry this along. Mom and I had a long discussion—"

"I would call it more of a showdown," said Priscilla.

"Showdown works too. I now understand what my busybody parents were up to with the custody thing. Even though their methods were *horrible*, their goal was worthy. They wanted me to step up. Is that about right?"

Adam put his hand on hers. "More or less. But you wouldn't even talk to us."

"I know. I'm not completely sure I want to talk to you *now*. But I get the point you were trying to make. I need to be with Felix more, give him a more stable life. I agree. I talked it over with Felix, and I'm going to cut way back on my schedule, now that this drag-ass shoot is over. We're going to stay in Jupiter Point, at least for the time being. In our own place," she added quickly. "Most likely on the other side of town. When I'm on a shoot, he'll have both you and my parents for extra support."

"You're *staying*?" Julie's eyes went wide.

Savannah leaned toward her, saying something in a low voice Ben couldn't catch.

Ben shot a quick look at Felix, who seemed more interested in the gauges and controls than the discussion in the backseat. He cut the comms and spoke out loud to Felix. "You okay with that, kid? Last I heard, you thought Jupiter Point was boring."

"It's not boring anymore," Felix said. "I got kidnapped. And I'll be able to fly this plane soon. And I might help catch a murderer."

Ben laughed. "Very good points. So, you don't mind sticking around here and helping us out now and then?"

"It's okay. Especially if you pay me."

"We can probably work something out."

He turned his headset back on and checked the little mirror that showed him the passengers. Julie's hands were clasped under her chin and her wide blue eyes were misted over. "So everyone's going to be in Jupiter Point? Is this some kind of fairy tale?"

The others all smiled; her joy was infectious. "Are you kidding, after everything you've done for us?" Savannah squeezed her hand. "You deserve your fairy-tale ending. Felix and I would do a lot more than this to make you happy."

"Oh good, because I can think of so many things." Julie grinned wickedly. "If Ben plays his cards right, there'll be a wedding to plan, for one thing."

"Will you marry me?" Ben asked quickly.

"Yes," she answered, even more quickly. They grinned at each other, while Felix groaned.

"Do I have to help with the invitations?"

Everyone laughed, even the elder Reinhards. Julie soaked in the sound of it, her eyes shining. Ben's entire world lit up at the sight of her happiness.

"We can negotiate that part, Kiddo. Also, Savannah, there's one other little thing you can do for me..."

"I GOT CHILLS, and they're multiplyin'..." Ben sang softly to Julie as she put the finishing touches on her 1950s-style Sandy "good girl" costume, complete with swingy ponytail and sweet smile. A moment ago, he'd had his hand up her skirt, getting her all hot and bothered before he fingered her to a fierce orgasm that she'd muffled against his neck.

"You're the one that I love..." she continued, singing strong and loud, getting her voice warmed up for the stage. She'd gotten the call from the *Grease* director right after she'd been released from the hospital. The bed in the sleepover scene had collapsed, injuring the actress who played Rizzo.

Savannah had jumped at the chance to take a break from high-stress movie shooting. And she was playing the hell out of Rizzo. She had so much charisma that whenever she was onstage, she drew all eyes to her.

Well, all eyes except Ben's. Ben seemed to want nothing more than to watch Julie's every move onstage. As if she was the star, which, he kept reminding her, she actually *was*. In this production, and in his heart. Forever.

The old sappy, romantic Ben was back, almost as if he'd never disappeared.

"Next time I'm going to drag you onstage too," she warned him as she snapped the band around her ponytail. "You have a pretty good voice."

"Yeah, not happening. I've got my hands full taking care of my girl. It's a full-time job, you know. Work all day, make love all night. It's tough, but I'm up for it." He puffed out his chest.

"Oh, I know you're up for it." She danced her fingers up his thigh and gave him a naughty wink. "But if you want to prove it some more—"

Someone tapped on the door of the dressing room, which was one of the perks of being the star, even though it was only a converted closet. "Five minutes."

"You know, I could get used to this 'star' thing," she mused as she slipped on her shoes.

"Good, because I could get used to this 'stargazing' thing," he quipped. "Jupiter Point's specialty. But if you need a bigger stage somewhere else, I'll be there for that, too," he added quickly.

"No. This is all I need. Write my songs, play my music, be with my Ben." Add a happy Felix to the mix, and she really couldn't ask for anything more.

He cupped her face in his hands and they dove into one of those ocean-deep, sky-high kisses that she never wanted to end.

"Go shine, my superstar. I'll be waiting."

She smiled through her overflowing heart, because she knew the truth—that the waiting was over. Their time was now. And it was worth every second.

WANT MORE JUPITER POINT? You can find the entire series at JenniferBernard.net.

SIGN UP for Jennifer Bernard's mailing list at JenniferBernard.net and never miss a new release or a sale (not to mention giveaways)! You'll also receive a free fireman story as a 'thank you.' Please consider leaving a review to help other readers find books to love. Thank you so much for reading!

ABOUT THE AUTHOR

Jennifer Bernard is a *USA Today* bestselling author of contemporary romance. Her books have been called "an irresistible reading experience" full of "quick wit and sizzling love scenes." A graduate of Harvard and former news promo producer, she left big city life in Los Angeles for true love in Alaska, where she now lives with her husband and stepdaughters. She still hasn't adjusted to the cold, so most often she can be found cuddling with her laptop and a cup of tea. No stranger to book success, she also writes erotic novellas under a naughty secret name that she's happy to share with the curious. You can learn more about Jennifer and her books at JenniferBernard.net. Make sure to sign up for her newsletter for new releases, fresh exclusive content, sales alerts and giveaways.

Connect with Jennifer online:
JenniferBernard.net
Jen@JenniferBernard.net

ALSO BY JENNIFER BERNARD

Jupiter Point ~ Firefighters

Set the Night on Fire ~ Book 1

Burn So Bright ~ Book 2

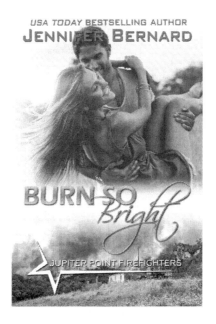

Into the Flames ~ Book 3

Setting Off Sparks ~ Book 4

Jupiter Point ~ The Knight Brothers

Hot Pursuit ~ Book 5

Coming In Hot ~ Book 6

Seeing Stars

(Prequel and Hope Falls Kindle World Novella)

The Bachelor Firemen of San Gabriel

The Fireman Who Loved Me

Hot for Fireman

Sex and the Single Fireman

How to Tame a Wild Fireman

Four Weddings and a Fireman

The Night Belongs to Fireman

Novellas

One Fine Fireman

Desperately Seeking Fireman

It's a Wonderful Fireman

Love Between the Bases

All of Me

Caught By You

Getting Wound Up (crossover with Sapphire Falls)

Drive You Wild

Crushing It

Double Play

Novellas

Finding Chris Evans

Forgetting Jack Cooper

ACKNOWLEDGMENTS

Thank you to Miriam Matthews for sharing her expertise on small planes. To my editor Kelli Collins, artists Dana LaMothe and proofreader Wendy Keel, thanks for all your great work. Most of all, to the Hot Readers and my Dream Team — I love you!

34758029R00188

Made in the USA
San Bernardino, CA
04 May 2019